THE DEATH TRAP

She crouched near the sludge pit. As she kneeled, her weight shifted and a long tree branch pushed up out of the water. With it came a pale hand which slowly rose straight at Sunny's face.

She screamed, a ragged sound that cut through the quiet night. She couldn't look away from the hand which she now saw was attached to an arm, oily water dripping slowly off the transparent fabric clinging to it.

She tried to get away, lost her balance, and slipped, splashing into the water, knocking against the body. As it popped to the surface, Sunny screamed again and started to slide toward the inert form. Halfway into the sludge pit, she felt horror rise within her. Her legs were under the body, now bloated, swollen, slick, and dark with oil, but still recognizable as a woman.

She gagged and tried to scramble out of the pool, then plunged farther into the pit. She realized she was drowning, and there was no help nearby. If she died, she might not be found for days, or maybe never. Was that what had happened to the woman floating nearer and nearer to her?

PINNACLE'S HORROR SHOW

BLOOD BEAST (17-096, $3.95)
by Don D'Ammassa

No one knew anymore where the gargoyle had come from. It was just an ugly stone creature high up on the walls of the old Sheffield Library. Little Jimmy Nicholson liked to go and stare at the gargoyle. It seemed to look straight at him, as if it knew his most secret desires. And he knew that it would give him everything he'd ever wanted. But first he had to do its bidding, no matter how evil.

LIFEBLOOD (17-110, $3.95)
by Lee Duigon

Millboro, New Jersey was just the kind of place Dr. Winslow Emerson had in mind. A small township of Yuppie couples who spent little time at home. Children shuttled between an overburdened school system and every kind of after-school activity. A town ripe for the kind of evil Dr. Emerson specialized in. For Emerson was no ordinary doctor, and no ordinary mortal. He was a creature of ancient legend of mankind's darkest nightmare. And for the citizens of Millboro, he had arrived where they least expected it: in their own backyards.

DARK ADVENT (17-088, $3.95)
by Brian Hodge

A plague of unknown origin swept through modern civilization almost overnight, destroying good and evil alike. Leaving only a handful of survivors to make their way through an empty landscape, and face the unknown horrors that lay hidden in a savage new world. In a deserted midwestern department store, a few people banded together for survival. Beyond their temporary haven, an evil was stirring. Soon all that would stand between the world and a reign of insanity was this unlikely fortress of humanity, armed with what could be found on a department store shelf and what courage they could muster to battle a monstrous, merciless scourge.

Available wherever paperbacks are sold, or order direct from the Publisher. Send cover price plus 50¢ per copy for mailing and handling to Pinnacle Books, Dept.17-271, 475 Park Avenue South, New York, N.Y. 10016. Residents of New York, New Jersey and Pennsylvania must include sales tax. DO NOT SEND CASH.

THE SPIRIT STALKER

NINA ROMBERG

PINNACLE BOOKS
WINDSOR PUBLISHING CORP.

This is a work of fiction.
All the characters and events portrayed
in this book are fictional, and any resemblance
to real people, living or dead, or incidents
is entirely coincidental.

PINNACLE BOOKS

are published by

Windsor Publishing Corp.
475 Park Avenue South
New York, NY 10016

First printing: October, 1989

Printed in the United States of America

To Dean,
for being there

To Lydia,
for making it possible

Nothing escapes my Web.
　　—Spider Grandmother

Prologue

WEDNESDAY, JULY 20
2:29 A.M.

Under the light of a waxing moon, an oil well pumped, its humped back moving steadily up and down, drawing black blood from deep under the sandy soil of East Texas. Pineco Well Number 87 had been pumping for years and had earned a fortune for its owners.

But the land around it had not fared as well. Where green grass had once flourished, the land was now bare, except for the cement, black machinery and silver pipes that made up Well Number 87.

A nearby sludge pit with dead trees reaching blackly into the sky from its center was used as a dumping ground for oil production waste. Over the years, death had spread from the pool and now marked the land around it with decay.

An owl hooted in a tree close by, safely above the spreading death of the land. The sound of a car passing on a nearby two-lane, farm-to-market road disturbed the quietness of the night, and the owl took flight, its wings beating noisily against the warm, muggy air.

The car turned off the road and slowly followed a one-lane blacktop, which led to the producing oil well. East Texas was crisscrossed with roads dead-ending at wells, many now capped, no longer in production. The car stopped near Well Number 87. A man got out, shut the door, stretched, looked around, then walked to the other side of the Ford Taurus.

He opened the door, and the inside light softly illuminated the interior. He pulled the limp, inert body of a woman from the front seat. Grunting with effort, he threw the body over his shoulder, then walked across the oil-darkened land to the stagnant pond. Moonlight gleamed off the black slicks that covered its surface.

Trying to keep his feet out of the muck around the sludge pit, he lowered the body into the water. For a moment it floated, then oil began to collect around the pale face and darken the once bright red hair. Sinking slightly, the woman still remained visible. The man cursed, then snapped off a dead branch from a fallen tree. He poked the body over and over. Finally black liquid darkened the lifeless face as the body sank into the watery depths, caught on something, and stayed submerged.

Satisfied, he dropped the stick near the sludge pit, then started back toward the car, his greasy footprints camouflaged in the oil-soaked dirt. He hesitated beside the pumping oil well, the steady, rhythmic sound reminding him of the woman's heart before he had stopped it forever.

2:32 A.M.

Billy Joe James sat on the back porch of his ramshackle house drinking beer. Life had passed him by fifteen years before, when he was seventeen and the star quarterback of his high school football team. He could still hear the cheers and smell the perfume of the prettiest girls in school. He'd had it all then. And with the blind faith of youth, he had blithely taken the best offer of a college scholarship and gone

8

back East to a university nobody in Texas had ever heard of.

Now he wished he'd never heard of it, either. He absently rubbed his ruined right knee. Doctors had patched it up, but it had never been right, not after the second season. He'd gotten a couple years of free college, then he'd been dumped out on his ass. They only paid if he played, and those he'd thought were friends suddenly didn't know him anymore. They brought in a new star, and Billy Joe had packed his bags and gone home to East Texas.

It'd been all right at first. The jobs hadn't been much, but working as a roustabout on oil rigs paid pretty good, even if it could be hazardous. He'd lost his best friend one summer in high school on a rig. He never could forget the scream as his buddy was smashed in oil-greased machinery.

He shuddered, took another long draw on his beer. Some nights he just couldn't sleep. Too many memories. Too much water under the bridge. The worst thing was, he'd never wanted to do anything but play football and be a star forever. He'd thought he was well on his way to being a pro, with visions of winning the Heisman, then being picked by the Dallas Cowboys or the Houston Oilers after college. Took just one damned play, a wrenched leg, and a bum knee to put him out of action forever.

He shook the can, checking to see how much was left. Gazing at the label, his thoughts continued to twist back in time. He'd gotten married once. Pretty little nurse with a cute rear end and a sweet nature. Problem was she spent too much time with the doctors, and he spent too much time with the booze, trying to forget. First thing he'd known, she was having her jollies with a doctor, and then the divorce had come.

Just as well. What would he have done with a houseful of brats, car payments, house payments? He looked back at the wooden house slowly decaying behind him. Parents had

9

left it to him. Problem with being born to forty-year-old people, they went and died off just when you needed them again. Well, they'd left him the house, anyway.

He knew he should do something to repair it, but it'd gone so far now he didn't know if it was worth the effort. Maybe he'd go into Longview and try to pick up a construction job the next day. He needed the money. There wasn't much work on the oil rigs anymore, not with the oil slump. Construction was damned hot work in July, but he could still hold his own with the younger guys.

His muscles hadn't left him yet, even if he had got a beer paunch that hung a little over his belt. But what did that matter? No girl to see him. No girl in a long time. Too long. One day he'd have to get up to Dallas, just over a two-hour drive on the interstate. They had women there who'd do anything for the right money, and it took a little more for him now than it used to.

But Dallas was far away when you had a '69 pickup with soft brakes and no money to fix it or to pay a hooker to make you feel like you were seventeen. Seventeen. He wasn't sure he could remember what it felt like to be seventeen. But he knew it felt a damned sight better than thirty-three.

Anything had to feel better than a thirty-three-year-old busted-up ex-football star. He used to like it when someone'd recognize him and say, "Hey, are you Billy Joe James?" When he'd reply positively, they'd get all gushy and start remembering fabulous plays he'd once made. He couldn't take that now. He had to get out fast if anybody recognized him, not that they did much anymore. He just couldn't take the memories. Not now.

He heard a car go by out on FM 203. He checked the luminous face of his cheap digital watch. Just past two-thirty. Damned late for somebody to be out on the road. But it was none of his business. He'd learned long ago to stay out of people's business back in the piney woods of

East Texas. East Texans were damned independent, and if they didn't want something known, it was better not to know it. Still, funny business, a car on 203 this time of night.

Then he laughed, rubbed the stubble on his face, and thought back to those fast-paced days of high school when he and his friends would jump in their cars and beat a fast track to some gasoline plant, where they could get drip from a spigot if they were damned clever. Oh, and they were clever. Damned clever. Damned drip was about half-processed gasoline and would rot out a car's innards pretty quick. But they didn't care. It was free and they were young. There would be plenty more cars, plenty more drip.

He took a long drink, swallowed wrong, coughed, and shook his head. Damned kids. Somebody ought to warn them. Let them know that life didn't play by any rules but its own. And it won. He laughed out loud. Yes, life always won, and you got death in the end. In the meantime, you got a living death that you began to think just might not be much better than death itself.

But for now he hung on. He'd been a star once; maybe he could do it again.

Then he laughed, coughed, and finished his beer.

2:34 A.M.

Struggling awake, Sunny Hansen fought to reorient herself. She was damp with sweat. Her heart beat fast. She was surrounded by black, twisted tree limbs reaching out to pull her down into darkness. The sound of a sludge pit, sucking something into its depths, reverberated through her.

She desperately fought off the sensation, trying to pull herself out of the dream. As she reached for the light beside her bed, she knocked over the digital travel clock. The alarm went off, jarring her completely awake.

Snapping on the light, she glanced around. There were

11

no tree shapes, only the faded, peeling wallpaper of an old house, a scarred dresser, and her sagging double bed. And there were no sounds, other than those of the crickets and frogs outside.

Home. All safe.

She'd just had another nightmare, nothing real to fear. She threw the sheet aside, swung her legs over the edge of the bed, and pushed back her damp hair. The wood floor was cool beneath her feet. She picked up the alarm, and shut it off. Gazing at the changing luminous numbers, she thought of happier times.

The clock had been a high school graduation present. Her parents had been alive then, and her dreams had been all bright and shiny. Now her dreams were dead, along with her mother and father in their smashed car on I35 near Dallas. Even though their deaths had occurred almost two years ago, she still hadn't gotten over the loss. Maybe she never would.

Her parents hadn't left much of an estate, not even enough to bury them properly. She had worked six months paying off the pale yellow coffin for her mother and the pearl gray one for her father. And that was after selling almost everything in their rented house to pay off the debts and funeral expenses. She'd been left with a few mementos and, most important, the memories. But that was all.

Now she was all that remained, her parents' hope for the future, the one to finally break out and live well above the poverty level. Not that it mattered to them anymore. They were gone, and she was alone. Still, she owed it to their memory to survive and do the best she could, and she owed it to herself.

But there was no point in thinking about the past. She had to deal with the present, with the nightmares. She jerked on a faded, stretched, oversized T-shirt and stood up. Every muscle in her body felt cramped and sore. She must have been sleeping tense again.

Nothing new.

Still, she wouldn't sleep more now. Too many shadows, too many memories were just around the corner, ready to reach out and grab her. Now she needed all the lights on in the house, regardless of the electric bill. She'd find some way to pay it later.

The window air-conditioner in her bedroom was struggling to pump out cool air, but it didn't stand much of a chance against the hot, humid weather of East Texas in July. She wished again, as she always did, for the cold, dry air of a new home or apartment, but she couldn't afford that.

She hit the switch in the small living room, watching the dim light of the forty-watt bulb illuminate the threadbare furniture that had come with the house she rented cheap. It might not look like much, but it was still home and all she had.

In the old-fashioned kitchen, she pulled a Pearl out of the ancient refrigerator. She popped the top, then let the cold, soothing beer slide down her throat. Taking a deep breath, she looked around. She walked through the living room, flipped on the porch light, glanced at the small pool of yellow light in the darkness outside, saw nothing, then turned back.

Everything was fine. Still, she couldn't get rid of the uneasiness the dream had spawned. She glanced around the room. Small shadows took on threatening shapes. She shook her head, determined to fight down the fading effects of the nightmare.

Work would help. She flipped on the light in her small studio. The lamp over her natural wood drawing table illuminated the white surface of an illustration board taped down securely around every edge. Bright red push pins held a piece of vellum to the board. She cast an experienced eye over the small illustration of a toaster and laughed hoarsely at her once grand dream of being a celebrated illustrator.

13

That'd been a long time ago, or at least it seemed like a long time ago. Six months. Seven days. Four hours.

No Dan for all that blessed time.

She'd run from him, all the way from Dallas to East Texas, a two-and-a-half-hour drive on the interstate. She wished it could have been farther, but she hadn't had enough money to finance a longer trip and no one to go to for help, fearing Dan would hurt anyone who aided her. At least there was no way he could harm her parents, and since she hadn't told any of her friends her plans, there was nothing he could gain from hurting them.

There'd been money once. Dan's money. He'd been a super-salesman when Dallas had been a boomtown, and he'd bought her furs, jewelry, a fancy car. He'd been a big fat cat, living high on the hog, spending money to improve his image, impressing friends and strangers alike.

She'd been twenty years old and impressed, just like a lot of people. She'd never had much and had worked hard after high school for everything she did have. So the money Dan had spent on her had made her feel good, special, loved. Looking back now, she realized Dan had bought her, just like he'd bought everything else.

But what she didn't think he had ever understood, or was capable of understanding, was that she'd really loved him: loved his boyish charm, his extravagant ways, his enthusiasm for life. Now she realized she'd been too young, too innocent, and in the end it had all come down to him being an egomaniac.

When he'd lost his job a year ago, he'd run through their savings, then sold her furs, jewelry, and car in an attempt to maintain his lifestyle, along with all the friends the money had bought. He'd hated the idea of her job supporting them, and his violence toward her had gotten progressively worse until finally her love had died, and she knew she had to escape.

But he couldn't stand the idea of anything he owned leav-

14

ing him and that was the way he looked at her. Property. To be used, abused, or destroyed. At his whim. He'd warned her that if she ever left him, he'd hunt her down and kill her. And she believed him. Because the night before she'd finally run, he'd almost done it.

She'd taken the money she'd taped to the bottom of a drawer in her dresser and driven to East Texas, where she'd once vacationed among the piney woods and beautiful lakes. That had been a good time, for it had been happy, carefree, safe, and isolated. Those memories had fueled her decision to hide out there.

But Dan's legacy was still with her, and she lived in terror that he would find her. She wasn't ready to face him yet, although she knew that someday she would have to go back and get a divorce. But she didn't have the strength or courage to do that, and didn't know when she would.

Dan knew well how to terrorize her. He was a master at it. She shivered. She didn't want to think about him. But even now, when he was not with her physically, he was in her dreams, in her mind. Was there no way to be free of him?

Forcing him from her thoughts, she glanced around the room, then down at her drawing table. She had a job to do, and she'd been lucky to get it.

There weren't that many jobs for artists, especially away from the big cities. East Texas had several large towns, and she'd answered an ad in the paper, offering to work cheap with no benefits and provide her own supplies and an office at home. They'd snapped her up.

Now she illustrated products for the monthly sales catalog of Speedy Fix-It, a Longview-based hardware company. It was not her dream job, but she was grateful to have it because everything was handled through the mail. That way, there was no one to see her, and that's what counted. With no one to recognize her, it'd be harder for Dan to find her.

15

All she had to do was continue living quietly and frugally in her small, rented home. And at the moment that was all she wanted to do, although it was far from what she'd planned to be doing at twenty-four. She didn't even want to think of a happy home and family. Dan had killed her dreams.

She resolutely completed her illustration, pulled the push pins free, set the finished art aside, and looked at the next catalog item to be illustrated. Fishing poles. She gritted her teeth, screwed the cap off a #1 Rapidograph drawing pen, then stopped.

Strange. She could hear a car on FM 203, and she'd never heard one go by this late at night before. The engine had the deep purr of a big car, just like the one Dan used to drive. She trembled and bit her lower lip.

Then she reminded herself that Dan couldn't find her. She was safe. She had been for six months. The car meant nothing. It was just somebody going home after a party, or returning from a trip, or anything. She was not going to let herself start connecting Dan to every unexplained event in her life.

She was smarter than that.

Gripping the pen hard, she drew the first line of a fishing pole.

2:37 A.M.

The Reverend Isaiah Mulhaney did not have fears. He had beliefs, strong beliefs. He believed in God, the powerful, kind, omnipotent being who could be stern, even unreasonable on occasion, but always God and therefore to be worshiped. He thought a lot about God, especially when he woke in the middle of the night with pains in his chest. God comforted him. He knew that he would go to heaven, where he would reside forever in heavenly glory

16

by the side of God. It made him feel loved and needed and secure.

Ministers needed security because their lives depended on the whims of congregations and peers and established churches. After being abruptly uprooted several times for reasons he believed to be spurious, he had decided that God wanted him to establish his own church. He had run out of gas in East Texas, and when given a half-tank by a kind-hearted soul in a small town called Gusher just south of Longview, he had decided to found his ministry there.

A lonely widow had willed his ministry two oil wells at her death. She had been very grateful for his kind support during her long illness, and he believed he had helped her achieve great peace of mind and spirit before she passed over to enjoy the pleasures of heaven. He was also sure her generous contribution had aided her quick ascent to God. Now he liked to picture her with a shining halo, sitting on a silver cloud, playing a golden harp.

With the money from the oil wells, he had constructed an impressive edifice in God's honor. The church was made of pink brick and floored with lilac carpet. Hand-carved wood and fiery stained-glass windows completed his little heaven on earth. He had also constructed a small parsonage next to the brick structure and moved in with nice, comfortable Early American furniture.

His congregation grew rapidly, bringing their families out of the piney woods. Now they no longer had to go into Gusher or Kilgore or Longview. They had their own beautiful church. They felt sorry for those who still had to attend church in wooden buildings or travel to town, but Christian charity kept them from saying so in public.

No one thought anything of the fact that Reverend Mulhaney had built the church just in front of the two pumping oil wells that had financed it. Everyone was used to seeing oil derricks mixed with the tall pines, and in fact, would have been hard pressed to notice the sound of the constant

17

pumping of black blood from the earth. They had lived with the sound all their lives. It was as natural as the wind in the trees.

With the arrival of the specially constructed organ all the way from Italy, Reverend Mulhaney and his flock felt that they had arrived at the pinnacle of grace on earth. They worshiped fervently on Sunday mornings, Sunday evenings, and Wednesday nights. The rest of the time they felt sufficiently holy not to worship at all, unless it was necessary to have God intervene in their favor.

Reverend Mulhaney was not fond of July. He did not like the incessant noise of insects, frogs, and crickets. Only the sound of the pumping oil wells soothed him at night. The cacophony of insects had kept him awake for an hour when he finally rose and pulled on his blue cotton robe initialed with a golden cross. Putting on soft leather slippers, he stepped out the back door.

He stood for a long moment smiling benignly on the two oil wells, their black backs pumping up and down, up and down, the shafts going in and out, in and out of the earth. For a moment he was shocked as he felt himself start to harden. Horrified, he began to walk, willing away the feeling.

Early in life he had decided the Bible was right in that women were the spawn of all evil, and it was man's place to subdue their errant ways. It was not an easy task, of course, but he had spent a lifetime doing God's will, and he had helped many women take the first steps on the path to salvation and glory.

But tonight he did not want to think about women. He wanted to sleep, but could not. The moon was waxing, becoming a round white globe which beckoned like the full breast of a woman aroused. He stopped again. What was wrong with him? His mind was getting dangerously close to being taken over by the devil. He could not allow that, or he would never get to heaven.

He began to walk more vigorously, his backless slippers clip-clopping in the still night. Dew covered the ground, and wet grass stained his shoes and dampened the edges of his light blue pajamas. He did not like the constant humidity or the summer heat. He wished his car had taken him farther. He was never quite comfortable, even though he had built his church there fifteen years before when he was thirty-six. But it was probably God's way of testing him, so he accepted his physical discomfort with a kind of holy resignation.

He left the grass for the parking lot, passed around the white line markers as if he were circumventing a maze, and felt his body respond to his attempts at self-control. Good. The devil would not get him this night.

Then he heard a car on FM 203. Surprised, he glanced down at his gold analog watch. 2:37 A.M. He could not remember hearing a car pass at that time of night before, but he comforted himself by thinking that he was normally asleep and would not hear the traffic on 203. There was something faintly sinister about the heavy engine purring down the quiet country road.

Shaking his head, he retraced his steps through the parking lot, noticing how the moonlight made the white stripes seem to dance. He pushed one more fanciful thought from his practical mind, and went inside to make himself a cup of herbal tea.

2:41 A.M.

Miriam Winchester was an older-woman by anyone's reckoning, but she still retained the sharp power of her mind, and her body had not been bowed by time. Always a strong, sensual woman, age had not changed her personal magnetism. With a long, sliver braid down her back, slanted green eyes, and skin stretched tightly across her combined Indian and white facial structure, she inspired admiration and fear, depending on the person.

But she didn't see many people anymore. She had outlived many of her contemporaries, and now preferred the company of her forest friends. Birds, squirrels, frogs, rabbits, and snakes would listen tirelessly to her tales of the past and demand nothing more than the sound of her voice and a little food.

Miriam frequently did not sleep at night, partly from age, but mostly from wanting to hear the soft whisperings of the wind as it moved through the limbs of the fragrant pines around her.

There was much to be learned at night, for even at seventy-three she knew she had not discovered nearly all there was to know. So she listened to the wind, to the earth, and to her forest friends as she watched the seasons change in natural order.

But tonight as she sat outside her small, wooden, well-cared-for house, she looked worried. Her green eyes sparkled with concern. There had been a car on FM 203 around 2:40 A.M., and as it had passed she had felt a cold, ancient wind, dangerous and deadly, move with it. She was glad when the car had gone on, but she had been left with a feeling of anxiety. Not for herself. She was too old for that. It was for the land, the trees, the forest creatures, and the people who lived in the shade of the tall pines.

She was Comanche-Caddo and close to the land, with medicine knowledge passed down through her grandmother. She would watch and wait. She was used to waiting. She had done a lot of that in her years. It was not wise to move unless the time was right or a sign was found.

Yes, she would watch and wait. But as she settled back in her wooden rocker, a shiver ran through her, and she wished once more for the innocent security of childhood when she could have turned to her parents for comfort and understanding.

But her parents were dead, her wise grandmother, too, and there was no one to turn to but herself. So she took a deep breath and said, "Whatever's out there, be warned you trespass on guarded territory. You may be dangerous, but so am I. And I'm Comanche."

1

Sunny Hansen awoke with a dull headache between her eyes. Rubbing them didn't help. She stumbled from her bedroom to the bath. Yawning, she turned on the faucet in the claw-legged tub, waited until the rust-colored water turned clear, then stepped in and jerked the pink plastic shower curtain shut. She pulled a knob, and hot water sprayed down on her.

It beat against the back of her neck. Hard. She smiled in pleasure, then massaged her neck, rotated her head, and felt the headache begin to recede. She'd worked too long the night before bending over her drawing table. She was pushing herself, working too many hours, but she needed the money.

She shampooed her short auburn hair. Until six months ago, she'd worn it long. Dan had liked it that way. But she'd had it cut, straight and shaggy, partly to disguise herself, partly in rebellion. Now it was just easy and comfortable.

But there she'd gone again, thinking of Dan. As much as she tried to keep her mind off him, she just couldn't seem to.

Sighing, she picked up the washcloth and soap and worked up a good lather. She ran the soapy washcloth over her body, noticing she was getting more muscle tone, even though she spent so many hours sitting at a drawing table. She supposed it was due to her long walks, something she'd never done in Dallas. Dan would be surprised if he could see her, but he wouldn't ever again, not like this.

She was five feet five, with a short waist and long legs, long arms, long hands, long feet. She chuckled. And a long nose. Other than that, she was about average.

Turning off the shower, she stepped out and looked at herself in the small, darkened mirror of the medicine cabinet over the white, porcelain sink. Her eyes were her best feature. Pale gray and slanted. Dan had like to watch their expression change. First with passion; then later all he'd wanted to see was fear.

Six months after they had begun dating, she'd heard gossip that he was known to be forceful with women. She was surprised, for he had always been the perfect gentleman to her—loving, kind, and considerate. By the time a more experienced woman had taken her aside and asked if Dan was starting to push her around yet, she was already deeply in love. She had ignored the warning, thinking it was jealousy, rather than one woman's concern for another woman who might be getting herself into trouble. Now she knew better.

But she wasn't going to let thoughts of Dan ruin her day. Grabbing a yellow towel, she began briskly rubbing herself dry. She toweled her hair, shook it out, then pulled on a pair of faded jeans and a gray, cotton T-shirt. Done. She'd never found dressing so easy in Dallas. But there she'd gone to an office every day.

Just out of high school, she'd persuaded a Dallas suburban newspaper to hire her as an artist. They'd been resistant to her age, her sex, and her lack of a degree, but she'd convinced them she could do a good job. And she had. In fact, she'd made it possible for other young people to be hired there.

She'd also proven that she could get a college degree. After being hired, she'd immediately started taking night classes at the University of Texas at Dallas and had kept them up until six months ago. She'd left town before the new semester started, telling no one, certainly not her boss or friends at work and college. Everybody was safer not knowing where she was going, and she was safer that way, too. Who knew what methods Dan might use to find her?

In the kitchen she started a pot of coffee, then set out a box of granola. As she poured some into a bowl, there was a knock at the back door. She set down the box, walked over to the door's window, and cautiously looked outside. Miriam Winchester smiled at her.

She quickly unlocked and opened the door, then the screen. As Miriam stepped across the threshold, Sunny smiled at her older friend, no longer surprised at Miriam's long morning walks. She had decided to attribute Miriam's amazing strength and health to her Indian blood and positive lifestyle.

Miriam was the only friend she had made since arriving here, and it was Miriam's persistence which had led to that. She now felt safe with her because Miriam never asked questions about her past. She was just beginning to realize how much Miriam's friendship had helped her survive when she'd first moved to East Texas.

"Morning, Sunny. See I caught you in time for breakfast. I just picked some blackberries. Want some?"

"Thanks. If you'll set them in the sink, I'll wash them. Want granola?"

"Don't mind if I do."

Sunny set another place, then washed the blackberries, noticing that Miriam had carefully picked them without getting any bugs, stickers, or leaves mixed in with the dark, juicy berries. In a moment, they were both pouring milk over their bowls of granola and blackberries.

After several bites, Miriam looked up. "Hear anything last night?"

"Like what?"

"Were you up around 2:30?"

"As a matter of fact, I was. I couldn't sleep, so I did some work."

"You're going to ruin your eyes."

"That's what you keep telling me, but so long as I can see to do my art, that's all that matters."

"Youth! Wasted on the young. About last night, did you hear anything?"

Sunny thought as she crunched a sweet-tart blackberry between her teeth and began crushing the small seeds determinedly. She swallowed. "I woke up from a dream about then. I felt uneasy so I looked outside, but I didn't see anything unusual."

"There was a car out on 203 about then."

"That's right. I did hear a car. It sounded like it had a big engine. But why would you ask about it?"

"I didn't like the feel of that car, Sunny."

Sunny raised a brow. Miriam's "feelings" made her uneasy. Problem was, Miriam was usually right; but there was always a rational explanation, too. In this case she thought it was probably Miriam's homemade blackberry wine talking. But she had been raised to be polite, and asked, "What kind of feeling, Miriam?"

"A cold, evil wind, and ancient, came with that car. I think maybe we're in for some bad times."

"Want some more coffee?" Sunny stalled.

"Yes, thanks. I can use the warmth."

Sunny poured them fresh mugs of coffee, but couldn't stop the shiver that ran through her. The last thing she wanted to hear about was evil, especially connected to a car that had reminded her of Dan. "Are you sure, Miriam?"

"I know what you think about my "feelings," but I had to warn you, anyway. Be careful. And if you notice anything strange, be sure and tell me. We'll take care of it together."

For a moment Sunny thought her friend might somehow know about Dan, then shrugged away the thought. It was just a car and just blackberry wine. Dan was far away in Dallas. He had no idea where she was. "All right, Miriam. I'll watch, but I don't want to think about anything evil."

"Neither do I, child, but you can't ignore the warnings—and survive."

"That's true." She had ignored Dan's true nature almost too long. Miriam was more right than she realized. "Just don't tell me any Comanche ghost stories."

Miriam chuckled and drank deeply of the dark brew. "Never planned to, Sunny. But if you notice anything, come over and tell me."

"I wish you'd get a phone installed, Miriam. It's not safe to live so cut off anymore. Anything could happen."

"I'm too old to change now. Besides, those things make me nervous. Wouldn't talk on one if I had it. Can't trust these new fangled devices."

"Phones aren't exactly new, but if something happens, come over here. I'll call for you."

"Thanks, but I'll be okay. It's you I worry about. You work too hard. You need to play more. Enjoy your youth, Sunny. You won't always have it."

"I know, but I've got to pay the bills."

"Maybe a bottle of blackberry wine'd help relax you."

"Probably would." Sunny chuckled.

"Good. I'll bring one over soon. Got to go now. Birds'll be wanting their breakfast." Miriam stood up and walked to the back door.

"Tell them hello," Sunny said as she followed her friend to the door.

Miriam smiled and nodded, then walked briskly into the woods and disappeared among the pines.

Sunny shut and locked the door. Sighing, she poured another cup of coffee. Miriam had just had too much blackberry wine the night before. That was all. There was no point in thinking about evil winds or strange cars. Besides, she had plenty else to think about today. She needed to get the illustrations packaged, then drive into Gusher and mail them. The sooner she went, the sooner she'd get paid. She was always short of money.

She sighed and carried the dirty dishes to the sink. Some lucky people had dishwashers. She had a stained porcelain sink and a leaky faucet, but she was glad to have that. She couldn't have afforded the electricity to run a dishwasher, anyway. In a moment the dishes were draining on the scarred counter top, and she was ready to package her illustrations.

Not long after, she started for town in her '74 Volkswagen Bug. She'd bought it cheap just before leaving Dallas, knowing it would be hard to trace since Dan had never seen it.

The Bug had obviously been in several small collisions, the paint was faded red, and the interior was tattered. But it ran, and she knew it was the cheapest transportation she could get. She didn't drive much, but she lived in fear that the car might develop some major mechanical problem she couldn't afford to fix. She drove carefully as she turned onto FM 203.

She lived only a few miles from Gusher, a small town that boasted two filling stations, one grocery store, a drugstore, a dimestore, a barber shop, a hair salon, and a few other assorted businesses all strung out along FM 203. Frame houses sparsely dotted the oil roads that crisscrossed both sides of the highway.

Sunny passed the town's one source of entertainment, other than gossip, and smiled. The aging drive-in theater showed a wide variety of B movies that continued to draw a pretty good crowd on Friday and Saturday nights. The marquee read CHEERLEADER REVENGE, and Sunny couldn't help but continue smiling. The title somehow put everything in perspective.

Parking in front of the small, brick post office built during the Kennedy expansion years, Sunny got out of her car and went inside. The postmistress looked over her package carefully, determined to find any flaws in the paper or tape or address that would be unacceptable to official U.S. Postal regulations. Unable to find anything wrong, she carefully stamped it "priority" with ink so pale it was almost invisible.

"Saving ink?" Sunny couldn't help asking.

The postmistress squinted behind round glasses, then frowned and stamped once more. Harder. It didn't help. She continued, carefully weighing, pulling levers, and finally sticking a dirty piece of white paper with faint red lines indicating the amount paid on the envelope. It didn't stick. She pushed at it. The paper popped up. Finally, she carefully measured off a short length of tape, then applied it to the paper.

Satisfied, she looked up at Sunny in triumph.

"Think it'll make it to Longview?" Sunny asked.

"Certainly, young lady. Rain or shine, the U.S. Mail goes through."

Skeptical, Sunny thought of all the times her mail had been mysteriously lost or late. But that train of thought brought her back to Dan. During the last six months before she left him, he had frequently hidden her mail, even going so far as to throw it away. For a long time she had blamed the postal system, and maybe it had lost a few pieces, but finally she realized her lost mail was a form of harassment by Dan. He had thought it very funny when she had gotten upset.

"Thanks," she said, pushing thoughts of Dan out of her mind. She paid the ever-increasing amount and walked out.

Driving to the local market, she thought about groceries being a little cheaper in Kilgore or Longview. But she liked the small-town store in Gusher, even if the food wasn't always quite fresh. It still saved her gas and wear and tear on her car. Besides, she didn't eat much. She couldn't afford to.

After buying beans, rice, oatmeal, milk, and cheese, she placed the small bag on the floor in front of the passenger seat. So much for her town outing. Maybe she'd just splurge on a vanilla Dr. Pepper at the drugstore, which still had an old-fashioned soda fountain.

Just as she backed out, she heard a loud crunch and felt her back bumper grate against something. Throwing on the brakes, she turned off the engine, pulled up the emergency brake, and jumped out, furious.

A tall, muscular man with a slight paunch was just stepping out of his faded blue pickup. The surprise in his dark brown eyes turned to speculation when he saw her.

She recognized the look, for she had seen it too many times in men's eyes at school, on the street, or in grocery stores, prime pickup spots in Dallas. "What do you mean running into me?"

He took off a stained cowboy hat, revealing thick, dark brown hair worn slightly long. "I didn't hit you. You backed into me."

"I did not. I looked carefully behind me before I backed out. You weren't there. You must have roared up and—"

"I can't do much roaring in this old Chevy. Besides, as your insurance company will tell you, it's the one backing out who's considered at fault."

"I don't care. You hit me."

"That's a matter of opinion. My pickup's not hurt, but your car looks a little bent here and there."

"Those are old. That's the new scar." She pointed at a scratch and dent in the right fender where his bumper had struck her car.

"I'm sorry, but I stopped as quick as I could. My brakes probably aren't what they should be."

"Driving a hazardous car! Now that certainly won't go over well with your insurance company, or the law."

"Look here, no harm's done to my truck and your Bug just has another scratch. Why don't we let it go? I'll even

29

take you over to the drugstore for a drink. Cool us both off. My name's Billy Joe James. What do you say?''

''I don't have time for a drink, and I'm cool enough. I bet you don't have insurance. Well, you could at least offer to pay for the damage.''

''Like I said, I'm not at fault. Besides, fixing a little scratch like that could cost a few hundred dollars. I don't have that kind of ready cash.''

Sunny quirked a brow at him. She'd seen him around, even passed him a few times on the streets of Gusher. She looked at his faded jeans and plaid shirt more closely, then back at the worn-out truck. He didn't look in much better condition than she did. But that didn't mean much. There were quite a few oil-rich Texans who were too tight fisted to buy themselves a decent meal, much less clothes or a car. But she had a feeling he was telling the truth.

She shrugged. ''All right. We'll let it go, but it wasn't my fault.''

''Mine, either.''

''All right. It wasn't anyone's fault. Happy now?''

''I'd be a whole lot happier if you'd come have a drink with me in the drugstore.''

''No, thanks. I don't have time.''

''What's your name, anyway?''

''There's no need for—''

''Hey, aren't you the woman who moved into the old Squire place? You don't live too far from me. Sorry, I never met you before, but I don't socialize much.''

''Neither do I.''

''Let's see. Name's Sunny, isn't it? Sunny Hansen. I remember because it sounded happy.''

''Happy. That's me, all right.'' She was horrified that her name had spread around the community, but she supposed it was something that couldn't be helped.

''I say something wrong?''

''No. It's nothing. Look, I've got to be going.''

30

"Maybe I'll stop by sometime to be neighborly."

"I'm really in a rush so if you'll just back up, I'll leave. You can have the parking place."

"All right, but there's plenty more besides that one."

"I know," Sunny said, surprised she could still joke, then slid behind the wheel.

Just before she started the engine, Billy Joe called, "Might stop by sometime."

She turned the switch and gunned the engine.

Billy Joe got into his pickup and backed up.

Sunny drove quickly out of town, thinking that the last thing she needed was for some lonely cowboy to come sniffing around her. Men were not high on her popularity list, and this one hadn't helped his situation by running into her poor little Bug.

Muttering to herself, she pushed the man from her mind and thought of a long afternoon nap.

2

Sunny gave up trying to nap around five. She was tired, but too tense to do anything about it. For some reason the car out on FM 203 the night before had really set her mind to spinning about Dan, and she couldn't see to stop it. Miriam's talk about evil hadn't helped any, either.

She laced up her hightop running shoes, an extravagance leftover from her Dallas days, latched the Velcro tabs, then picked up her oak walking stick. It was late for a walk, but the sun wouldn't set for several more hours, and she should be safe in the woods around her house. Normally, she didn't have much fear about taking a long walk, but after last night she felt a little uneasy.

She carefully locked the back door, then let the screen bang shut. Slipping the key into the pouch on her right shoe, she hit her favorite trail. She inhaled the scent of evergreen, feeling pine needles cushion her feet, and thought about the bugs that were thick in the forest. Chiggers, spiders, and other crawlers wouldn't bother her much so long as she stayed on the path.

But mosquitoes were a different matter. Miriam had taught her to deal with them by not eating sugar. For some reason, the lack of sugar made humans less tantalizing to mosquito palates. Since she couldn't afford much sugar anyway, she'd gotten used to relying on wild blackberries as an inexpensive sweet treat. She'd even frozen some for winter.

As she walked, sweat began to bead her forehead. The temperature hovered around a hundred degrees, and the humidity was high. But she wasn't going to think about the heat, or anything else for that matter, except her favorite blackberry patch.

With Miriam's help, she'd watched the blackberry bushes begin blooming in the early spring. First there'd been white flowers, which became green, then orange, red, and finally black. The berries came in varieties, first the dewberries, then finally the last in the heat of the summer, blackberries. She'd found they were all good, and had watched the progression of the season by their growth.

Following a narrow trail, she reached the patch, pulled several ripe ones off a shrub, careful to avoid the orange and black wasps who had built a nest in its center. She could have killed the insects, but preferred to leave them alive since she'd developed a reverence for life after moving to the country and didn't want to kill anything unless it was potentially deadly to her.

After eating the fruit and staining her fingers and lips blue, Sunny turned onto a little-used oil road that led to a sludge pit. She periodically checked the pit, just to see how badly it was encroaching on the land around it. She hated to see the land poisoned and killed now, just as much as she hated to see animals hurt or killed.

She had changed. Living in the woods and hearing Miriam's tales of the forest and its creatures had made her feel akin to them. Like Miriam, she had taken to putting out birdseed. It meant she ate a little less, but the singing of the birds near her home always cheered her and made her feel less lonely.

The day was so hot the oil road had softened and her running shoes sank into the surface, leaving a patterned trail behind her. There was no doubt the back roads crisscrossing East Texas were good. Sunny had learned that oil and dirt were combined, making a thick mixture, then poured and smoothed over a leveled surface. It made a road strong enough to support oil industry rigs, construction crews, and maintenance vehicles in most weather.

Although she knew how important the oil industry was to the area's economy, she still wished the land hadn't been so badly scarred by pumping huge quantities of oil and gas out of it.

The heat of the oil road sent hot shafts through the soles of her shoes into her feet. She continued to walk, but as she neared the sludge pit, the heat grew so intense she finally had to step off the road under the shade of a tree.

While waiting for her feet to cool, she wiped the sweat from her brow and fanned away the tiny insects buzzing around her face. Glancing down, she noticed that thick white foam clung to a tall grass stalk, and remembered Miriam laughingly telling her she'd thought it was snake spit when she was a child. What it really was, Sunny still didn't know. Snake spit was probably more interesting than the truth, anyway.

When her feet had cooled some, she resumed walking. She wasn't far from the sludge pit now. She glanced up. It was a beautiful day. The sky was a clear blue with puffy, white thunderheads. Tall, green pines towered overhead, and the scent of wildflowers filled the air.

She passed a pumping oil well and came to the sludge pit that lay like a black hole of pestilence, surrounded by nature's beauty and bounty. Dead, blackened hulks of trees rose from its center. Oil slicks glistened and undulated over the dark surface. Flies swarmed everywhere, and the land radiating several yards out from the pit was dark and diseased, tainted and twisted.

But it didn't seem to have spread. That relieved Sunny. No more land to be gobbled up by the sludge monster. She almost chuckled at that thought. It reminded her of the comics she'd read when she was younger. Monsters. No monsters here. Except the human variety. And those you couldn't control.

She walked nearer the pit, but didn't get too close. There was no point in getting oily muck on the bottoms of her shoes. As she stared at the black pool, she could hear the oil well she'd passed pumping in the background, over and over, endlessly sucking the oil out of the earth. Pump. Pump. Pump.

She glanced over the black surface of the pit, then let her eyes travel to the edge near her. Everything looked normal. Then she hesitated and looked closer.

There seemed to be a face under the water, with open, staring eyes.

She stepped back, blinked, then looked again. Now there only seemed to be dark water. She started to step closer for a better look, then decided against it. There was no point in messing up her shoes for nothing. There simply couldn't have been a face under the water. It was just a trick of the light, or her imagination working overtime.

She turned away and started walking back toward the pumping well. She needed some rest. A good night's sleep and there would be no more faces in sludge pits. She re-traced her steps on the oil road, noticing the pattern of her shoes now paralleled, coming and going.

It was hard to forget the face as she walked back toward her house. For a moment it had seemed so real, but she had to have imagined it. Maybe if she concentrated on other things, the face would go away.

But hours later, it hadn't. Sunny lay in bed, listening to the feeble attempts of the air-conditioner trying to cool her room. It didn't help much, as usual, and sweat trickled between her breasts and ran down her sides.

But it was more than the heat of the room making her sweat. She couldn't forget what she'd seen in the sludge pit that afternoon.

She shivered, despite the warmth, and wished for the hundredth time that she could forget that face. But it wouldn't go away, and she'd finally remembered something. The face hadn't been her own reflection or her imagination imposing her own features on the surface of the water. The face had belonged to a stranger—a woman.

She shivered again. Who or what was in the water of the sludge pit?

That was something she didn't want to think about, and had been trying not to think about for hours. Turning over, she glanced at the illuminated face of her alarm clock. 1:45 A.M.

She was exhausted. She needed desperately to sleep if she was going to work the next day, but she couldn't. The woman's face was haunting her.

Finally, she threw back the covers, snapped on the lamp beside the bed, and sat up. She had to still her mind. Somehow she had to stop the thoughts. She got up and paced back and forth across the room several times.

What if someone had been murdered? And the body had been dumped in the sludge pit?

Then she thought of Dan. What if he found her, killed her, and hid her body in the sludge pit? She felt renewed terror gnaw at her. If there was a woman in the pit, it could just as easily have been her. She could be walking through the woods, and Dan could jump out, covering her mouth so she couldn't scream for help, not that there would be anyone near enough to hear. Then he could do whatever he wanted with her, maybe even rape her before strangling her, knifing her, or shooting her.

She paced faster, the images more real, more vivid than she could ever have thought possible. She didn't want to think about dead women or Dan, but she had to. She had to know the truth. If there was a dead woman in that pit, she had to find out. It could be vital to her own safety and to that of other women in the area.

Of course, she knew she was being irrational, even paranoid, and she had good reason. Six months before, Dan had beaten her so badly he would have killed her if a neighbor hadn't interrupted. And she had yet to get over the terror of that one moment when she realized death was so close.

One night a year ago, after Dan lost his job, he had gotten drunk and come home and hit her, spoiling for a fight, wanting to smash and hurt. The verbal abuse had been horrible. He'd deliberately tried to destroy her confidence, her ability to deal with her job and her friends. And he'd continued undermining her spirit, adding more and more physical punishment to the mental abuse. Once, he'd even raped her.

For a long time she'd remembered the love and the good times, hoping he'd change, until finally all her feelings were dead, and she had run for her life. But if Dan found her, he'd kill her, and she could end up dead in a sludge pit.

Suddenly she couldn't ignore the question that had plagued her since leaving Dallas. Would Dan finally find her hiding place and finish his game of toying with her life?

She shivered again, then tried to convince herself that her imagination was working overtime. She was safe. She had been for six months.

Jerking open her closet door, she pulled on faded jeans and a black T-shirt. She decided to put on a pair of old boots instead of her expensive running shoes, since she didn't want to chance ruining them.

Hardly able to believe her decision, she strode into the kitchen. It was ridiculous even to contemplate going back to the sludge pit at night alone. But she knew she'd never sleep unless she proved to herself that the woman's face had been some sort of reflection in the water, or just a product of her imagination, spawned by thoughts of Dan.

Shaking her head at her own folly, she grabbed a flashlight from a kitchen cabinet, then let herself out the back door, locking it behind her. She turned on the flashlight, flicked the pale light over the trail she'd taken earlier, then started down it. She walked rapidly, knowing her way and not wanting anything to distract or impede her.

To fill her mind while she walked, she thought of what she planned to begin the next day. She wanted to do some new drawings for a portfolio that would be good enough to show to New York illustration agents. It was the first time in six months she'd felt able to do more than just the hardware art necessary to survive.

Since the night before she'd felt as if she hadn't run far enough away from Dallas, but the money she was making on hardware illustrations wasn't enough to take her anywhere else. She'd have to make a lot more money in order to move across the country, leaving no trail behind. Then maybe she could get Dan and sludge pits and dead faces out of her mind.

She'd hate to leave Miriam, but she didn't want to get her involved in some deadly game, either. It'd be safer for them all if she moved. She only hoped she was good enough to attract the attention of a New York agency. Although she'd have to be prepared for rejection, she would give it her best shot. She'd start the new illustrations as soon as she got some rest. But to do that, she first had to visit the sludge pit.

Walking faster, she flicked the flashlight back and forth across the trail. All seemed peaceful. But still her skin prickled with anticipation, and her heart beat fast.

She left the woods for the blacktop road, and turned off her flashlight. She could see fairly well in the waxing moonlight, and there shouldn't be anything on the road to trip her. The blacktop was still soft from the day's heat, and she could feel the heels of her scuffed cowboy boots sinking into the surface as she walked. But tomorrow her footprints wouldn't be there, for the hot road always leveled out again.

Her boots were well past their prime, reminders of the days when she had first met Dan, and they had gone out to the Longhorn Ballroom, the bastion of country-western dancing to big-name bands in Dallas. But Dan had ruined dancing for her, since you needed a partner to two-step, and a partner she didn't want.

She came to the oil derrick and watched its black back pump up and down for a while. For some reason, she felt reluctant to continue on to the pit. There could be snakes, or spiders, or any number of other creatures, but the sludge pit didn't attract much, and it killed everything it touched. Rationally, she knew that, and yet she felt fear curl in her stomach.

She looked back over her shoulder, but couldn't see anything. A chill ran through her. She suddenly felt terribly alone. The sound of the oil well pumping should have comforted her, reminding her that humans had left their mark here. But it didn't.

Nevertheless, she wouldn't let fear overcome her. She had worked hard to hang on to what little she had left of her life. She wouldn't let wild fears take over now. Resolutely, she passed the oil well, walking through its long, menacing shadow toward the sludge pit.

She stopped. The pit looked almost pretty. Moonlight reflected off its dark surface invitingly, attracting fireflies who occasionally plunged to their doom in its dark depths.

Taking a deep breath, she moved closer, feeling her boots slide into oily dirt. She turned on her flashlight. It reflected nothing but dark water.

She took several steps closer, tried the light again. Nothing. Frustrated, she looked behind her, feeling as if something or someone was sneaking up on her, but still saw nothing. She stepped right to the edge, then suddenly feared being pushed in, or dragged under its surface.

Taking a firm grip on her emotions, she crouched down, hoping she'd be less likely to fall in and perhaps could finally see into its depths. As she kneeled, her weight shifted and a long tree branch pushed up out of the water. With it came a pale hand which slowly rose from the surface, straight at Sunny's face.

She screamed, a ragged sound that cut through the quiet night to carry deep into the surrounding forest, then clamped down on her lower lip. Anyone could be listening. She was unable to look away from the hand which she could now see was attached to an arm, beads of oil dripping slowly off the transparent fabric clinging to it.

In a panic she tried to get away, lost her balance, slipped, slid, one foot splashing into the water, knocking against the body, dislodging it.

As the entire body popped to the surface, Sunny screamed again and started to slide toward the inert form. She desperately clutched at the bank, but her fingers slid through the grimy dirt. She reached again, panting, and found a heavy tree limb. Grabbing it, she finally stopped her descent.

Half in the sludge pit, feeling the oily water soak through her jeans clear to her hips, she felt horror rise in her. Her legs were under the body, now bloated, swollen, slick, and dark with oil, but still recognizable as a woman.

Sunny gagged, cut off a scream, then tried to scramble out of the pool, slipped, and slid farther down until the syrupy sludge extended to her waist. She realized she was in danger of drowning, and there was no help nearby. If she died, she might not be found for days, or maybe never.

Was that what had happened to the woman floating nearer and nearer to her?

Sunny fought her fear. She was not going to die, not here, not now, not like this other woman. Feeling the water slowly start to overtake her, she clutched at the tree limb and pulled. Her hands, now black with slick muck, slipped, but she clawed at the branch again and again until finally she crawled out of the pit onto the bank and collapsed.

Her heart thudding painfully and her mind whirling, she knew she had to do something about the dead woman. But

40

she didn't want to go to the police. There'd be too many questions, too much attention, and the news media was sure to get involved, all of which could lead Dan straight to her.

Had the woman simply drowned? She found that hard to believe. Few people came here, and it wasn't likely they'd get close enough to fall in the pit and accidently drown. It looked like murder, and if she didn't go to the authorities with her information, another woman might be killed, even her.

Suddenly she struggled to her feet, feeling renewed terror pulsing through her. She had to get away. What if the murderer was watching? She couldn't be more alone or vulnerable.

She stopped thinking and began to move, purely on instinct. Crouching low, she ran from the sludge pit into the forest, listening for any strange sounds. She heard nothing except the pumping of the oil well.

But that didn't mean she was alone.

3

When she could run no more, Sunny stopped and leaned against the trunk of a tall pine, her breath ragged, sweat dripping down her face. She didn't know where she was in the woods; she had just run blindly, perhaps even in circles.

Now she was beginning to feel rational again. She had found a dead woman, but that didn't mean she was being watched. It was just an accident she had found the body in the sludge pit.

She fought for control, breathing deeply until her heart slowed. There was no need to panic. She would be calm, cool, collected. Pushing away from the tree, she stood straight and brushed her damp hair back from her face.

It was dark in the woods, and she suddenly realized she had lost her flashlight. But that was all right. She could pick it up later, or do without it forever. Right now, she needed to deal with the body she'd found.

As she stepped away from the tree, she thought she heard the sound of an automobile engine. Surprised, she stopped and listened more closely. Yes. A car was getting nearer, coming down FM 203. But that was strange. It was so late. Suddenly she remembered the automobile she'd heard the night before and Miriam's words about evil.

She chewed on her lower lip. There was no need to be

frightened or to think this car had anything to do with the one she'd heard the previous night, and certainly no need to think it had anything to do with Dan, or the dead woman.

The automobile slowed, and turned down the blacktop road toward the pit.

Sunny felt chilled. It was strictly coincidence. There could be several rational reasons for someone to be using the blacktop late at night. It was just hard to think of any, especially since it dead-ended at the sludge pit. An oil and gas analyst wouldn't be checking the pumping well at night. Maybe young lovers seeking a quiet spot?

Or had someone heard her loud flight from the pit? Had someone been watching the area? Did they know she was still nearby? Were they coming for her?

No. She would not let her mind run wild.

By the sound of the car, she realized she'd run in circles and was still near the oil road. Just to prove how wild her thoughts had been and that her fear was totally unfounded, she decided to watch the automobile. Whoever was in it had been too far away to have heard her running through the woods earlier, anyway.

She edged toward the noise of the engine as it purred closer.

Headlights splashed bright light through the trees as the automobile made its way slowly down the road. Sunny ducked as the lights passed her, then edged toward the car, staying hidden by the woods and undergrowth.

The car stopped near the oil well. The engine died, the driver's door clicked open, the inside light came on briefly, then darkened as someone stepped out and shut the door. Moonlight illuminated the tall shape of a man wearing an overcoat.

A coat in July? Sunny shivered. Wrong. All wrong. She remained very quiet, wishing she had been able to see more when the car's interior light had come on. But it had been too quick, and there had been too much shadow to make out any details of the person's appearance.

The man walked around the back of the car to the passenger's side.

Sunny felt a surge of relief, realizing nothing was wrong. He simply had a sick passenger and had decided to find a quiet spot where the person could recover peacefully. They might need help. She started to step from the trees to offer assistance.

The man opened the door. The dim interior light came on. There was no movement inside. No sound. Then he leaned down and lifted a limp form in his arms. When he straightened, he obviously held a woman, skirt pulled high around bare legs and long blond hair flowing free. Then he pushed the car door shut with a foot.

Sunny crammed a fist in her mouth to keep from crying out. Another body! No wait. Maybe it was just someone who was sick. But Sunny didn't move to offer help. She held her breath, and waited.

The man carried the inert form down the blacktop toward the sludge pit.

Suddenly Sunny tried to remember how she'd left the pit. Was the dead woman still floating on the surface, or had she slipped back into the watery depths when Sunny had pulled herself free?

Or perhaps her mind was making all of this up. Maybe in a moment she'd awaken and be safely in her own bed. But when she heard the splash of water, she knew she wasn't asleep. She knew she was witnessing a terrible crime. She knew the man had not been aiding a sick woman, but disposing of a dead or wounded one. If only she could have seen more in the car's feeble light, but the man had been all dark shapes and shadows.

Then she realized there was nothing she could do to help the hurt woman. She was no match for the man's size, she

44

had no weapon, not even a flashlight. Yet something had to be done.

She heard the gurgle of water as the body was pushed under and felt sick. She swallowed hard, tried to keep the nausea down, and saw the man walking back toward her. She only hoped she was concealed by the dense brush, or that he was very sure of himself and not expecting an audience. If he didn't see her, she might be able to get to the woman in time after he'd left.

But he was observant, swinging his head from side to side as he quietly strode down the road. Moonlight cast him in black and silver relief, but revealed no details. Sunny could only tell that he had short hair and a large build.

When he stopped by the driver's side of his car, he looked back down the road toward the sludge pit. Then he opened the door, and quickly got in, shutting the door firmly behind him. A moment later the engine purred to life and he backed out, the lights of his car spotlighting the oil well as it pumped back and forth, drawing out the lifeblood of the earth.

Sunny didn't breathe again until the car had turned onto FM 203 and roared away. She took a deep breath and dashed for the sludge pit. If the woman was still alive, she might have a chance to save her. She ran down the road since it was quicker, but kept looking back over her shoulder because now she was completely exposed, and if the man had returned once, he might again.

She hurried to the edge of the pit, sliding in her haste, grabbing a tree limb to stop her descent, then looking desperately into the water. She couldn't see anything. She glanced hastily around for her flashlight, but couldn't find it.

If the woman was still alive, she had to be saved quickly. But Sunny couldn't see her. The woman was probably unconscious, trapped under the surface. Gritting her teeth, Sunny kneeled and bent over the oil-slick water, then plunged both hands into its depths. She shuddered as small slimy objects slid past her hands, but endured the horror as she groped in the muck. She had almost lost hope when she finally touched fabric. Clutching it, she pulled.

A body bobbed up, floating free, and the form of a young woman streaked with oil emerged. Sunny felt sick, and swallowed convulsively as she slowly pulled the limp form to shore. In the moonlight she could see it wasn't the body she'd found earlier, but the woman with long blond hair.

Although Sunny couldn't detect any sign of life, she pulled the body onto the bank, knelt over the young face, then noticed the terrible dark marks around the woman's throat. Strangled. But perhaps still alive?

The body was still warm. Hope against all hope, Sunny pried open the woman's lips, closed the nostrils, then began giving artificial respiration, desperately ignoring the acrid taste of oil in her mouth. Over and over she repeated the process. Inhale. Exhale. Inhale. Exhale. Until finally she had to admit that life was gone from the woman she held.

Hot tears came then, cascading down her cheeks onto the dead woman's face. Maybe she had somehow hoped she could atone for her personal fears, for Dan's destructiveness, or a crime against nature by saving this woman. But it was not to be. There was no salvation, only death.

After a time, she closed the woman's mouth, tried to clean some of the greasy oil from her face, then realized what she was doing and stopped. There was nothing she could do, and what if she was found with a dead woman? What if she went to the police and told them she'd found two dead bodies in the sludge pit?

The publicity could alert Dan to her whereabouts, and she could end up in the sludge pit just like these two women. She shuddered, revolted at the thought of the killings. Inhaling sharply, she faced death alone, seeing it, touching it, wanting somehow to comfort the dead woman she still held.

46

But there was no reaching the young woman, and abruptly she realized she was trying to help an empty husk.

Suddenly she stood up and stepped back from the body. Profound shudders shook her, tears stung her eyes, and she looked around, as if there was some help to be had, someone to right the wrong. But there was nothing, nobody, just darkness, quiet, and her.

She looked back down at the body. The woman could so easily be her. If they exchanged places, the dead woman would be standing here, mourning as she was. But still they would be caught, trapped, in the same web. One dead, one alive, and yet their lives entwined, separated by so little. She shook her head, knowing she must be rational, not fanciful. And yet she could be the one lying so still, so silent. Dead.

What was she going to do? She ran over her options quickly. If she went to the police, she would have to request her name be kept confidential. That would mean explaining to total strangers, probably men, much of the sordid details for the last six months of her marriage to Dan. And if they agreed to keep her name anonymous, could they? Once the news media learned of the murders, they would be desperate for more information. Top security files could be breached. The idea of her name, maybe even her picture, splashed over the front pages of newspapers or TV screens terrified her.

Maybe she could get a protective court order to keep Dan from coming near her, but how many women had been found dead with just such protection? Besides, that would require time, plus lawyers, judges, and courts. Could she expect constant police protection? She didn't think so. Anyway, that would call even more attention to her, as if walking into a police station wouldn't expose her face enough.

Shivering, she glanced down, her thoughts returning to the first victim. She still didn't know if the body had been visible when the murderer arrived. If it had been, had he pushed it back down, along with the new body? And if he had, did he think it had surfaced naturally? Or did he suspect someone had discovered the evidence of his crime?

No. She didn't think the murderer would have dumped the second body if he'd thought his hiding place had been found. She breathed a sigh of relief. Then caught her breath. Perhaps he had suspected and left the second as bait? She glanced around uneasily. Something had to be done. The man must be stopped. If he had killed two, he might kill more.

Yet what could she do?

She could push the second body back into the sludge pit. It would give her time to think of a plan, something that didn't involve her. She hated to do that to the poor dead woman—the pit was a terrible place—but she couldn't just leave the body lying out to be found by anyone, perhaps a child, or to alert the killer if he returned.

Slowly she began to drag the corpse toward the water. The body splashed over the edge, repeating the same sound the murderer had made when he had tossed the woman into the pit. What if someone was watching her? What would they think? She'd be the guilty one then. No. She wouldn't think that way, wouldn't turn around and look behind her. She was buying time. That was all.

She used the heavy limb to push the body under. At first the dead woman wouldn't sink, and she had to push again and again, her stomach churning with every movement of the tree branch. Finally, when the body caught on something and stayed submerged, she threw the limb down and ran for the woods. She threw up in a clump of bushes, then couldn't get the taste of bile out of her mouth, or the smell of death and oil out of her nostrils.

Finally, she stood up, brushed back her short hair and faced the sludge pit again. She had to cover her tracks if there were any. She walked back to the pit and smoothed down the churned up dirt, splashed oily water over it, then tried to make it look natural by scoring it with the tree branch. It looked fairly normal in the moonlight. By day, she had no idea how it would appear.

Then she remembered her flashlight. If the police got involved, it could be used as evidence. She had to find it. Glancing around, she didn't see it near the pit. She must have dropped it in the woods. Using a tree branch, she began to destroy any footprints she might have left as she made her way to the forest. Again she looked for the flashlight, but it was too dark under the trees to see much. She'd have to come back the next day and find it.

But for now the flashlight wasn't her main concern. She needed to get away from there. The killer might come back anytime. But she didn't want to go home. She couldn't stand the idea of being alone, and she needed to talk to somebody. There was only one person she trusted. Miriam. She was usually awake at night, and she was smart. Besides, Miriam had told her to come by if there was any trouble, and this catastrophe certainly qualified.

Sunny glanced one last time at the sludge pit. It looked calm and peaceful, even pretty in the soft, silver moonlight. Then she headed down the trail toward Miriam's house.

4

Reverend Isaiah Mulhaney watched his flock make their way to their cars, a benign expression on his face. He hoped they had truly understood his message this Wednesday night. He did not mean for the men to go home and beat their wives and children. But women were the root of all evil. It said so in the Good Book. Therefore, they must be counseled and taught to obey men so they would not sin any further or corrupt their children, especially their daughters.

Girls had to be taught piety and servility early in life, or they could easily be led astray by the devil. If that happened, they had to be punished, and no man wanted to punish his wife or daughter. However, in some cases it was the sole way to their salvation, and if salvation could only be acquired with a rod, then a little pain was better than eternal damnation.

Reverend Mulhaney smiled to himself. Yes, he felt sure his flock had understood. He noticed one of the fathers swat a little girl on her bare legs as he coaxed her into their station wagon. The Reverend nodded sagely. Yes, they had taken his message to heart. Spare the rod and spoil the child, especially the girls.

He locked the front doors, then walked back through his

church, turning out the lights, checking the lilac carpet for stains or dirt. Then he picked up his well-worn black leather Bible from the pulpit. At the back door, he gazed proudly over the church he had built for his Father, then turned out the lights.

Outside, the two oil wells pumped steadily. He paused, watching their humped backs move up and down, up and down, then glanced up at the heavens. He thought of God, the stern Father who would not hesitate to discipline his naughty children if they needed to learn the error of their ways. Yes, his sermon had been divinely inspired.

Stars twinkled in the clear night sky, and the moon shone its silvery light down on his beautiful church. He felt sure his heavenly Father was well-pleased with him. It had not been easy bringing this church into being and this congregation together, but he had done it and felt sure God understood and accepted the necessary sacrifices.

Still smiling, he entered his parsonage, thinking of a cup of tea warmed by a little medicinal brandy. After such a fiery sermon, he needed help relaxing, and he felt certain God understood that, too.

Much later he was awakened by the ringing of the telephone. His head felt fuzzy as he pushed himself upright in the big easy chair where he had fallen asleep. He must have added more brandy than he had realized to the tea. As he picked up the phone, he checked his watch. The time was just after 2:00 A.M. It was already Thursday morning. He felt stiff and cramped from having slept in the chair so long.

"Hello. Reverend Mulhaney speaking." His voice was thick with sleep.

"Reverend, I had to call and tell you what a powerful sermon you gave tonight. I heard it on the radio."

"Thank you. It was inspired by God," the Reverend replied, trying to feel meek, but not succeeding very well. He was thrilled to know that the money he had recently decided to spend on broadcasting his sermons over a local

AM stereo station selling airtime cheap to stay alive in the market was paying off. If he developed a strong enough following, he might soon be on television.

"Fact is, I first heard you speak Sunday night, and I've been thinking of your words ever since. I almost called you last night, and after your sermon tonight, I couldn't wait. You've inspired me to stay in the area."

"I am glad to know you were touched, my son. Will you come to our church next Sunday?"

"I'd like that. I hope I can 'cause I think we're a lot alike. You know, I've had to discipline my own women."

"To keep them from evil ways?"

"Yes. And tonight I need some advice."

"I am always ready to help one of God's children in need, but I could be of more service to you if you would come to the parsonage. Over tea, we could discuss whatever it is that concerns you."

"The phone'll do for now, Reverend. I just want some guidance. Sometimes I can't remember so good anymore."

"You should see a specialist then. A doctor. I could recommend someone."

"No! I need spiritual help."

"What is your name?"

"Doesn't matter. Names don't matter. It's what a man does that counts. Isn't that right?"

"Yes. God will judge a man by his actions."

"What was it you said in your sermon tonight about girls and the devil?"

"I spoke on the necessity of guiding our children correctly, of making them see the error of their ways, especially girls who can be so easily misled by the devil."

"That's right, Reverend. I learned that good. You have to punish evil, don't you? You've got to weed out the bad from the good. Right?"

"That is correct. Do you have children?"

"No. But I know about the evil in women. You have to take control sometimes and save them from themselves."

"Yes, but it is better in God's eyes if an ordained minister handles problems like these. If you know someone who needs guidance, please bring her to me, and I will be happy to counsel her."

"You're a good man, Reverend. If I meet a bad woman, I'll try to put her on the right road. But sometimes they're stubborn about their badness."

"That is the devil speaking through them. They are more susceptible to the devil than men, and so we are the rightful ones to help them if they become possessed."

"That's what I've always thought. But sometimes it's hard to make a woman realize the devil's in her. How can I help them if they don't want it?"

"I know what you mean. It is a problem, but I am trained to handle situations like that. You could bring the woman to me, if she was willing. I would be more than happy to counsel her," the Reverend offered.

"What if it took more than counseling?"

"What do you mean?"

"Well, sometimes they won't listen to reason."

"I understand. In that case, you do your best, and it is all you can do," Reverend Mulhaney stated firmly.

"Right. You do your best to cleanse them, and God will understand."

"Yes, that is right. God always understands."

"Thank you, Reverend. I knew you could help me."

"I am glad, my son. Is there anything else?"

"Not now."

"Call again if you need me, or call and we can discuss the scriptures."

"Thanks. I'll do that. I wish I could talk longer, but I've got to go now. I'm feeling tired, and I've got to find a place to sleep."

"You mean you are without a home?" the Reverend asked, anxiety lacing his voice.

"I'm out of work right now, but I'm looking. Something'll turn up."

"You poor man. So many in need of God's help. Perhaps I could find a place for you to stay among my flock."

"That's okay, Reverend. I'll make it. Got to go now."

"I will pray for you . . ."

But the phone went dead before the phrase was finished, and Reverend Mulhaney carefully replaced the receiver as the man on the other end hung up and looked around. He had used a pay phone at a closed filling station just north of Gusher.

The moon was riding high in the sky. It was getting late. He stared down at his hands. They were smudged with oil, and he looked around in confusion. He didn't remember fixing a flat, or changing oil, or even getting gas, but he must have. As he'd told the minister, he didn't always remember so good anymore.

But he didn't want to leave the phone dirty from his hands, so he pulled out a white handkerchief and carefully wiped it clean.

Then he glanced down at his car. He couldn't remember where he'd gotten it. Probably some woman gave it to him. They were always coming on to him, dirty little sluts. If he'd do what it took to make them wet, they'd give him things, anything he wanted. But it was dirty business. He hated their nasty bodies, always trying to suck him up into them and devour him. But they paid. He always made them pay.

He didn't like the car. Didn't want it. There was something dirty and evil about it, and he had to stay clean. That was most important. Being clean. Women were dirty. Bad. Men were clean. Good. It was that simple.

Using the handkerchief, he carefully wiped at one hand then the other, but the oil stains wouldn't budge. Horrified, he rubbed harder until the skin turned red, then hot, but the stains remained.

He thought of getting the oil off with gasoline, but the tank was almost empty. He began rubbing again, horror growing in him. He had to get clean. The world had to be cleansed, and he couldn't do that without clean hands.

Finally, he got in the car and left the door open so the interior light would stay on. He opened the glove compartment and found a small, red utility knife. He pulled out a blade, checked its edge, nodded in satisfaction, then slowly began scraping the stained skin from his hands. It was fairly easy on the right hand since he was left-handed, but harder on the left, and he left a ragged, bloody mess when he was done.

He grinned in satisfaction, wiped off the knife, closed it, then tucked it in a pocket. The job had been painful, of course, and now his hands stung, but it had been worth the pain, for he felt clean again. However, he didn't like to see blood because it reminded him of women. He closed his hands into fists, hiding the wounds.

He hadn't originally known blood was dirty, but when he'd learned that women leaked it once a month, he had discovered the truth. Dirty women. Dirty blood. The worst of it was a man never knew when a woman was bleeding. She kept it secret just so she could surprise him. Dirty. Disgusting. He'd been looking a long time for the best way to cleanse women, and it seemed like he'd finally found it. Only he couldn't remember it right now, but it'd come back to him. The good things always did.

He didn't recognize anything in the car. He felt slightly sick when he noticed lipstick-stained tissues on the dashboard. It reminded him of blood, of women, of dirt. Had he let a woman in his car?

He couldn't remember for sure, but it seemed like there might have been some slow-talking woman from Louisiana. She'd stopped on the interstate to give him a ride, but he'd known that wasn't the kind of ride she'd really wanted to give him. So he'd . . . but he couldn't remember now. She'd been dirty. He must have cleansed her. That would have been the godly thing to do.

The good Reverend would agree with that. He liked Reverend Isaiah Mulhaney. He was a good man, a learned man who reminded him of his own father. Right now he couldn't remember his father, but he must have been like the Reverend.

He would join Reverend Mulhaney's church sometime soon, but first he wanted to get really clean, find a place to live, and get a good job. When he was presentable, he would go to the reverend, and they could become better friends and discuss wonderful passages from the Bible. He looked forward to that.

But for now he didn't want the car. He'd just leave it for somebody needy. The Reverend would like that, knowing he had helped some poor soul. But he'd clean it up first. He wouldn't want to leave it dirty.

In the small pool of light inside the car, he very carefully began going over the interior, feeling deep in the cushions for any stray material, using his handkerchief to wipe every single inch inside the car, being careful not to bloody anything, then he turned his efforts to the outside.

But he needed something bigger than a handkerchief. He noticed he was wearing a dark overcoat, but it was too big to use. He carefully laid it aside, glad he had something so nice to keep him warm on cold nights. It seemed like he was cold a lot. Then he took off his shirt. It was just the right size.

He spent a long time meticulously shining the car. When he was done it gave him a great sense of satisfaction. The car looked almost new. Then he glanced at his shirt, saw its dirty condition and sadly shook his head. It would be terrible to put so much dirt against his body, but it was sinful to show your flesh. He hesitated, then slowly slipped on the shirt, shrinking from contact with the dirty material. He covered it up with his overcoat, tucking his dirty handkerchief in a pocket.

Satisfied that the car was clean and he was covered, he glanced down at his hands. Somehow he'd gotten dirt ground into the jagged cuts. He felt sad. It was so hard to keep clean. He'd have to find someplace to wash up, but not anywhere his naked flesh could be seen.

Unclean, ugly, and tainted, the body had been made from woman and was forever damned. It should never be shown. He kept his own covered except when he bathed or was forced by dirty women to expose it to their lust.

He shuddered at the thought of revealing his flesh, then glanced back at the car. He smiled, well-pleased. The clean, late-model Plymouth was his gift to a needy person. If the price was a soiled shirt, he would pay that price, knowing the Lord loved a man who helped others.

In the meantime he would take a walk through the countryside, find a job and some clean clothes, then he would call Reverend Mulhaney again.

Whistling softly, he started down the road.

5

As Sunny walked through the woods toward Miriam's house, for the moment faced with no new horror, the terrible reality of her situation began to sink in. Her legs felt weak. Her head thumped painfully. She wanted desperately to run away to a safe place, someplace where she would never have to deal with the pain of life again. But she couldn't do that, and knew it.

Bugs buzzed around her face, attracted by the oil sludge all over her. She absently waved them away, then realized how she must look. She tried to wipe some of the oily muck off her face, but couldn't tell if it did any good. She combed her fingers through her hair and drew out oil-coated twigs. Running her hands down the front of her T-shirt to straighten it, she realized just how awful she looked and smelled. Like some sludge monster.

But this time she didn't laugh at that thought. Sludge monsters had suddenly become very real, and she didn't want to scare Miriam, coming out of the woods in the middle of the night looking like this.

Continuing down the path, she listened for any unusual sounds, anything that might indicate she had been followed or that someone was lurking nearby. But the night seemed calm and peaceful. Here, it was hard to believe what she had just seen at the sludge pit. Here, the world seemed normal. Maybe she could forget it all and go on about her business. Then maybe it would all go away.

But she knew she was kidding herself, knew it had come to her, all the fears and frustrations finally combining in one awful experience, forcing her to confront her own terrors. She knew she couldn't let any more women be killed if she could help it, couldn't let any others be as terrified as she had been of Dan. Somehow she had to stop and fight, but she didn't know if she had the strength. No, she knew she didn't. She had to have help from someone older, wiser, and stronger. Miriam.

Thoughts of her friend coincided with a view of Miriam's back yard. Sunny stopped at the edge of the forest, suddenly hesitant. She no longer felt safe simply walking up to the house. What if the killer had been there?

She trembled, then scoffed at the idea. Miriam was fine. The only thing she had to worry about was not surprising her friend. There were no lights on in the house, none on the back porch, either. But that didn't mean Miriam was asleep. She was frequently up at night. Then there was a flicker of light on the back porch and Sunny smiled, relief washing over her.

Miriam had just lit her pipe. She was awake. Help was near. With that thought, all the braveness seemed to seep out of Sunny, and she felt like a child who wanted to run and bury her head in her mother's lap so that all her hurts and ills would be healed. She started to step forward, then remembered her appearance. She mustn't scare Miriam.

So instead of running to the safety of the back porch, Sunny cautiously called, "Miriam."

There was no response.

"Miriam," she called louder.

Still no answer.

"Miriam, it's me, Sunny!" she yelled.

"Sakes alive, child, come on up here. What are you doing out in the woods this time of night?"

"Miriam, I've had an accident and I wanted to warn—"

"I'll be right there."

"No. I'm all right. I just wanted to warn you I'm covered in oil."

"Oil! Just a minute."

Sunny walked into the backyard. Soft yellow light suddenly illuminated the back porch as Miriam lit a kerosene lantern, then hurried down the stairs.

"I'm filthy," Sunny said, stepping back from Miriam's outstretched arms.

"What happened? Are you sure you're okay?"

"Yes, but it's a long story."

"I was afraid something bad would happen and afraid you'd be involved. But don't worry, we'll take care of it together. Come on up to the house."

"Miriam, I'm not going in. I'd track oil all over the place, and you'd never get it off."

"Sit down then on the steps if you won't come in the house." Miriam picked up her kerosene lantern and held it near Sunny. "You look like you fell in a sludge pit."

"I did."

The light wavered as Miriam's had shook. "You're lucky to be alive."

"I know, but that's not nearly the worst of it."

"You look pale. I'll get you some blackberry wine. And I'm going to bring out a can of kerosene and some old rags to clean this mess off you. Then we'll talk."

Miriam bustled inside, and Sunny sat down on the top step, trying hard not to cry, trying hard not to break down in front of her friend. All the emotions she had kept at bay for so long were threatening to overwhelm her. Still she mustn't burden Miriam with the fear Dan had instilled in her, and yet she felt dangerously close to bursting open, all the little pieces of her that made up the whole falling apart

60

until there was no more Sunny Hansen. And maybe it was what she wanted. That thought scared her most of all.

"Here, drink this," Miriam said, shutting the screen door behind her.

Sunny took the jelly jar of wine, and drank quickly. The sweetness and heat hit her stomach, then spread outward. It made her feel more stable, and she smiled at Miriam. "Thanks."

"That's the least I could do. Now I'll help you off with those boots, and we'll get you cleaned up."

They removed the boots, then the jeans. Miriam put them aside, then began helping Sunny rub the oil off her body with kerosene-soaked rags. Soon the smell of sludge was replaced by the strong scent of kerosene, but Sunny preferred that smell by far.

"You can come in the house now. There's plenty of hot water if you want a shower."

Sunny laughed grimly. "You don't have to ask twice. Between the sludge oil and the kerosene I can hardly breathe."

Miriam opened the screen door, and Sunny followed her inside, carrying a kerosene-soaked rag.

The small living room was dim, revealing dark shapes, but Sunny knew her way around. The room was filled with collector's items that would make an antique dealer's heartbeat quicken with joy, but for Miriam, it was just old, comfortable furniture handed down in her family for years.

"While you shower," Miriam said, taking Sunny's jelly jar, "I'm going to set out some food. If you need me, call. I'll be in the kitchen."

"Thanks, Miriam."

"It'll all look better with a clean body and a full stomach," Miriam replied.

"I hope so."

But Sunny didn't really think so as she shut the door to the bathroom behind her, flipping on a light switch. The room was very similar to the one she had at home, and she noticed Miriam had set out a cotton day dress for her to put on when she was clean.

As she removed the rest of her clothes and finished cleaning off the sludge, her mind kept returning to the horror of the pit. Somehow it didn't seem quite so real now. As she turned on the shower and stepped under the hot, stinging spray, it was hard to believe anything other than the comfortable life she had known in East Texas could be real.

Or maybe that was what she wanted to believe.

But she couldn't stay in the bathroom forever. She had to do something about the dead women. Something that didn't involve her going to the police. Something that didn't involve her at all, and she had to do it soon.

She began to wash herself with a bar of strong-smelling soap, and the sheer pleasure of being clean again made her feel better, more sure, but she knew it was an illusion. Her safe world had been shattered, and she didn't know how to put it back together again.

She turned off the shower, then quickly dried herself with a flower-patterned towel that looked like it might have come from a package of detergent, back in the days when manufacturers did that type of thing.

Finally, she pulled on the flowery print housedress and buttoned it up the front, feeling as if she had suddenly stepped back into another age. It was time to share what she knew with Miriam, and yet she dreaded doing it, for who knew how it would affect their lives.

She took a deep breath, left the bathroom, and walked into the kitchen. Miriam was waiting for her at the table. Sunny sat down. There was fresh-baked bread with butter and blackberry jam; plus, her jar of blackberry wine had been refilled.

"You look better. Sit down and eat," Miriam said, then took a sip of her own wine.

Sunny didn't feel hungry. In fact, she felt like her world

had collapsed and she would never eat again. But Miriam was right. She had to keep up her strength. She buttered a piece of bread, feeling so tired she could hardly go on, and spread jam on it. Her throat was tight, but she took a bite and swallowed, anyway. She knew the food was delicious, but she had lost all sense of taste.

Still, she forced down several more bites, drank some wine, then looked into Miriam's concerned face. It was now or never. Taking a deep breath, she blurted out, "I found two dead women in the sludge pit near here."

Miriam's face paled, and she clutched her jar of blackberry wine. "So it's come to us then, that cold, evil wind I felt."

"A murderer's come to us, Miriam. No wind."

"There are many powers on the earth, Sunny. Many of them we hope never to see or feel or know, but we can't deny them when they touch our lives."

"I'm not denying anything. I found two dead women. Don't you understand?" Sunny felt hot tears sting her eyes.

Miriam suddenly looked contrite. She stood up, and pulled Sunny against her warm body. "I'm sorry. I must have sounded like I didn't care, but I do. More than you know. Tell me about it. Can you?"

"That's why I came to you. I didn't know where else to turn."

Miriam nodded, then pulled a chair close to Sunny and took her hand, holding it firmly. "We're safe here, for now. Tell me what you know."

"I went for a walk earlier today. I thought I saw a face in the water. I convinced myself it was my imagination and went home. But I couldn't sleep. I kept seeing that face, and it wasn't mine or anybody I'd ever known."

"So you went back."

"Yes. And there was a dead woman in the pit. She had red hair. I almost drowned trying to find her."

"Sunny, you came so close to joining her. Do you feel it around yourself?"

"Miriam, please! Don't go spooky on me. You're making me shiver, and I'm already scared enough. I'm all right now. I got away." Sunny couldn't deny to herself that Miriam had voiced exactly what she'd been thinking about Dan.

"But death hovers around you. I can feel it, sense it."

"No!" Sunny clenched Miriam's hand. "This is a simple case of somebody murdering women. Nothing more. It has nothing to do with us. We aren't reading a New Age book or a Stephen King novel." She took a quick gulp of wine.

Miriam nodded but didn't look convinced. She pulled her small, meerschaum pipe out of a pocket and began filling it with tobacco, the sweet scent filling the kitchen. "Go on, Sunny."

"After I found the body I got scared and ran into the forest. I mean, the killer could still have been lurking around. That's when I heard the sound of a car with a big engine. It drove up, a tall man, or at least I think it was a man wearing an overcoat, got out and carried a woman down to the pit and pushed her in with the other one.

"This woman had long blond hair. I tried to save her when he'd gone. She was still warm. I gave her artificial respiration, but it didn't help. She was dead."

Sunny pressed her arms hard across her stomach, suddenly shivering, seeing her own face where the dead woman's had been. Miriam pulled a faded old shawl from the back of a chair and wrapped it around Sunny's shoulders, then held her close. Sunny took deep breaths, trying to control herself as Miriam slowly stroked her head.

"You've been very brave, Sunny, but you can cry now if you want. You have good reason."

Sunny suddenly jumped up, determination in her gray eyes. "No. I cried all I'm going to, a long time ago. Nobody's going to make me cry again." But she knew that didn't mean her terror was over.

"I wish life was that simple, Sunny, and decisions that easy to abide by, but they aren't. Here, drink some more wine."

Sunny picked up her wine, and Miriam relit her pipe, absently stroking the bowl which had been hand-sculpted in the shape of a sea horse, the meerschaum having turned dark and luminous over long years of use.

Trying to appear in more control than she felt, Sunny took a sip of wine. "Something has to be done. The police have to catch the man who's doing this. But I can't go to them. Anybody could see me enter the police station, and even if the police promised to keep my name secret, it might somehow get out."

"You want to tell me about it now, Sunny? I've known since you arrived that you were hiding something, but I didn't press you then and I won't now. Still, if I'm going to help you, if we're going to help the women around here, I need to know what we're up against."

Sunny shivered and drank more wine, hoping it would bolster her courage, though she was feeling more terrified by the moment. Somehow it seemed that if she told anyone about Dan it would conjure him. Suddenly he would be there, bigger than life, ready to hurt her, kill her, and she couldn't face him. Not now, maybe never.

Still, something had to be done.

"There's really not a lot to tell," Sunny stalled. "Some-body might be looking for me, and I don't want them to find me."

"Then what are you going to do about the dead women?"

"I've been thinking. I could make an anonymous phone call tonight. The police could find the bodies tomorrow morning when it's light, then go on with the investigation. They don't need me. I didn't see anything that would help. I mean, I didn't get a good look at the man or his license plate or anything."

"Is it so bad you can't trust the police?"

"Yes!" Sunny paced back and forth. "All right. I'm scared this man—my husband—will find me and kill me."

"Why would he kill you?"

Turning haunted eyes to Miriam, Sunny stopped and whispered, "Because he's already tried." Then something seemed to break in her, and all the walls she had so carefully constructed came tumbling down, and tears began to trickle down her cheeks.

Miriam quickly took Sunny in her arms, murmuring, "It's all right. Had he hurt you before the attempt?"

"Yes, a few times." She nodded, feeling her throat tighten and tears burn her eyes as the old pain and fear welled up in her, as fresh as if it had just happened yesterday. She sobbed once, then swallowed hard. "If I'd been stronger, if I'd done something different, if . . ."

"You couldn't have helped it. The fault is not yours, child. You must believe that. Some people, some men simply want to hurt someone, for whatever reason. You're innocent. You must believe that, too. The women who were murdered were also innocent. And we must keep other innocent women from being hurt as you were hurt, as those two dead women were hurt."

"Maybe I deserved it, maybe . . ."

"Sunny, stop!" Miriam shook her slightly. "You don't believe that, do you? Think!"

"It's true Dan—my husband—had abused other women before me. But I wanted to make him stop it somehow, make him want to stop it, make him love me like he had in the beginning."

"You saved yourself, Sunny. That was the most you could do."

"But now it's come to me all over again. Maybe Dan will find me. I know he wants to kill me and—"

"Sunny, you're safe with me," Miriam crooned, rocking Sunny gently in her arms. "I'll take care of you, and we'll

66

find out who murdered those women. We'll find a way. We'll do it together."

"Truly?" Sunny looked deeply into Miriam's eyes.

"Yes. Evil has come to us and we must not hide from it. That's what it wants, what it hopes for, but we must be strong."

"I don't feel strong."

"But you are. Only a strong individual could have endured all you have and survived."

"I can't go to the police. I just can't."

"All right. We'll go to your house, and you make your phone call."

"What if the police don't believe me?"

"We'll watch the sludge pit. If they don't show up by midmorning, we'll make another plan."

6

"Miriam, I just don't think I can trust a man, especially not this one," Sunny objected as they hurried down an oil road just south of Miriam's house around ten the next morning.

"I know how you feel, but we waited near the sludge pit, and the police didn't show up. Whoever took your call must have decided it was a crank and forgot it. I imagine they get plenty of crank calls they ignore. Now, if you'd walked into the police station or given your name, it would have been another matter."

"I couldn't do that, and you know it."

"Yes, but, Sunny, you asked for my help, you asked for my advice, and Billy Joe James is the best I can come up with."

"But he ran into my car, and I didn't like the way he looked at me. Besides, he's a man."

"I admit Billy Joe has always been a little wild, but I knew his parents and I've known him since he was born. He's a good man. Take my word for it."

"But why would he help me?"

"He's alone. He doesn't have much to do. He needs the distraction."

"Some distraction! I still don't think he'll do it, and I

hate to ask him. I'd feel better if you'd tell the police for me."

"Sunny, we discussed that. You know how much faith they'd put in a half-Indian woman over seventy, especially with my reputation for seeing and hearing things nobody else does."

"I suppose you're right, but still—"

Miriam stopped in the middle of the road and stared hard at Sunny. "You've got to pull yourself together. Either do this and do it right, or let's forget it."

Sunny took a deep breath, looked around at the thick stand of pines around them, smelled the scent of wildflowers, and decided she was overreacting. How bad could Billy Joe James be? Anyway, maybe he wouldn't be home. "Sorry. I'm not myself."

Smiling, Miriam squeezed Sunny's hand. They started walking again. "No wonder. But you're going to have to start trusting a few people again."

"I guess you're right, but it's hard to do after what I've been through."

Sunny glanced around, feeling sweat bead her forehead as the day heated up. "I wish we'd at least taken my car. We'd have been there by now."

"This is safer. If you don't want anybody knowing what we're doing, a walk near Billy Joe's place will look like a walk, a car will look like a visit."

"I guess you're right. If anyone saw us drive to his place, they might later put two and two together and involve me with the murders. I just wish I had this over with."

"Don't worry. We'll be there soon, and you'll see how easy it is," Miriam reassured her.

When they came to Billy Joe's house, it was apparent there had been little work done around the place in a long time. A narrow stone path led from the road through tall grass to a wooden porch which was overgrown with shrubs.

Ancient trees of pine and oak and sweet gum dominated the yard, their limbs twined together over the roof of the house.

Sunny stepped onto the path, immediately feeling the cool relief of the shade. As she walked up to the porch, she felt more strongly than ever that she shouldn't have come. But what else could she do?

She started to push her way past the vegetation overrunning the porch, but Miriam touched her arm and beckoned. She followed Miriam along an almost invisible trail that wound around the side of the house to the back.

Billy Joe James sat on the steps of the most rickety-looking porch Sunny had ever seen. He was wearing faded jeans and a blue T-shirt. Without glancing up, he said, "Hello, Miriam. You bring me company?"

Sunny was surprised, and a little impressed. Without looking, how had Billy Joe known it was Miriam, or that she had brought someone with her? Good ears, she supposed.

"Sure did. How's that old coon dog of yours?"

Billy Joe chuckled and glanced up as he scratched behind the ears of a quite elderly bird dog sprawled at his booted feet. "Buck's fine." Seeing Sunny, his eyes lit with surprise and speculation. "Well, hello, Sunny Hansen. I didn't expect to see you at my place."

"Hi," Sunny replied, biting her lower lip to keep back a sharp reply. "Miriam thought we should come over."

Billy Joe suddenly stood up. "But here I am forgetting my manners. Believe it or not, my parents raised me to be a gentleman, a Southern gentleman."

"Had a lot of use for it?" Sunny retorted, then chewed on her lower lip. Why was she so antagonistic toward this man? But it was not just this man, it was any man. And Dan had played the role of the perfect gentleman, too. For a moment she remembered vividly his insistence on her "please and thank you" for the pain he gave her. She shuddered and refocused on her surroundings.

Billy Joe and Miriam were both looking at her expectantly and with a certain amount of concern. Had she missed a question or something?

"I told Billy Joe I'd have a beer," Miriam said. "Do you want one too, Sunny?"

"Yes, thanks." Sunny privately thought it was a little early for drinking. But it was a hot day already, and it was probably a choice of cold beer or warm water. She didn't expect Billy Joe to have ice-cold lemonade, and she didn't want to experiment with water from his well, if that's where he got it.

While Billy Joe went inside, Sunny glanced around. There was a tire swing hanging from a massive branch of an old elm in the back yard. Not much grass was growing, but there was a wide variety of overgrown scrubs. Two large gardenia bushes covered with sweet-smelling white flowers stood sentinel on each side of the porch. Bees buzzed determinedly around them, and for a moment Sunny was almost lulled into forgetting her real reason for being there, for the backyard seemed like something out of an older, gentler time.

Billy Joe came back, a beer in each hand and two under his arms. "Here you go." He handed one to Miriam, tossed one to Sunny with a critical eye to her catch, then sat down on the top step. "Go ahead and take the rockers."

Sunny eyed the grayed wooden rockers with sagging seats apprehensively. If she dared sit down, she didn't know which would go first, the chair or the porch. Right now, she preferred to keep her feet on firm ground. She was already feeling unsteady enough. "Thanks, I think I'll stand."

"Suit yourself." Billy Joe popped the top of a beer and downed half of it.

Miriam sat next to him and took a sip of her own beer. "How you been getting along, Billy Joe?"

"You know, fair to middling."

"You've got some beautiful trees here," Sunny said, walking around the backyard as she built up the courage to talk to Billy Joe about the dead women.

"Thanks. Mom planted a lot of things, but I don't keep it up like she did." He finished the can and threw it, a perfect overhand curve, to land exactly in the center of a pile of empty beer cans. Then he popped another top.

Sunny looked at the pile of cans thoughtfully. "You sure know how to throw them."

Billy Joe laughed derisively. "I ought to. I throw enough."

"He's being modest, Sunny," Miriam explained. "Billy Joe made Gusher High famous all over Texas when he quarterbacked the team."

"You're *that* Billy Joe James?" Sunny asked, impressed. Since football was frequently called the state religion of Texas, almost everybody was vitally aware of players and statistics from grade school on up. "I thought you were playing pro or something."

Billy Joe laughed again, and took a long swallow of beer. "In my mind, but that's the only place."

"He got a bad knee injury in college, Sunny," Miriam explained.

"I'm sorry."

"Don't be. It was a long time ago." Billy Joe gave Sunny a hard stare. "And if you aren't going to tell me, I might as well ask why you two ladies decided to visit me this morning."

"We need your help, Billy Joe," Miriam replied. "Isn't that right, Sunny?"

"Yes."

"It isn't to get that Bug of yours fixed, is it? Because if it is, I still haven't got any money."

"No," Sunny quickly denied. "It was just another little dent, anyway. The fact of the matter is, I don't know many people around here. I didn't know who to turn to, and Miriam suggested you."

"What do you want?" Billy Joe watched Sunny appreciatively as she paced. "You got rats in your basement or something? I can't think of anything much more serious than that ever happens around here."

"No, Billy Joe James," Sunny replied, stung by his attempt at humor. "We have dead women in a sludge pit."

There was a moment of silence, then Billy Joe chuckled. "That's a joke, right?"

"No," Sunny said.

Silence.

"You expect me to believe that? Dead women in a sludge pit?" Billy Joe asked, his voice full of skepticism.

"Yes," Sunny insisted. "I found the bodies last night. And I'm fairly sure they were killed by one man. You think I would kid around about something like that?"

"It's the truth, Billy Joe." Miriam looked grim.

"Did you see them?"

"No," Miriam replied.

"And you expect me to believe it when some smart-mouthed city girl tells me we've got a murderer around here?"

"She wouldn't lie. I know her," Miriam defended, then took a drink.

Billy Joe looked at Miriam for a long moment, obviously coming to a decision, then glanced at Sunny. "Shit!"

"I agree." Sunny finished her beer and tossed it at the pile of cans. It veered off to one side and bumped down to the ground. So much for her throwing skills. Billy Joe had made it look easy. She walked back to the porch and sat down. Miriam stroked her hair.

"So, did you call the cops?" Billy Joe asked.

"Yes," Sunny replied, "but it was an anonymous call, and they didn't show up at the sludge pit this morning."

"Prank call," Billy Joe interpreted the lack of police interest. "That the pit near here?"

Sunny nodded.

"So what're you doing here instead of beating down the door of Sheriff Barker's office?"

"Sunny has a problem," Miriam put in quietly.

Billy Joe turned narrowed eyes on her. "What kind?"

"She's hiding out from a violent husband."

Billy Joe's head swung toward Sunny, his eyes questioning.

"Dan will kill me if he finds me," Sunny explained, keeping her emotions tightly under control. "He already tried."

A soft whistle came from Billy Joe. "You're afraid if you go to the cops, this husband will find you?"

"Yes," Sunny agreed.

"You can insist they keep your name confidential," Billy Joe explained.

"I know," Sunny said. "But even if the records are sealed, even in the best of departments, information can get out. When this hits the news, you know the media is going to go wild. I'm terrified of Dan finding me."

"I think our cops are better than that," Billy Joe defended.

"Even if they're the best in the world, I just can't get involved with them. I'll be the first to admit I'm being paranoid. But when you've been that close to death in the arms of someone you . . . you know well, then—"

"It's all right, Sunny," Miriam interrupted, patting her shoulder. "Billy Joe, we came to ask if you would call Sheriff Barker and tell him you found two dead women in a sludge pit while on a walk. He'll believe you and get right out there. We've got to stop these killings!''

Billy Joe glanced over Sunny's trim body again, then back at Miriam. ''That's asking a lot. Besides, can we really believe anything this woman says is true?''

Sunny stood up, strode several paces away, then turned back and focused on Billy Joe. ''Okay, don't believe me, don't trust me. I don't care. But please call the sheriff and tell him about those bodies. If he dredges the pit and finds nothing, what have you got to lose? But if he does find those dead women, then you'll have helped their families and maybe saved the lives of other women, as well.''

Billy Joe gave her a long, hard stare. Sunny Hansen was a smart-mouth, all right. Clever. And he'd been too long without a woman or he wouldn't even be considering getting involved in this crazy scheme. If not for Miriam, who was usually solid as a rock, and not for the itch he'd had since running into Sunny's car in Gusher, he'd have told the city girl to go to hell.

As it was, he knew he was getting himself into trouble. And for some stupid reason he felt a burst of adrenaline like he hadn't felt in years, like he used to feel on a football field with the bright lights, the cheers, the pretty girls.

Pretty woman. Roy Orbison had made that number famous, and he'd never hear it again without thinking of Sunny Hansen. ''All right,'' he agreed, watching her eyes light up with relief. ''I'll do it.'' Later, he wanted to see her eyes light up with something else, something just for him.

''Oh, thank you,'' Sunny said, grasping his hand and shaking it briskly before turning to hug Miriam. Maybe if she couldn't save her own life, she could at least help other innocent women.

Billy Joe stood there watching the two women, feeling too tall, too rough, and too damned hot. Why was it that women always made him feel, except when he had them under him, like they had all of life's answers, if you could only get them to tell you.

But at the moment he didn't care. After all, they'd come to him for help, and for the first time in a long while he didn't fell like a complete loser.

7

Sheriff Nate Barker was pretty skeptical when Billy Joe James, who was known for his occasional hard drinking, had called in with a story about two dead women in the sludge pit near Pineco Well Number 87, just off FM 203.

However, it was the second call about dead women in a sludge pit, and that was two calls too many. The first call had been anonymous, and therefore had been put at the bottom of the investigation list. With severe staff cutbacks because of the oil bust, they had established a new order of handling business—with anonymous or prank calls coming last. But with Billy Joe's call, the sludge pit had moved up to top priority.

Sheriff Barker was going to check out Billy Joe's story, but he didn't expect to find any dead women. That kind of thing just didn't happen in his county. He was never sure if it was because of his law enforcement effectiveness, or because the people in his area were just plain dull. When he was being honest with himself, he thought the latter.

But two dead women in a sludge pit was not dull. In fact, it was an affront to his county. They were peace-loving people, and he couldn't think of anybody he knew who could possibly have done such a deed, if in fact Billy

Joe hadn't seen the whole thing from the bottom of a bottle of beer.

Still, it had to be checked out, and he'd called in an assistant and an ambulance, just in case. He'd also told Billy Joe to meet him at the pit.

Nate Barker was a big, blond man who'd reached forty with just a small beer belly and most of his hair. He was proud of his full head of hair, the large moustache he sported, and the way his crisp, starched gray uniform fit him snugly. He liked the weight of the revolver on his belt and wore his authority as county sheriff proudly. He also wore expensive black lizard cowboy boots, which weren't strictly regulation, but made him feel like the Texas sheriff he was.

As Sheriff Barker made his way down 203, Deputy Price Simmons followed, thinking back to the woman he'd screwed the night before. She'd had damn fine legs, long, firm, and strong when they'd been wrapped around him. Too bad he couldn't see her again, but he had to be careful. His wife took other women hard. She bawled to other cops' wives and eventually word got back to the sheriff's office. The department didn't like that. They wanted family men if they were married.

He loved his wife, loved their two children, but that didn't mean he had to be hog-tied and shackled the rest of his life. Besides, he never could resist a pair of long legs. Maybe it was just as well he would only see the women once, because more than that could turn monotonous fast, and women could get clingy even faster.

Price was a short man, and very aware of that fact. He worked out at a gym in Longview and was determined to make up in breadth what he could never achieve in height. With every movement, his muscles strained against his uniform. He liked that feel, liked knowing he was strong. Women liked it, too, and they liked the way he was hung. He secretly thought of himself as a stud bull. Other men might have height, but he didn't need it with what he had.

He rubbed his short, dark hair, then glanced at the trim legs encased in nylon which belonged to Nan Shubert. Nan had insisted on coming along. She was always sticking her long nose into everybody's business. Problem was, technically she had the right.

Nan had recently been put in charge of woman matters covering several counties. He'd never bothered to find out what her official title was. He just knew that if it had anything to do with rape or sexual harassment or children, whether abused, runaway, or sexually molested, Nan was called; or more likely she was there before you even knew what'd happened. She had to have spies everywhere to know so much.

She also had too much education as far as Price was concerned. She had several college degrees and some high-powered experience with some female programs back East. She was too fancy to be sticking her nose into East Texas business, but everyone was careful around her. Nobody wanted to be stuck with racist or sexist problems. Price disliked everything about her except her legs. He'd invited her to ride with him so he could look at her long, athletic legs.

What he didn't do was listen to her. She'd been going on about some new Supreme Court decision about blacks, or women, or gays, or some such stuff, and he'd just tuned her out like he'd learned to do with his wife. If her mind hadn't been ruined with so much education, she might have made a fine woman. As it was, he just looked at her legs and forgot the rest of her.

Nan Shubert watched Price Simmons watching her legs and smiled grimly to herself. The man thought with his dick, nothing else. But perhaps he had nothing between his ears to help out. Still, he might be useful sometime, so she

79

tolerated his glances and kept him in place. Men could be so difficult, but then so could women.

She just wished the people she worked with and dealt with could really, truly understand the plight of women, children, and minorities in their society. But lip service was the best she got, except on occasion when some truly grisly occurrence would make everyone sympathetic.

The possibility of two women, murdered, perhaps raped, and dumped in a sludge pit in East Texas made her sick. It also made her determined to see that their killer was quickly brought to justice; not just because it was right, but also because the sooner the murderer was stopped, the sooner women in the area would be safe again. There was little doubt in her mind that the perpetrator was male, if the deed had been done, for statistics stood solidly behind male violence.

She hoped, but hardly dared believe, that the phone call alerting Sheriff Barker had been a hoax. Too many women were hurt, murdered, beaten and abused daily in the United States for her to really believe that's all it was. So she had come along, ready to help the dead women and possible future victims by being on the scene, or to have her hopes proved right.

The two police vehicles and one ambulance pulled off FM 203 onto a narrow oil road. They followed it in single file to Pineco Well Number 87, then stopped behind an old Chevy pickup.

Billy Joe James stepped down from the truck, then tossed a flashlight onto the torn fabric on the front seat. Damn good thing he'd gotten there early. Sunny's flashlight had been just at the edge of the woods and would have been found right away. Now she was safe, at least for the moment.

"What's this danged nonsense about two dead women, Billy Joe?" Sheriff Barker called as he opened the door of his car and carefully stepped onto the road. He didn't want to get oily muck on his expensive, lizard-skin boots.

"Just what I told you on the phone. I was taking a walk last night, came by here, looked in the sludge pit, and you know the rest."

"Funny business," Sheriff Barker said, then motioned his deputy forward. "Get down there, Price, and see what's in that sludge pit."

Price hurried toward the pit, always anxious to impress his superiors. He was twenty-eight and looked forward to a long, successful career if he played his cards right.

"Just a minute, Price. I want to look at whatever's in there, too." Nan Shubert hurried after Price.

"Who's that?" Billy Joe asked.

"That's our new special investigator. Women and Children's Affairs."

"Women's what?"

"Slut Corps, Price calls her," Sheriff Barker said, his voice low. "Careful around her. She hates men."

"Why?"

"Who knows? One of those women-libber types. I'll introduce you, but don't get too close or your voice might get high." Sheriff Barker laughed at his joke, then added, "But don't quote me on any of this. Officially, she sticks her nose into anything that has to do with women, kids, even minorities."

"Then she'll be helping out on the investigation?"

"If there is one. You sure you didn't have too many beers last night, Billy Joe?"

"Wish that was all it was."

"Hey, Sheriff!" Price called. "Better get down here."

Sheriff Barker gave Billy Joe a hard stare, as if he had suddenly come under suspicion, then took long strides toward the sludge pit.

Billy Joe followed him, suddenly realizing why Sunny had wanted to stay far away from the problem. "Slut Corps?"

That sounded just like Price Simmons. But why was Sheriff Barker so skeptical of his new colleague? Departmental politics, he supposed.

"Hell and damnation!" Price exclaimed as Sheriff Barker and Billy Joe arrived at the pit. "Ever see anything like that?"

Price was standing on a tree branch which extended into the water. Raised by the pressure of his foot, the branch held aloft the slim, white, oil-streaked arm of a women.

"You weren't kidding, were you, Billy Joe?" Sheriff Barker said.

"Good eyes," Nan Shubert observed.

Billy Joe turned to look at her.

She stared back, her brown gaze cool, appraising. She looked to be about forty, stood five feet five, was solidly built, and wore a gray business suit and her gray-brown hair in a pageboy.

For the second time Billy Joe felt he was being put under suspicion, and he didn't like it.

Before Billy Joe could reply, Price exclaimed, "Sure he's got good eyes! That's Billy Joe James you're talking to. He's the best damned quarterback ever to come out of Gusher High."

"Is that so?" Nan asked, her left brow lifting slightly. "So you're used to noticing small details, anything unusual in a setting."

"Damn, Nan! You're talking to Billy Joe James," Price interrupted, obviously insulted for the community legend.

"Price, why don't you get some body bags down here and alert the ambulance to our situation," Sheriff Barker said, stopping what he considered an explosive situation.

"Sure, Sheriff. I'm on my way, but wait for me before you do anything. All right?"

"Okay, Price. Just get on with it."

Billy Joe looked at the dead woman's arm, glad he hadn't

82

seen more. Sunny was a tough city girl, all right. Middle of the night. Dead bodies in the sludge pit. Murderers running loose. Hair raised on the back of his neck. He didn't like any of it and wished he hadn't agreed to her request. But it'd been easy this morning with her so needy, easy before he'd actually seen the body and dealt with the police. And he knew why he'd done it. Matter over mind.

"Billy Joe?" Sheriff Barker lit an unfiltered Camel, then held out the pack.

"No, thanks." Billy Joe remembered how he'd given up smoking the first time it'd interfered with his running ability.

"Let me introduce you to Nan Shubert," Sheriff Barker said. "She may have some questions for you. She'll be helping with the investigation, won't you, Nan?"

"Couldn't keep me off this one, Sheriff. I'm sure you realize the implications of this murder."

Sheriff Barker took a long drag on his cigarette, trying not to look confused. Implications?. Why did the woman even use words like that? He guessed she'd paid a lot to learn them, so felt obliged to use them. "Sure."

She nodded briskly. "Then we'd better get on it right away."

"We are on it," he said coldly.

"I mean the publicity. We probably shouldn't let the news media know the exact location of the sludge pit. The authorizations. I wonder what reaction Pineco's executives will have? And, of course, we'll want a rush through lab."

"Nan, we're doing nothing till we know exactly what we've got here." Sheriff Barker was now thoroughly irritated. "We don't even know if there are two bodies in the pit. I only see one. How'd you know, anyway, Billy Joe?"

"It looked like two last night. There wasn't much light. I could be mistaken."

"Probably are. You're just trying to beef it up, make it

83

more than it is," Sheriff Barker concluded. "Civilians! You watch too much danged TV cop shows."

"I don't have a TV," Billy Joe replied.

"Too much imagination then," Sheriff Barker insisted.

"You men! That doesn't matter in the least. What we have here is at least one dead women. Statistics tell us that the probability is extremely high that she was murdered, probably raped by a man. That leads us to the horrible conclusion that if this man has done it once, he will do it again, and probably soon. You know mass murders are on the rise."

"Of course we know all that," Sheriff Barker replied. "We've got to get our facts straight first, though. We don't want to go off half-cocked, Nan."

"That's fine with me. Here's Price, anyway."

Price was followed by two ambulance attendants with body bags and two stretchers. Price hurried over, looked back into the water, then nodded, pleased when he saw nothing had been disturbed. They'd waited for him.

As the ambulance attendants looked at the hand reaching out of the water, silence fell over the group. A crow cawed nearby, then all was silent once more.

Sheriff Barker dropped his cigarette, then crushed it out with the toe of his boot. "We might as well get on with it."

"Are you going to get equipment out here and dredge the pit?" Nan looked determined.

Sheriff Barker gave her a hard stare. "I know my job, Nan. First things first. I want this body out and to the coroner, then we continue. Now you be quiet a minute and let us do our work."

Nan nodded, and stepped back.

A short time later, the body of a small Caucasian woman with red hair, estimated to be in her early twenties was zipped into a body bag, then lifted onto a stretcher and taken to the ambulance. Sheriff Barker and Deputy Simmons pushed around in the water with tree limbs for several minutes, but couldn't find another body.

"Guess we'll have to dredge the pit," Sheriff Barker concluded. "Price go call in some equipment. While we wait, I want to talk to you, Billy Joe."

"All right, but I've got things to do. I can't hang around here all day."

Sheriff Barker looked at him suspiciously, knowing damned well Billy Joe worked on and off whenever he felt like it. But he couldn't blame him for wanting to go. He wanted to leave, too. The bloated body of the woman had made him sick. He wished he hadn't eaten such a big breakfast. "I'm not going to keep you all day. I just want you to answer some more questions."

As the two men walked away, Nan Shubert stood alone by the edge of the sludge pit, looking at the oily water. How many more bodies would they find down there? How many women had already been killed and hidden in the pit? Was the murderer out stalking again? Or had he killed and found a new hiding place?

She shivered, even though it was hot and growing hotter by the moment in the fierce Texas sun. Whoever was doing this had to be stopped, and soon. But who could it be? Hopefully the dead woman's body would hold clues to the killer's identity.

What about Billy Joe James? He was an obvious suspect. How had he found the body? Why did he say two? There was something not quite right about his statement, or his eyes. She didn't like the way his eyes slid away whenever he was questioned about the bodies. Could he have done it and called the sheriff to point the authorities away from him?

Possible. But there were plenty of men who could have done it. Amazing how normal a killer could look and act. She wouldn't even put it past Price Simmons. The deputy sheriff was not quite balanced where women were concerned, but what man was?

Thinking about all the dead and hurt women of the world, she clenched her fists and vowed softly, "I'll find this murderer and stop him before he commits any more atrocities."

Then she quickly retraced her steps to the cars. She wanted to help question Billy Joe James.

8

Death. Billy Joe had seen it before. One of his buddies had died in high school on an oil rig. His parents had died. He'd done his share of hunting animals when he was growing up, killing them with little thought. But none of that had prepared him for the sight of the dead woman in the sludge pit.

Maybe it was because he was older now, and life meant more. Or maybe it was just the grisly sight of murder, if that's what it turned out to be, and he didn't see how it could be anything else. Murder. Practically right in his own back yard.

And Sunny Hansen. Who'd ever have thought a pretty woman like her could be married to a man who beat her so bad she was hiding out from him. And who'd have thought she'd be the one to find the dead woman's body. It was a surprise anybody'd found it at all.

Sunny. Hansen. Was her last name hers, or his? For some damned reason, he hoped like hell it was her birth name, not her husband's name. He was more interested in her than he should be, knew it, and couldn't seem to stop it. She was married. That was trouble enough. And she was evading the law. That was worse yet.

Still, he hadn't had a woman affect him like Sunny in a

long time, too long. Every time he thought about her husband hitting her, even trying to kill her, for Christ's sake, he wanted to beat the man to a bloody pulp. And if he ever got the chance, he'd damn well do it.

What was he getting himself into? Murder. Cops. A married woman with a crazy husband. Damn! Maybe he was just plain old bored. But he knew better than that. It was Sunny Hansen, and all she represented. She was scared, all right, but she was fighting back, doing the best she could, and she'd won Miriam's respect, which didn't come easy.

Maybe he was feeling like a whiner. Here he'd been complaining about a busted knee for over ten years, drinking and trying to forget, and he hadn't come anywhere near his own death. But Sunny Hansen had, and she was fighting back.

Maybe it was time he did, too. At least, he had to fight for her. You couldn't let a scrapper like Sunny go down without some help. It wasn't fair. And you couldn't let any more women get hurt. That wasn't right, either. After all, weren't men supposed to protect the fairer sex? Wasn't that the way he'd been raised? Isn't that what a Southern gentleman did?

What had the world come to when women were running for their very lives from the people who were supposed to be helping and protecting them? If this was the way it was going, then women were better off depending on themselves and nobody else. It made him mad, really mad, in a way he hadn't been mad in a long time.

Well, this was one woman who wasn't going to be hung out to dry if he could help it. And if he got a bit of a smile or a little trust from her in the bargain, then he'd consider himself lucky and rewarded. Of course, he wanted more and would try for more, but after what she'd been through, would Sunny Hansen ever be able to give more to a man again?

That made him mad all over again. Damned stupid husband of hers! What the hell was wrong with him, anyway? If he ever got his hands on the man, he'd kill him, or at least give it a damned good try.

Billy Joe gunned the engine of his Chevy and pulled into Sunny's front yard. He turned off the motor and took several deep breaths, determined to calm himself. He couldn't go into her house all hot and bothered. The last thing she needed was another wild male around her. But, if it was the last thing he did, he was going to keep her safe.

He picked up her flashlight off the front seat, opened the pickup door, and stepped down. His right knee caught, and he grimaced with pain as he rubbed it. When the burning had eased, he walked, limping slightly, past Sunny's faded red VW and up to her house, a small white frame building that had seen better days but was still in a lot better shape than his own home.

Stepping up on the wooden porch, he knocked, then glanced around. A wild yellow rosebush stretched its tendrils across one of the front windows, and the scent of roses in bloom had drawn bees who buzzed and flitted from flower to flower. Some of the roses had already reached their peak and had dropped single yellow petals that had been caught by a breeze and scattered over the wooden porch. There they lay curling and slowly dying.

Death. Suddenly the scent of roses reminded him of funerals, of cemeteries, and of caskets. His mother's favorite flower had been a yellow rose, and he'd had a huge spray of them made to place on her coffin.

Death and roses. The sweet smell suddenly made him feel like gagging.

Where was Sunny, anyway? He knocked again. Hard.

She suddenly peeped out the small square window in the front door, nodded, quickly unlocked and opened the door, then repeated the process with the wooden screen.

"Hi. Come on in," she invited, but her·voice was a little unsure.

"Thanks."

He followed her into the house, trying not to appear too obvious as he looked around, wanting to get more of a feel of her, how she lived, what she liked. But none of it seemed to fit the image he had of her, for the house was dim inside, and too warm. Also, the furniture was all wrong, and there were no paintings, prints, or posters on the walls. Nothing anywhere that could be related to Sunny Hansen at all.

Had she left it all behind then . . . her past, her memories, everything that'd had meaning for her? There was a lot more he wanted to know about her, but knew he wouldn't, couldn't, ask yet.

"It's hot," she said, standing awkwardly in the middle of the small living room.

"Yes," he agreed, staying near the front door. She really was afraid of men, he suddenly realized. And to have a stranger in her house must take a lot of courage.

"The air-conditioners don't work very well. Would you like a beer?"

"Thanks."

"I only have Pearl. It's made in Texas, you know."

"Yes, I know. I'll take one."

"I know you like Bud, but—"

"Pearl is fine."

"All right." She turned, and quickly left the room.

He started to follow her into the kitchen, then stopped. No, that would make her even more nervous. He didn't want her to feel trapped or cornered. He sat down on the sagging couch and tried to relax. Touching the on/off switch of the flashlight, he spotlighted sections of the room. She kept a damned clean house, but she revealed nothing of herself.

He heard her step back into the room and glanced up.

She was carrying a beer in each hand and a couple of white napkins tucked against one. She looked good, and the beer even better.

"You found my flashlight," she said, stopping beside him, relief in her voice. "Thanks." She handed him a beer.

He set the flashlight on the coffee table and took a long draw on the Pearl.

She sat down across from him, pushed a napkin near him, then carefully placed one on her side of the coffee table. Finally, she placed her beer in the exact center of her white napkin. Then she picked up the flashlight.

"You talked with the police?" she asked, rolling the light back and forth in her hands.

"Yes. They found a body in the sludge pit."

She set down the flashlight, shut her eyes hard, then focused on him again. "I don't know whether to feel relieved or scared or both. At least the police know now." She took a sip of beer. "Thanks for taking my place. I just couldn't have done it."

"I was glad to help out."

"You know, while I waited today I kept hoping it was somehow all my imagination."

"I did, too. But they found the woman."

She frowned. "One? But I saw two. There was a woman in the pit, then the killer carried another one down there. "What color hair did the woman they found have?"

"She was covered in oily sludge, but I think her hair was reddish."

"The woman I tried to save had long blond hair." Sunny looked confused. "I don't understand."

"Neither do I. But the police are going to dredge the pit. The other body is probably snagged on some old tree stumps."

He swallowed more beer, then glanced at her.

She twisted her napkin, now damp from the condensation

91

of the beer can, and tore it. She carefully pieced it together, then looked up. "Billy Joe, did it go all right? I mean, did the police believe you and everything? I don't want you getting into trouble."

"As far as I know, it went okay. Sheriff Barker was skeptical, but he always is. Price is just after his pension. But they had a woman out there, too."

"Who was she?"

"She's a special investigator for women, children, minorities. Far as I can tell, her job covers several counties, and she was suspicious of me, maybe of all men."

"Do you think she believed you?"

"I don't know, but I wanted to warn you. She'll probably be around asking questions. They all will, I guess."

"And I don't know anything except what you came over and told me."

"But you don't know me, Sunny. I wouldn't have told you anything."

She frowned. "I don't understand."

"That's something I wanted to talk to you about. This is a damned small community. If we knew each other, then everybody would know, and nobody knows that."

"I see."

"I had in mind that, if you thought it was okay, we could go out to the drive-in in Gusher Saturday night."

"Drive-in?"

"We're in this together, and we've got to talk about it. People are going to notice."

"There's the phone."

"You want to depend on it all the time? Besides, I'm here right now, and people'll know that, too."

Sunny set down her beer and stood up. Pacing several steps, she came back and looked down at him. "But what does the drive-in have to do with any of this?"

"Because there's not a soul in this area who'd believe we were just friends. They're going to think we're dating."

Looking away, she wrapped her arms around herself. "I don't think the drive-in's necessary. In fact, I imagine this is all over for us. The police will handle it from here." She quickly sat back down.

He finished his beer. "It wouldn't be a real date. We'd just go to the drive-in so we could be seen. What's that going to hurt? You got other plans?"

She shoved fingers through her thick hair and bit her lower lip. "No. It's just that I thought if you took care of the police it would all be finished for me."

"Maybe it is. Maybe they'll catch the killer today. But what if they don't?"

She hesitated, then looked at him hard. "I guess you're right. We should plan for the worst."

"And hope for the best. Anyway, will it be so bad to spend a few hours with me?" He toyed with his empty beer can.

"I don't know." She suddenly smiled. "Will it?"

"I haven't gotten a lot of complaints yet."

"I'm sorry. I don't mean to be rude. But my life ceased to be normal a long time ago."

"So did mine. What's normal, anyway?"

"TV?"

He laughed. "If it is, we're all in trouble."

She smiled again.

"I think they may be playing *Return of the Killer Tomatoes* at the drive-in. But the main thing is the concession stand. It's probably one of the few places in the old U.S. where you can still get real drive-in food like fresh-popped corn, curly french fries, cut and fried right before your eyes, and the hot dogs are the greasiest best I've ever had. And the pop is real."

Sunny couldn't help but laugh. "It does sound good. You know, it's funny, but there's a lot of food I don't really enjoy anymore because they've changed it and I remember the way it used to taste. It was better then."

93

"Like Dr. Pepper in little bottles?" Billy Joe asked, smiling.

"Right."

"I guess that's age for you."

"Yes, but if it's this way now, what's it going to be like when we're eighty?"

"I don't know. Maybe we should ask Miriam," Billy Joe suggested, his smile growing.

"Maybe so. You know, you've made this drive-in sound so good, I can't help going. But I'll pay my own way." She tapped the top of her beer can for emphasis.

"No. It was my idea, so it's my treat. I'll just work a couple of extra days."

She hesitated. "Okay, but next time it's on me."

Billy Joe nodded. "And it'll give us a chance to discuss any new clues we've heard about."

"Do you suppose you can get Sheriff Barker to let you know what's going on?"

"I don't know. He's pretty closemouthed, but I'll try. You still want to stay out of it?"

"Yes. I must," Sunny insisted.

"Okay, but you may have to tell your story sometime."

"I hope not, but I'll worry about it then, if I have to." She finished her beer. "Right now, I've got a lot of work to do if I'm going to pay my rent."

"What do you do?"

"I'm an illustrator."

Billy Joe looked blank a moment. "You mean you're one of those creative types?"

"Not really. Not unless you'd call drawing an exact replica of a refrigerator, or a hammer, or a lawn mower creative. I do the illustrations for Speedy Fix-It catalogs."

"I'm impressed," Billy Joe said.

"Impressed?" She looked at him in surprise for a long moment, then felt really good, better than she had in a long time. He meant it. The fact that she could draw meant something to him. "Thanks, Billy Joe, I appreciate your saying that."

"I mean it. I can't draw a straight line." He shrugged.

"Neither can I. I have to use a ruler, just like you," Sunny said, winking at him.

"Well, it was just an expression. I meant I can't draw."

"I understand. I was just making a joke. You see, most everyone says that to an artist, and really an artist can't draw a straight line, either. We just have professional instruments that help us. But, thanks. You made me feel more like a real artist than I have in quite awhile. Sometimes I forget, living so isolated."

"I know what you mean. I guess I never got over being a quarterback, but I can still throw a long, straight pigskin. There's just not much use for it, anymore."

"It's still nice to have the skill."

"I guess so." He stood up. "But I'm keeping you. You've got work to do, and I want to make some extra money for Saturday night."

She stood, too. "Thanks again for the help."

"You sure you'll be okay here alone? There's a killer out there."

"I'll be fine. I've learned to take care of myself."

He looked skeptical. "Call if you need anything."

"Thanks, I will."

Walking to the front door, he stopped and turned back. "I'll see you Saturday night about a half hour before dusk."

"Okay. And, Billy Joe, be careful."

He hesitated, looked at her a moment, then nodded. "You, too."

He quickly opened the doors, stepped outside, and walked to his pickup. He got in and slammed the door shut. As he drove away, he glanced in the rearview mirror. Sunny had stepped out onto the porch, and was holding a yellow rose as she watched him drive away.

Death and roses.

He grimaced, but kept on going.

9

Nan Shubert watched the dredging process, glad Pineco had been cooperative in giving its permission to investigate the sludge pit. She hoped Billy Joe James had been mistaken, hoped there would be no second body, or a possible third or fourth.

But even if there were no other bodies here, there were other sludge pits in East Texas. And checking them would be a lengthy process. If they could even find them all—and it was unlikely anyone would invest the necessary time, money, and energy to do that—it just wouldn't be profitable to dredge them at this point in the investigation.

Besides, it wouldn't be easy to get permission from the numerous oil corporations and holding companies. Eventually, they were bound to start getting nervous about the funding, cleanups, and reporters, for they were naturally very aware of their image and legal liabilities.

Anyway, she didn't know if dredging endless sludge pits would help. There might not be a man on a killing spree, for the death could have been an isolated incident. Perhaps someone had lost their temper and gone too far. Manslaughter, not premeditated.

But she didn't really believe that. She believed Billy Joe James. She believed, deep in her gut, that there was something bad going on, and that it would continue until they found and stopped the person committing the crimes against women.

So far they had turned up little evidence. The initial report was that the red-headed woman had been in her early twenties, white, and dressed in medium-priced clothes. She had been strangled, then raped.

Nan shivered despite the heat of the day. Yes, that was right. The man had killed his victim first, then raped a corpse.

It was evidence of a very sick, perverted mind. At least it was sick and perverted to her. Maybe some people could rationalize or make excuses for murderers, but she wasn't going to get into that type of mind game. It was a trap that could end up sucking away all the righteous anger needed to see a case like this through.

She was definitely not going to be sympathetic to the murderer. It was the victim, and future victims, who needed help, sympathy, and understanding. As far as she was concerned, the murderer could take all his problems and neuroses and shove them, for there was simply not enough concern for the feelings, stress, and problems of the victim, from a simple automobile accident to the most horrendous crimes of all.

No, she didn't care about the killer. She was going to find him and stop him, no matter what it cost. And she would use any of the resources at her disposal to achieve her end. Until women were no longer viewed as potential victims by males and establishments in their society, someone had to look out for them.

And she was being paid to do it, although she didn't know how long her job would last now that women's programs were being continually cut by the government. But until they stopped funding her job, she was going to do all she could to help women. Of course, even if they stopped paying her, she knew she would go right on doing what she could to help.

She just wished there'd been some help for her sister when she'd needed it. However, that was water under the bridge.

"Looks like we've come up empty," Sheriff Barker said, halting the dredging process. "No need to keep pushing it. There's just not another body down there."

Nan nodded in agreement. "It was late when Billy Joe discovered the body. He could have been mistaken." She was relieved there wasn't another victim, which meant it might have simply been a case of manslaughter, after all.

"He must have been," Sheriff Barker agreed. "This takes care of it then. When we get the final coroner's report, we'll know more."

"What are you going to do now?" Nan asked.

"What can we do?" Price replied. "I mean, until we get the final autopsy report, what have we got to go on?"

"We'll question the people living in this area," Sheriff Barker said. "Maybe they saw something, or heard something that'll help the investigation."

"Do you really expect to learn anything that way?" Nan asked.

"No," Sheriff Barker admitted. "But I want to find that killer as much as you do, and I'm going to do everything in my power to do it." He lit a cigarette, and inhaled deeply. "There's never been a murder in my county before, and so far we don't have much to go on. There's been no missing persons report, so it's beginning to look like this woman wasn't from around here. Somebody traveling through could have hidden the body in the pit and driven on."

"How would a stranger have known about the sludge pit?" Nan asked thoughtfully.

"He could have just taken a back road and stumbled onto it," Price suggested, glancing around the area.

"Possible," Nan replied, "but it seems like too much of a coincidence, especially if there is a second body."

"But there isn't a second body," Sheriff Barker reminded her.

"Not here," Nan said.

"Now, don't go making this worse than it is." Sheriff Barker flicked ashes off his cigarette.

"I'm trying not to, but—"

"Let's deal strictly with the facts. We've got a dead woman on our hands. We've got to find out who she is. We'll send out an inquiry through police channels, and maybe we'll get that cleared up pretty quick. In fact, we should get some reports back tomorrow. And maybe the autopsy will tell us more. Until then, about all we can do is question the people who live around here and try to keep the newspapers and TV stations as low-key as possible."

Nan knew Sheriff Barker was right, that he was following good police procedure. Still, she wanted to see more done. "I agree with your tactics, Sheriff, but I'd like to do a little poking around myself."

"I can't stop you, but be careful, and don't get in the way of my people."

"I won't. I'm a pro."

"Yes," Sheriff Barker agreed, "but this is different, and I don't want anything botched up."

"I understand. Your job on the line on this one?"

"Damn sure is. I've got to be reelected in a couple of years, and something like murder has to be solved and solved quick or they remember."

"Don't worry, Sheriff," Price said. "We'll have this solved and the murderer behind bars in a week. Just you wait and see. You've got the best staff in the area."

Sheriff Barker looked at his deputy a moment, then shook his head. "Start making the rounds of the houses around here, Price. And be polite. Don't scare anybody. We want this conducted with as few hysterics as possible."

"Got you. I'm the man for the job."

"I'd better head back to the office," Sheriff Barker added. "This isn't the only case we've got."

"Why don't I go along with Price, Sheriff," Nan suggested. "That way you'd know for sure I'm not disturbing the evidence, and there's no point in covering the same ground twice."

"That all right with you, Price?"

"Sure, why not? Give me some company driving around these back roads."

"Okay, Nan, but take it easy on Price. He's still wet behind the ears."

"I am not," Price protested.

Nan smiled at Sheriff Barker. "Sure, Sheriff. I'll go easy on him."

"See you two later."

As Sheriff Barker and the dredging team drove away, Nan looked out over the sludge pit again. She had a feeling there was a second body, and she wished they'd found it. The case would have been approached differently then. Nevertheless, she was going to handle the case as if there were two bodies and time was of the essence because the killer might strike again at any time.

"You can leave your car here and ride with me if you want, Nan," Price offered.

"Thanks, but I'll follow. That way I can leave whenever I want." She didn't want to abandon her car at the sludge pit. She also didn't want to ride with Price and endure him looking at her legs.

"Okay, if you're sure."

"I'm sure."

Nan slid under the wheel, once more glad she'd selected the white exterior with a cool gray interior. When purchasing her new car, she'd inquired at the dealership as to which color was seen best by other motorists. The reply had been yellow first and white second.

Yellow she couldn't live with, but white was acceptable,

101

and now she'd grown to like it. There were a lot of other colors she might have selected for pure pleasure, but she had seen the police deal with so many horrible motor accidents caused mainly by drivers not seeing each other that she was determined to avoid any potential accidents by making herself as visible on the road as possible—especially since the Fox, although a solidly build car, was a subcompact.

She followed Price away from the sludge pit, past the pumping oil well, then back on to FM 203.

10

By the time Nan pulled up behind Price's car in front of a small, white frame house, the sun was beginning to set. They had talked with a lot of people in the piney woods around the sludge pit that afternoon, but nobody had seen or heard anything that seemed to help the investigation. The day had been long, but all the days were going to be long until the murderer was safely locked away.

She parked next to Price, then followed him up to the porch. A beautiful wild yellow rosebush was in bloom, and yellow leaves were scattered across the porch.

Price nodded at her, then knocked briskly. When no one answered, he knocked again. "Police!"

A young woman with short auburn hair and pale gray eyes opened the door.

"I'm Deputy Price Simmons and this is Special Investigator Nan Shubert. You're Sunny Hansen, aren't you?"

"Yes."

"We'd like to ask you some questions." Sunny unlocked and pushed open the screen door.

Price stepped inside, and Nan followed, shutting the screen door behind her.

"Have a seat," Sunny said, motioning toward a sagging couch. "Can I get you something to drink?"

"No, thank you," Nan replied, not wanting to be obligated in any way.

Price sat down, and Nan joined him. Sunny sat cautiously across from them.

"There's no easy around this, so I'll give it to you straight," Price explained. "We found a dead woman in Pineco Well Number 87's sludge pit near here."

"I know the place," Sunny replied, wondering why he mentioned only one dead woman. Hadn't they dredged the sludge pit yet?

"You don't seem surprised," Price added, looking at her more closely.

"I'm not. Billy Joe James stopped by here earlier and told me. It's a terrible thing."

"You and Billy Joe?" Price looked surprised, gave her body a quick once-over, then nodded in approval. "I hadn't heard about the two of you."

"I don't believe that's part of the investigation," Sunny replied.

"Maybe not, but it's big news." Price grinned. "Guess old Billy Joe's still got what it takes."

Sunny forced herself not to show any emotion. Now she knew exactly what Billy Joe had meant when he had insisted everybody would think they were dating. Actually, it was obvious they were going to think it was much more than dating. But what could she do? She simply couldn't let the police know about her involvement with the murders. Gossip about her liaison with Billy Joe was preferable.

"If you've seen or heard anything unusual, we really need to know," Nan explained, drawing the conversation back to the investigation."

"I'm sorry, but I can't help you." Sunny tried to keep her voice steady.

"You're new around here, aren't you?" Price asked.

"I've been here about six months," Sunny replied,

wished she had something to do with her hands, for she kept trying to clench them.

"What kind of work do you do?" he continued.

"I do the illustrations for Speedy Fix-It catalogs."

"That outfit in Longview?" Price questioned.

"Yes."

"I've seen those. They're good. Never thought about who drew them. Did you, Nan?"

"Could we see some of your work, Ms. Hansen?" Nan asked, obviously skeptical.

Sunny tensed. "Yes, of course. Just a moment. I'll get some." She quickly left the room.

"You didn't believe her?" Price looked at Nan in surprise.

"It's always a good idea to verify information. Don't you agree?"

"This is East Texas, not back East," Price replied hotly, then looked up as Sunny walked back into the room.

"Here are a few illustrations I'm working on for Speedy Fix-It, and you might be interested in these charcoal drawings I've done of Miriam Winchester." Sunny set the pieces of art on the coffee table, then sat down, wiping her palms against her jeans.

"You're very good," Nan complimented, quickly scanning the drawings. "I especially like your portraitures."

"They're just sketches of Miriam," Sunny explained. "I started doing them because she's such a wonderful subject."

"Real good," Price agreed.

"If you have the time," Nan said, glancing at Sunny, "I'd like for you to draw a portrait of me for my parents."

Sunny hesitated, knowing the request was probably Nan Shubert's way of getting back into her house to ask more questions. She was very afraid of that.

"Why don't you get a fancy picture made in Longview," Price suggested. "Those people can make you look real good, and it'll be in color, too."

105

"That's not what I want," Nan replied. "My parents have all kinds of photos of me. Their anniversary is coming up and I know they'd really treasure a portrait. What do you say, Ms. Hansen? I'd be happy to pay."

"I'm not sure, and I'd have no idea what to charge."

"What about an even hundred?"

"A hundred dollars!" Price exclaimed. "I didn't know a few pencil lines were worth that. Maybe I'd better start drawing." He laughed at his own joke.

"I'd be happy to pay half on acceptance of the commission," Nan pushed. "Then the second half on completion."

"Better take her up on it," Price winked. "Probably best offer you'll get."

Sunny hesitated, thinking. She could certainly use the money, but she didn't want to work with Nan Shubert. She didn't trust her or her sharp eyes. It would be an easy hundred as far as work was concerned, but it could be a hard hundred if the woman questioned her the whole time, which she fully expected. Still, it was quick cash, and she needed it. "All right. I accept."

Nan smiled. "Thank you." She opened her purse, pulled two twenties and a ten out of her billfold, then set them on the coffee table.

"The portrait won't take long," Sunny explained. "A couple of sittings should be enough."

"I work days, so could I come in the evenings? Or would you prefer daylight?"

"I'd like sunlight. Could you come this weekend?"

"Sure."

Sunny didn't have any plans except to go with Billy Joe to the drive-in, and somehow this put a damper on that. In fact, this put a damper on a lot of things. She didn't want Nan Shubert nosing around, but she didn't see any way out of it now. Still, if she could get the portrait done in a couple of days, satisfy Nan Shubert's curiosity, and make a hundred dollars at the same time, it would be time well spent.

"Wait'll the sheriff hears about this," Price said. "Imagine a hundred bucks for a few pencil lines."

"Maybe it'll catch on around here," Nan responded. "I'd think a lot of people would like to see an artistic interpretation of their child or loved one. A good artist can capture the essence of the whole person. Why don't you ask your wife if she'd like original drawings of your children? I imagine your thoughtfulness would please her."

"You think so?" Price's mind quickly raced down that possibility. This could make him look like he was thinking of her and the children when he was away from them. The folks would like it, too. He didn't know anybody who had original drawings of their kids. It was kind of highfalutin, and he liked that.

"So, what do you think?" Nan pushed. She had a feeling Sunny knew more than she was saying, and if she helped her make another commission, she might be more willing to trust her and talk openly.

"You could be right, Nan," Price finally agreed. "You and Sunny have got class. No doubt about it. I'll mention it to my wife. Will you charge a hundred if I get one of these portraits of both the kids?"

"She should charge more for two," Nan quickly insisted. "Isn't that right, Sunny?"

"It would be more work. Maybe for two in the same drawing I could charge one hundred fifty," Sunny replied, becoming more reluctant all the time. The last thing she wanted was to be drawn into any closer contact with the law, even if it wasn't part of the investigation.

"Okay," Price agreed. "I guess I'd still come out cheaper than if I had two done. Seems damned expensive, but I guess you artists can get away with it. I'll talk with my wife and let you know."

"All right," Sunny replied. "No rush."

"And expect to pay cash," Nan added, tapping a piece of art with the tip of her finger.

"Okay," Price agreed again. "But it's time to head home. It's been a damned long day."

"You go ahead, Price. I want to talk to Sunny a moment about the portrait."

"Oh? Well, okay. I'll see you later then." He nodded at the women, did a quick once-over, then left the house.

Nan and Sunny sat on the couch watching each other, calculating, judging, waiting. Soon they heard Price's car pull away, then head toward FM 203.

"Actually," Nan broke the silence, "I want to talk to you alone." She pushed a hand through her hair.

Sunny's heart sank. Had she somehow given herself away? She carefully stacked the pieces of art, trying to appear nonchalant.

"Since we're going to be working together, I'd like you to call me Nan. It'd make things easier, don't you think?"

"Yes, of course." Sunny took a deep breath. "And you must call me Sunny."

"Thanks. I'd like that." Nan hesitated, then gave Sunny a hard stare. "Price mentioned he wasn't going to bother questioning an older Comanche woman who lived somewhere in the area, but I'd like to see her. I don't think we should skip anyone who might possibly have seen or heard something potentially important to the case. Don't you agree?"

Relief rushed through Sunny. "Yes, of course. But Miriam Winchester has the reputation of being a crazy old woman. They might not accept her opinion."

"But a lot of clever, intelligent, insightful older women are called that, aren't they?"

"I really don't know," Sunny responded cautiously, expecting a trap.

"What I mean is, it's sometimes a misconception applied

to older women simply because they are older and a woman."

"I see what you mean," Sunny replied, wishing Nan would leave and take her rhetoric with her. It was all starting to be too much, and she simply wanted to lie down, try to stay cool, and forget the horror going on around her.

"Anyway, knowing how that can happen with older women, older men, too, for that matter, I decided I might just drop by myself. Perhaps she would talk more freely with another woman."

"She might," Sunny said, thinking of Miriam. Just because Nan was a woman wasn't going to make her instant friends with Miriam. The Comanche judged each person on their own merits, not on any external physical characteristic. "In any case, she's a sharp woman."

"Excellent. We 'girls' have to stick together, don't we?"

"Well, since a woman's been killed, we're probably more at risk than anyone else."

"Definitely. I'm glad to know you understand the situation. It's the women still alive I'm concerned about."

"You mean you think the murderer will strike again?" Sunny was playing a double-edged game, knew it, and yet had to keep it up somehow without giving herself away.

"I'm afraid so. Did Billy Joe tell you he thought he saw two bodies?"

"Yes, but Price only mentioned one."

"That's all we found, even after dredging the sludge pit." Sunny paled. "But I don't understand."

"Billy Joe must have been mistaken, or where could the second body be?" Nan ran a hand through her hair again. "Until we know for certain that this is simply one isolated murder, the women in this community should take extra precautions."

"Yes. Still, I think it's odd. Billy Joe is usually very dependable.'' Sunny shuffled her art, unaccountably alarmed by the news that another body hadn't been found.

"So I've heard. But in this case we'll just have to wait and see, won't we?''

"Yes, I suppose so.''

"Look, I don't want to keep you any longer since I know you have work to do, and I'd like to stop by Miriam Winchester's place before it gets dark. Then I'll be back Saturday. What time would be convenient for you?''

"About ten.''

"Fine.''

Nan got up and walked to the door. Sunny followed her, trying to figure out what had happened to the other dead woman. She knew she had seen two, so how could only one have been in the sludge pit? They'd dredged the pit, and that should have been that. But it wasn't.

"Sunny?'' Nan asked at the door, obviously repeating herself.

"I'm sorry. What did you say?''

"Thanks for the help. And could you give me instructions to Miriam Winchester's place?''

"Of course. Just go back out to FM 203, take the first oil road to the right, then follow it back into the pines. Her house is the first on the left. You can't miss it.''

"Thanks. See you Saturday.'' Nan smiled, then stepped outside and walked to her car. She got inside, adjusted her seat belt, then waved as she drove away.

She liked Sunny Hansen, even if the young woman seemed to be hiding something, which might or might not have to do with the case. She couldn't press Sunny to confide in her, but she wished Sunny had trusted her a little more, especially if she needed help or had information about the investigation. Of course, Sunny had naturally been protective of her friend Billy Joe James, and a little reluctant to talk.

But that was all right. Sunny was simply a careful person,

110

probably with some bad scar from the past. Most women had them. She couldn't blame Sunny for protecting herself and her friends, as long as it didn't impede the investigation. But Nan had a feeling Sunny knew something that might help the case, and she was going to try to get it out of her.

Carefully negotiating the road to what she hoped was Miriam Winchester's place, she parked her car, then walked through a blaze of wild bluebonnets. The riot of color emphasized the fact that the house was very old, very weathered, and very picturesque.

As she lifted her hand to knock on the front door, it opened. She tried to cover her surprise as she smiled pleasantly at the silver-haired, green-eyed woman who gazed fiercely into her eyes.

"Ms. Winchester, I'm Nan Shubert. A dead woman has been found in a sludge pit near here. I'm helping with the police investigation, and I'd like to ask you a few questions."

Miriam eyed her for a long moment, then nodded. "Go around back."

Surprised, Nan simply stood there. "Pardon me? Did I understand you to say—"

"Go around back. We'll talk on the porch."

Nan started to reply, but the door was abruptly shut in her face and she was left alone on the small front porch. She raised a brow and glanced around. Well, no wonder the woman had a reputation. But she still needed to talk to her. Carefully stepping off the porch, she began walking through the lush vegetation that surrounded the house.

Around back, Miriam Winchester was sitting in a rocking chair on a wide porch, drinking from a mason jar. Once more Nan simply stopped and stared. It was like something out of an antique picture and she felt chilled, as if life had

111

suddenly swirled out of her control and into another dimension.

"Sit down, girl. Have some blackberry wine."

Nan very carefully climbed the rickety-looking steps and sat down gently in an ancient rocker. It creaked with her weight and she immediately stilled.

Miriam laughed. "We may all look pretty old and fragile around here, but take my word for it, girl, we're a long sight from falling apart."

"Oh, certainly. I never meant to imply by my actions anything to the contrary."

Miriam threw back her head and laughed, showing an excellent set of natural teeth. "You need a drink quick."

"I'm sorry. I'll be driving home soon and I shouldn't risk the possibility of—"

"Just a little to relax you," Miriam insisted and poured a small amount into a jelly jar.

Nan accepted the wine, hesitated to drink the concoction, then tasted a tiny amount. She was surprised at the fragrant bouquet and smooth palate. "Delicious."

"Ought to be. I've been making blackberry wine for over fifty years."

"Well, you've certainly had experience."

"Sure have," Miriam agreed, finishing her drink. She set the jar aside, and pulled her meerschaum pipe in the shape of a sea horse out of her skirt pocket. As she filled it with sweet-smelling tobacco, she watched Nan closely.

"But what I came to discuss was the possibility that you might have seen or heard something suspicious lately. Maybe even seen someone who didn't belong in the area."

"Wish I could help you, girl. But I'm an old woman. I don't get out much. Don't need to. Got everything I need right here in the woods."

"Then you haven't seen any strangers around here?"

"Just you."

"Oh. Yes, I see. Well, I had in mind a man."

"The murderer?"

"Yes."

"Can't help you. I didn't see him."

Nan paused. She had the oddest sensation that Miriam meant that although she hadn't seen the murderer, someone had. A chill ran through her. Could someone actually have seen the killer and be withholding the information? But why? And if so, who could it be?

"More wine?"

"No, thank you. I haven't finished what I have yet." Nan quickly drank the contents of the jar and set it down. "Any help you could give us to bring this killer to justice would be greatly appreciated."

"Count on me to do what I can." Miriam hesitated and lit her pipe, puffing hard several times until she was satisfied it would stay lit. "There's one thing. I felt a cold wind the other night. I think something bad has come, some ancient evil. You'd better be careful back in these piney woods."

Nan blinked. Ancient evil? Then she smiled, sort of, remembering Miriam Winchester's reputation. "Thanks for the warning. It was one I had planned to give you, too. In fact, I might stop back by this weekend in case you've thought of anything else, or just to check in."

"You can stop by, but there's nothing more for me to remember, and I'll be okay."

"I hope so. But I'll be spending some time at Sunny Hansen's place anyway, so—"

"Sunny?"

"Yes. She's going to draw my portrait Saturday and Sunday."

Miriam looked at her suspiciously. "What'd you want a portrait of yourself for?"

"My parents anniversary, and I thought it'd be a nice

surprise for them. Deputy Simmons may have her draw his children, too.''

''This portrait work have anything to do with the dead woman?''

Miriam Winchester was not only smart but very astute, Nan quickly realized. ''Actually, just a lucky coincidence for me. My parents will be delighted with the present, I'm sure.''

''Sunny's a good artist. They ought to be pleased with her work. She's a good girl, too.''

Suddenly, Nan felt as if she had been warned. What was going on out here in the pines? She definitely had the feeling that she wouldn't want to cross this woman. It was a silly feeling, for what power could someone so completely out of touch with the times have? Still, the feeling persisted, and she defended herself. ''I like Sunny Hansen. I'm going to pay her for the portrait. The deputy will, too.''

''That's only right.''

''Yes, it is.'' Nan stood up. ''Well, thank you for your help. I'd better be on my way. Perhaps I'll stop by over the weekend.''

''I'll be here. You can have some more blackberry wine then. If ever I saw a person need it, you do.''

Surprised and faintly insulted, Nan merely said, ''Well, thank you for your time and the wine.''

Miriam chuckled. ''Come back again, girl. You're quite a show.''

Nan inhaled sharply to keep from replying rudely, then carefully got out of the rocker and stepped as lightly as possible down the stairs. Once safely on the ground, she nodded, then turned and made her way back to her car.

Inside she quickly locked all the doors, fastened her seat belt, turned on the engine, then sighed in relief. There was something about Miriam Winchester that made her feel like a clumsy adolescent, and she didn't like the feeling. She had

114

worked long and hard to become a responsible adult, and she didn't like anybody shaking that confidence.

Backing out, she turned around and started up the oil road. On FM 203, she turned the air-conditioner on high, snapped in a cassette of the Eurythmics "Revenge", and started for home.

11

Alone again, Sunny paced her living room. Had Price and Nan believed she knew nothing more than she had admitted about the murder, or were they privately finding loopholes in her story? Nan was coming back for a portrait, and maybe Price, too, so that told her something and it wasn't something she liked.

But what else could she have done? She needed the money, and if she had turned down the work, she would have looked more suspicious. I'm trapped either way I turn, she thought with renewed tension. Somehow she had to stop the worry and the doubt.

She walked into the kitchen and popped the top on a Pearl. Letting the cool, soothing liquid slide down her throat, she paced the worn linoleum, thinking. There was no reason to believe Price and Nan suspected her of anything. They were simply doing their duty, and she was going to make some extra money. There was no point in imagining problems that didn't exist.

Taking another long drink, she felt a little better. The main thing to remember was that she was still safe from Dan, and she had to stay that way no matter what. Priorities. She must remember her priorities. Staying out of Dan's hands was at the top of her list, and it had to stay that way, despite some local murder.

She walked back into the living room and glanced around. Everything was just as it had been before the police arrived, except for the fifty dollars Nan Shubert had left. She would just consider that easy money and not let it spook her.

But still she felt uneasy. Dan had done that to her, and she wondered if she would ever feel completely safe again. Sometimes she tried to remember the good times they'd shared, hoping to blot out the later terror.

And there had been good times. There were the expensive restaurants with the differential waiters and guests. Dan would be dressed in a dark, expensive, silk suit, a white shirt, and heavy, gold cuff links at each wrist. He was handsome, big, imposing, and always in command. Slender, her long hair heavy, she had always dressed in silk and spike heels. He'd liked the fact that she was an artist, young, impressionable, and dependent on him. And she'd liked it, too, before he'd turned it all against her that last six months.

Of course, there had been early warning signs in the marriage. He'd wanted to completely dominate her, and almost had because she'd been young and so much in love. There'd always been that barely restrained temper of his, but it had been exciting when it had only been a vague threat.

But once he'd lost his job, the violence had become very real. She hadn't known they'd been living so far above their means until he had lost the income, the credit, everything needed to keep his little empire afloat. Her salary wasn't nearly enough to suit Dan's lavish tastes, and he couldn't stand the idea of his wife supporting him, anyway.

So he had begun to hurt her psychologically, undermining her confidence and embarrassing her in public or in front of her friends or colleagues. He would plot elaborate schemes to give her the utmost psychological torment. Suddenly she never looked good anymore, no matter what she wore or how she did her hair. And he began to put down

117

her art, trying to make her think she wasn't good enough to become an acclaimed illustrator, or even able to finish her college degree.

At first she had tried to explain his words away by his need to exert the lack of control he felt in his professional life with her at home. It was as if he thought she had too much power in their relationship by making the money, and he wouldn't give her any more power by loving her, or needing her, or giving her support, either emotionally, mentally, or physically. Soon there hadn't been any sex, except what he used to try and dominate her.

But psychological torment and emotional and physical withdrawal were soon not enough for him; within six months he had moved to physical violence. Once she had gone out with friends directly after work and didn't get home until around nine, laughing and happy. But that had only lasted a moment, for when she saw his face she knew she was in trouble.

In an explosion of rage, he had started busting up an antique armoire, the only legacy from her parents. He had hit it with his fists, and ripped it apart with his hands, throwing it across the room. Then he had started in on her clothes, tearing them apart, throwing them at her while screaming abuse. She had been so stunned and hurt she could only stand there and stare in terror and fear, until finally she had screamed back at him, defending herself as best she could. Then he had slapped her, thrown her up against a wall, and left. Later he had come back drunk. Much later he had apologized.

And once more she had tried to explain it all away. She had done that for a long time, until she had finally realized there was no going back to what they'd had. In fact, she was lucky to be alive, especially after that last horrible attack.

Shivering, she glanced around, drawing herself back to the present. She didn't want to think about Dan and the bad times. She had been trying to remember the good. But she was cold again, despite the heat. Dan would never have let her go if he'd had a choice. And now that she'd run away, she had no doubt he would kill her if he could find her. No, the police mustn't know about her. It was too risky.

She walked back into the kitchen and finished her beer. Throwing away the can, she checked the back door. It was locked tight. She tried the front door and found it locked, too. Safe. She was safe. What she needed now was to take her mind off Dan, murder, and the police.

Picking up Nan's fifty dollars as she walked across the living room, she felt a little better. At least someone seemed to think she could still draw fairly well. That helped to make her feel better. Maybe she was going to make it, after all.

She went into her studio and hid the money inside her pencil holder. Sitting down, she checked her list of Speedy Fix-It products to draw, then selected the correct Rapido-graph and got to work.

Some time later she heard a knock at the back door. Surprised, she glanced up and noticed it was dark outside. She didn't know how long she had been working, but it must have been several hours. Yawning and stretching, she set another completed illustration aside and got up.

The only person she could imagine being at her back door was Miriam, but she was well aware that deep down she expected to find Dan every time she answered the door. She hated that expectation, but didn't know how to stop it.

Walking into the kitchen, she flipped on the light and stepped to the back door.

There was another knock, and Miriam called, ''Sunny, are you awake?''

''Just a minute.'' She quickly unlocked and opened the door and screen.

Miriam smiled and stepped inside, carrying a large round object about a foot in diameter. ''How're you doing?''

119

"Okay. What have you got there?" Sunny locked the door behind her friend.

"A medicine wheel. I made it for you. For protection."

"I thought we had the police for that."

"Spiritual, psychic protection."

"Now wait a minute, Miriam. You know how I feel about that stuff. I'm an atheist. I believe in this one life and my five senses. Nothing else."

"Don't you think the wheel is attractive?"

"Well, yes, it's a beautiful piece of art. I didn't know you could do that."

"Neither did I, but I'm learning I can do a lot of things I haven't done before, or not since I was a child."

"That's good, but why did you make it for me?"

"A lot of reasons. We need to talk, Sunny. Can we do that, or are you busy?"

"Sure. I've been working and could use a break. Why don't I get us a beer and we can sit in the living room? While Sunny opened the refrigerator, Miriam carried the medicine wheel into the living room. She glanced around, checked the directions, and decided the wheel should be hung on the west wall, the direction representing death and resurrection, for she had decided Sunny needed to be protected from death and to obtain resurrection from her marriage.

The medicine wheel had been hard to construct because she had to protect Sunny on two fronts: Dan and the murderer. Also, she simply didn't have the medicine or shaman knowledge she needed to know she was doing everything correct. Her grandmother wasn't here to instruct her, so she had to rely on herself. It was something she had never in her wildest dreams imagined needing to do, not in their current world, but she was rapidly discovering that she had more shaman instincts and knowledge than she had even realized.

"Here's your beer," Sunny said, entering the living room.

"I think we should put the medicine wheel on this wall. You don't have anything else there, anyway."

"I don't want to take it, even though you made it for me." She set the beers on the coffee table. "If I accept it, it'll be as if I believe that some evil occult force is behind the murders. And that simply is not true."

Miriam set the medicine wheel down and leaned it against the wall. She walked over to Sunny and smiled. "I wouldn't try to force you to believe in something you don't. At this point, I'm not completely sure what *I* believe. If you'll let me put it up you don't have to believe in anything except my own personal determination to keep you safe. Is that too much to ask?"

Sunny hesitated, looked at the wheel again, then nodded. "No, I guess not, and my living room can certainly use some decorating."

"Good. Have you got a hammer and nail?"

"Just a minute."

While Sunny went back into the kitchen, Miriam picked up the medicine wheel again. She held it close and shut her eyes, imagining the center closing against any force that might try to enter Sunny's psychic dimension, her personal inner space. Then she chanted, a low, keening sound that made the hairs rise on the back of her neck. Satisfied, she glanced up as Sunny entered the room. "If you'll put the nail in about there, I'll hang the wheel."

"Okay." Sunny hammered in the nail, then stepped back. "I didn't know you could chant. You really sounded Indian."

"Native American. It's a more accurate term."

"Well, that's right. Columbus thought he was in India, and—"

"Named us Indians. The label may have stuck, but we don't have to accept it."

"No, of course not. I'm sorry, I didn't realize the difference."

"That's all right. A lot of people don't." Miriam carefully placed the medicine wheel against the wall, making sure it caught against the nail securely, then stepped back.

"It looks good."

"And most important, it'll protect you."

"If that's what you want to believe."

"I do." Miriam squeezed Sunny's hand and led her over to the couch. "Now, I'm ready for that beer." They sat silently for a while, drinking and looking at Miriam's crafted creation.

"Sunny, I want to tell you about this wheel. Perhaps it'll have more power for you if you understand the symbolism in it."

"All right, but I'm not promising anything."

"That's all right. We'll take it one step at a time."

Sunny drank more beer, wishing Miriam wasn't going to talk about things that would give her chills. But there seemed no way around it this time.

"As you can see," Miriam began, motioning toward the wheel. "It is an open circle, made of willow branch and wrapped in deerskin. You can think of the round shape as representing the earth, and I've stretched rolled strips of leather from north to south and east to west, indicating directions. Tied in the center is a medicine bundle, a square of leather wrapped around sage, cedar, lavender, sweet grass, and some protective herbs. It represents the Great Spirit."

"What are those colored beads for?" Sunny tapped the side of her beer can, more interested than she'd thought she would be.

"From each direction I've tied a leather strip and let it dangle free. Knotted into the strip are several beads in colors representing their element. In other words, yellow beads represent the element air and the east, red beads are for the element fire and the south, black beads are for water and the west, and white beads are for earth and the north. The blending of those elements gives shape and form to us and all we do."

"I see."

"The elements also have animal totems, which can vary from nation to nation. As an example, the earth can be represented by a turtle. In fact, North America is called Turtle Island by Native Americans."

"I didn't realize that. Is it because it represents the earth element?"

"Yes, partly. You're catching on quickly."

"I don't know about that, but it's beginning to make some sense."

"Well, maybe I'm explaining this better than I thought."

"But it's still very complicated, Miriam."

"Only while it's unfamiliar. I've done my best to be accurate, basing it on what my grandmother taught me and what I can remember. But you have to understand that she wasn't pure Comanche. She was also part Caddo. And that makes her teachings both Comanche and Caddo. Her medicine knowledge was based on several Native American cultures, and she primarily used what worked for her. That's what she passed down to me."

"So each medicine woman works differently."

"Yes, depending on her training, nation, tribe, and personal power. So, what I'm telling you might not be quite the same as you would hear in another part of the country. However, in essence it would all be similar."

"It's okay, Miriam. I'm not going to question you or go off trying to find a better teacher. Mainly, I just want to get on with my life and keep you happy."

Miriam smiled and drank more beer. "Thank you. I understand that. I think I'm trying to convince myself more than you, for I'm not at all sure about what I'm doing."

"Thanks! You're making me feel better all the time."

"What I mean is that my knowledge is sketchy, and my powers, if they exist, are rusty, at the very least."

"I don't care, Miriam. If you believe in this medicine wheel and want me to have it, then that's enough. I believe in you."

Miriam squeezed Sunny's hand, and tears misted her eyes. "Thank you for your faith. I'll try to be worthy of your trust." She swallowed hard. "Now, where was I?"

"I'm not at all sure."

Miriam laughed. "Neither am I, and maybe it doesn't even matter. We'll just do the best we can."

"I hope you aren't planning to test me on all this."

"No. I just wanted you to know about the medicine wheel. Another thing, the wheel is to remind us that life is a circle without beginning or end, and when broken into twenty-eight sections, it can be used as a moon calendar, with the twenty-ninth moon represented by the center."

"Well, the medicine wheel certainly seems to represent a lot of things."

"It can. Basically, it's like our science, where two or three letters represent a chemical element, or in the English language, where a letter represents a certain sound and several letters make up a word which will make a sentence. It's all a matter of communication."

"I see, but it still seems very complex."

"Not if you had grown up with it and it was a part of your culture."

"I appreciate your hard work, Miriam, and I wish I could believe more in the medicine wheel's power."

"When I made it, I chanted, visualizing strong protection around you. I believe it will help. I know all of this is hard for you to accept, and I don't even ask it. But I do know about my grandmother's power. I watched her bring the rain when we needed it. I saw wild animals walk right up and eat from her hands. And she could heal. She had power, real power. It's something you can believe in or not

124

believe in. But it doesn't matter much either way because it is still very real once it enters your life."

"But we don't know it has entered my life, or yours, or anybody's life around here. What we have is a dead woman. That's pretty simple."

"It's not simple." Miriam finished her beer and set down the can. "Based on all that my grandmother taught me, on all that I remember, on all that I feel now, this is not a simple murder. Somehow, and I don't know how, I think you're a key force in a struggle that is taking place around us. I've been thinking long and hard about these murders. The Caddo discovered oil in East Texas long before the whites. They used to bathe in springs and pools of it to drive away rheumatic pains, or they applied it as an ointment to cuts, burns, sores, and even drank it for medicine. But they never hurt the land, for they took only what was given."

"But that was a long time ago."

"Time is not what matters here. The whites came, but they had no respect for the earth. They took her black blood in huge quantities, they took her gas. The land has been denuded, bulldozed, twisted, polluted, and now it is being strip-mined. The earth hurts, and sometimes I feel her pain and the pain of the animals who try to exist here."

"But we're talking about simple economics. People must survive, and they need the natural resources to do it. I admit there has been terrible waste and destruction here, and surely there could have been better ways of taking the oil and gas, but still, people have to survive."

"I agree with you. But it doesn't change the fact that the land has been hurt. You have been hurt, and you came to this wounded land. Now another woman, or perhaps two, has been hurt and thrown back into the bleeding earth. Don't you think symbolism alone says something, Sunny?"

"No. It's all simply a matter of coincidence. I came here because I couldn't afford to go farther." She finished her beer and set the can down with a snap.

125

"You could have gone north, or west, or south."

"I vacationed here once, and it was pretty."

"Or your destiny drew you here."

"No, I'm here to hide from Dan. That's all I know. You can put your medicine wheel on my wall. You can chant in my living room. You can tell me interesting stories. But only because I've come to trust you, not because I think the wheel will do any good, or that there's anything but bad men to watch out for."

"Well, maybe you're safest believing that for now." Miriam squeezed Sunny's hand. "But I'm afraid a time is coming when you will have to recognize that there are forces converging around you that will lead you to believe in more than you ever have before."

"If that's the case, I'll worry about it then. In the meantime, I'm just trying to survive and not doing real well at that."

"You're doing very well, Sunny. Don't ever doubt that. I'm proud of you, and I'm here to help you."

Sunny squeezed her friend's hand in return. "I'm sorry. I don't mean to belittle what you've said or what you're trying to do. It's just that I'm already frightened, and all your talk is scaring me even worse."

"That's not what I meant to do. I'd hoped the medicine wheel would comfort you."

"If I believed in it, maybe it would. As it is, it's more likely to scare me in the middle of the night if I walk out here and forget it's on the wall."

Miriam laughed. "I hadn't thought of that." She shook her head. "Well, I'd better be off. I'm trying to remember so much of what my grandmother taught me. But when I was young, the world was changing, and I thought there would never be a need for it. How wrong I was." She stood up.

"Maybe you're wrong, and Nan Shubert will call us tomorrow to tell us the murderer has been caught."

They walked to the back door, then hugged. "Do you want me to walk you home, Miriam? Or I could drive you. You know you shouldn't be out alone at night with that killer out there."

"You're the one I'm more worried about. I'd rather you stayed here where you're safer. Besides, I can walk through those woods so that no one knows I'm passing. And I'd be out there, anyway. I want to get a feel of the night and try to remember."

"All right, but be careful."

Miriam smiled, then slipped through the door and disappeared silently into the darkness.

Watching at the door, Sunny wondered if she should have insisted on driving Miriam home. Then she realized that Miriam did as she pleased, and she could not have insisted on anything. Sighing, she shut and locked the door. She didn't like the idea of Miriam being out there alone, but she also figured her friend was safer than anyone else in the woods at night.

She walked back through the house and stopped to look at the medicine wheel. Surprised, she noticed a powerful feeling coming from it. Then she scoffed at the idea and turned away.

But she was left feeling more uneasy than ever. It had been bad enough hiding out from Dan, then finding dead women in a sludge pit. If she started believing in some unknown, unseen, uncontrollable evil power, how could she possibly fight it?

12

About 2:00 A.M. Saturday morning, a big, dark car drove slowly down FM 203, turned off on an oil road, then purred past Pineco's Well Number 87 and stopped. When the car's engine was turned off, the forest's silence was broken only by the sound of the pumping well.

A tall man got out, looked around, circled a Pontiac Bonneville, and opened the door on the passenger side. A crumpled form fell into his arms. He glanced around again, then lifted a woman's body into his arms.

The sludge pit beckoned under the light of a waxing moon, and he walked toward it, glancing occasionally at the head lolling back against his arm, the eyes wide and staring, the dark hair soft and shiny.

He hesitated a moment at the edge of the pit, then placed the body in the glistening water. She floated a moment, as oil began to stain her clothing, collect in her hair, and darken her face. He waited for her to sink. When she didn't, he picked up a fallen branch and began to poke at her, forcing her body to submerge.

When the body finally disappeared, he stood up straight, nodded in satisfaction, tossed the stick aside, and walked back to the car.

He slipped into the comfort of the Pontiac, turned up the

air-conditioner, found a religious radio station, then backed out. On FM 203, he drove slowly, enjoying the feel of the big, heavy, powerful car. He tapped the steering wheel in time with "Onward Christian Soldiers," then drove into Gusher. The small town was quiet and dark, obviously asleep.

He liked this time of night. It made him feel powerful and in control, as if he owned the world and could do whatever he liked.

The music changed to Stryper, one of the white metal rock groups. He snapped off the station. No matter what they said, he believed listening to any kind of rock and roll music, even if it was Christian, could lead you straight to the devil. He had spent a lifetime trying to avoid the devil, and he was not going to let some music trap him.

On the north side of town he noticed a closed filling station. It looked familiar. Then he remembered it was where he liked to call the Reverend Isaiah Mulhaney.

He turned off the road and parked near the public phone booth. Getting out, he felt in his pocket for a quarter. Fortunately, he found one.

He was glad the phone was in one of the older booths where you could go inside and shut the door. He liked that, liked the privacy, but he kept his foot in the door so the light wouldn't come on. He didn't like the bright light shining down on him, spotlighting him. No, he didn't like that kind of light. Hated it, in fact.

He shivered, glad he had the overcoat to keep him warm, and glanced around, wondering if he was being watched. Was there someone in that big car waiting for him? Where did it come from? He didn't remember seeing it before. Then he felt the keys in his hand. Car keys. It must be his, but he didn't remember owning a car like that. Pretty fancy for him, but then he deserved good things.

He felt better. He had a dial tone now and wanted to talk to the Reverend. He'd think about the car later. He dialed the number quickly from memory, then waited while it rang and rang and rang.

Finally, on the thirteenth ring, the receiver was picked up. "Hello," a sleep-rough voice said, "Reverend Mulhaney here."

"Reverend?"

"Oh, it is you. How are you?"

"I'm fine. I have a new car."

"Good. You must have found a job."

"A job?"

"The last time we talked you were looking for work and a place to stay."

"Oh, yes. I'd forgotten we discussed that. Well, I must be doing okay to have such a fancy car."

"What did you get?"

"It looks like a Pontiac. A big one."

"Well, if it looks like one it must be one." Reverend Mulhaney chuckled at his wit.

"Yes, that must be right. Reverend, I wondered what you thought of this new rock and roll religious music? I'm afraid if I listen to it, I'll go straight to the devil."

"Well, of course, I like the old standards best, but I understand they are trying to reach a bigger, younger audience."

"But is that right?"

"I do not recommend it to my flock, but we are living in a media-sophisticated world, and a lot of ministers are trying unusual methods to bring the good word to those poor sinners out there."

"But will it make them go to the devil, anyway?"

"I do not know, son. To be on the safe side, I would avoid it."

"Just what I thought. I hate it. I never listen to it. It's dirty. That's what I think. Dirty. Like women. When something's dirty through and through, you just can't get it clean."

"But we cannot stop trying, can we?"

"No, sir. I've been trying to do good all my life, but it's not easy with the devil out there tempting you all the time, especially with women."

"I know. The devil is clever. You have to beware of him all the time. And women must be guided and taught so they don't drag men down into sin with them."

"That's right. I do my best, but it's not easy, and it's hard to remember sometimes."

"As I get older, I sometimes have a little trouble remembering myself. Do not worry about it. I am just glad to know you have a good job and a new car. Would you consider coming to services on Sunday? I would be glad to have you meet some of the church members. I think you would make friends easily with my flock."

"That sounds good, Reverend. Maybe I will. I'd like to be part of your church. In fact, I feel like I already am."

"Thank you, son. So do I, and I appreciate your confidence in me. Do not forget to call any time you need to talk. I am always ready to help."

"Thank you. You're a good man, Reverend."

"I hope to see you Sunday."

"I'll try."

"Good. See you then."

"Bye, Reverend."

When Reverend Mulhaney heard the click on the other end of the receiver, he hung up, a concerned furrow creasing his brow. He was glad the man had found a job and bought a new car, but there was something about the stranger that disturbed him. Maybe if the man came to church on Sunday, he would meet him and feel better about the situation.

It was a hard world, and the devil was always busy. He just hoped this upstanding Christian man would join his flock. Joining a religious group always helped to stabilize a man and make him understand God's word more clearly.

With friends, this stranger would feel a part of the community and would not need these late-night calls.

Satisfied that it was only a matter of time before he had a new member of his church, Reverend Mulhaney started to go back to bed, but he was no longer sleepy.

He tried to read his Bible, but had already planned his Sunday's sermon and did not want to confuse it with other lessons from the good book. He put his Bible down and picked up the *Kilgore News Herald* which had been delivered that afternoon. The headline leaped out at him, ''Woman Murdered and Dumped in Sludge Pit.''

When he first read the article earlier that evening, he had been deeply shocked, and as he scanned the article again he felt the same horror grip him.

The report referred to a sludge pit in his own community. He had called the sheriff to find out the details, in case someone needed his help as a minister. Sheriff Barker had been reluctant to say much, but had given him the location of the sludge pit, warning him to tell no one else its exact location.

The sludge pit was not far away. He could drive over there and observe the scene of the crime. In fact, he felt sure it was his duty to see the place. When his flock came to church on Sunday, they would be worried, needing his reassurance and support about this grisly crime that had come into their midst. Yes, he should take a look at the sludge pit so he would know how to calm their fears.

The women in the community would be worried, frightened, and in need of direction. A man, especially a man of God, had to take control at a time like this. In fact, he should probably change his sermon, drawing on something from the Bible that directly pertained to women. The ''whore of Babylon'' came to mind, then ''suffer not a witch to live,'' and ''scarlet woman.'' But none of those seemed especially comforting, or exactly pertinent.

No, they would not do. He thought awhile, then he

132

smiled, feeling divinely inspired. He knew exactly what would work. He would talk about Mary, the mother of Christ. There had never been a better or more inspiring woman.

Yes, he would remind the women that if they were good wives and mothers, seeking only to help and serve others, they should not fear ending up dead in a sludge pit. He could even see how the news item could be used to remind women of their proper place in life and to comfort them at the same time.

He would indeed change his sermon, and everyone would feel much better. It was times like these that made him feel proud to be a servant of God. He would help others and serve his Lord at the same time. Nothing could be better.

But before he wrote the sermon, he should probably have a look at the sludge pit just to make sure everything was under control. He did not want any members of his church being frightened by unfounded rumors. He would also get back in contact with Sheriff Barker. He needed to be kept up on the case if he were to serve his flock and God properly.

Feeling very good about taking control, Reverend Mulhaney carefully dressed in old clothes, putting on galoshes just in case it was messy around the pit, and went out to his car. He sat down in the driver's seat of his blue Chrysler, then picked up his flashlight and checked to make sure the battery was still strong. Satisfied that all was in order, he locked the car doors and turned on the engine.

As he headed down FM 203, he checked his watch and noticed that it was well after two in the morning. He thought about how isolated and alone he would be at the sludge pit. He briefly considered returning home and waiting until daylight to examine the pit, but he wanted to be prepared if any church member called about the crime. He was determined that his flock could count on him to be in total control during any emergency.

He turned onto the narrow oil road leading to Pineco's Well Number 87. He stopped a little past the pumping well, shut off the engine of his car, then sat still for a moment.

Finally, he took a deep breath and opened the door. The night was quiet, except for the pumping of the well. The sound comforted him, reminding him of the two oil wells in the back yard of his church.

He was not afraid, of course. God was with him. But he did feel a flutter of excitement in the pit of his stomach. He quickly dismissed that as indigestion. Stepping out of the car, he turned on his flashlight and followed the small yellow beam down the oil road.

The night air was hot, moist, and filled with the scent of pine and wildflowers. He worried about his sinuses as his feet sank into the soft surface of the road, still warm from the heat of the day. He was glad he had worn his galoshes, since he did not care to ruin a perfectly good pair of shoes.

He stopped near the sludge pit. It did not appear in the least sinister. In fact, he found it hard to believe that a dead woman had been taken from there. With the moon shining on it, the dark water looked rather pretty in an austere kind of way.

Walking right up to the edge of the pit, he glanced around, casting the soft yellow beam from his flashlight back and forth across the surface of the stagnant pond. Everything looked perfectly normal, if one could call a sludge pit normal.

In fact, it really was difficult to believe a crime of violence had been committed here. He glanced up at the waxing moon, then around at the dark forest. Everything appeared peaceful, even placid.

He smiled, pleased with himself. There was nothing much to see, and certainly nothing to be afraid of. The best thing to do was say a prayer for the dead woman and go home. Had she gone to heaven or hell? He did not know, but he

134

would pray for her salvation and assent to heaven, rather than having to submit to the horrors of hell.

After a time of silence in which he prayed for the dead woman's soul, he added that he hoped the killer would be brought to justice, punished, and shown the error of his ways. If the murderer accepted Christ, then he could be forgiven and cleansed of his sin and join Christ in heaven at the right hand of God. He prayed for that, too.

Maybe his prayers would be answered and he would be given the honor of meeting and converting the obviously Godless killer. He would keep informed on the case, and as soon as the murderer was brought in, he would ask Sheriff Barker to allow him to minister to the errant soul.

He smiled. Yes, he had done the right thing by coming out here tonight. God had given him a message. He would help not only the dead woman, but save the killer's soul, as well. Feeling very satisfied, he glanced down, aiming his flashlight at the edge of the pit.

The light struck the vacant, open eyes of a woman just under the surface of the oily water.

Reverend Mulhaney choked, gasped for air, then grabbed his chest as he felt pain contract his heart and race down his left arm to his hand. He sank to his knees, face to face with the woman in the water. Horrified, he gagged, and opened his mouth repeatedly, trying to drag in air.

Dazed, he fell forward into the water, hitting the woman. Face to face, they were united for a moment before he managed to push himself up, using the dead woman's body for leverage, and hoist himself to the bank. Lying in the oily muck, his chest wracked with pain, he faced the pit unable to move, and watched helplessly as the dead woman popped to the surface, rivulets of black oil cascading around her slim body.

Again he gagged and felt bile rise in his throat. As his heart continued to squeeze out pain, his stomach emptied itself of its contents.

He could not move, could not control the pain in his chest, and could not stop watching the woman, whose dead eyes stared sightlessly up at the moon.

After what seemed an endlessly long time, the pain in his chest began to ease. His breath began to come more freely. He closed his eyes, blocking out the sight of the dead woman's staring eyes, oily hair, and body made brazen by the oil and water molding her short dress to her curves.

And while his eyes were shut, he told himself over and over that it was some trick of the devil. As a servant of God, he did not find dead women in sludge pits. In fact, perhaps it was not the devil at all. Perhaps it was a vision sent by God to test him. Yes, that sounded right.

There was no dead woman in the sludge pit. They had already taken her out. This vision was simply God testing his strength, reminding him of his own mortality and of all he had to do before his own ascent to heaven.

Satisfied with his explanation and feeling better, although exhausted from the experience, Reverend Mulhaney sat up, keeping his eyes closed, and edged back from the pit. When he felt reasonably calm, he opened his eyes again. A whimper began to come from his lips, growing louder and louder until he was moaning, "No. No. No."

The chanting grew louder until he leapt to his feet, screamed, "No!" at the floating body, then ran back down the oil road to his car. He threw himself into the seat, turned the key, ground the starter, pumped the gas pedal, but the car did not start. He pumped harder and harder, then smelled gasoline. He knew he was going to flood the engine in a moment, but couldn't stop his frantic movement. He had to get away.

He was caught in a nightmare. The worst ever. He had to get away before the woman got up out of the water, raised her long, wet arms, and came after him, putting her cold, blue lips against his, drawing his breath from his body, drawing his life into her, and sending him straight to hell and the devil.

It was no vision from God!

He ground the starter again and again, pumping the gas pedal, sweat dripping off his face. His heart began to cramp again. The pain raced down his left arm like the cut of a sharp knife. He glanced toward the sludge pit, expecting to see the woman coming up the road for him at any moment. He had to get away before she followed him. But the car would not start. She was controlling it. That was it. He had never had this kind of trouble before. She was a witch!

Terrified, he clutched his chest, his face turning bluish. Suddenly the engine turned over and purred to life.

He threw the car into reverse, careened off the road, and backed into a tree. Yelping in pain and terror, he shifted gears, and jerked away from the tree. He risked a glance back down the road. Yes, he could see her coming for him now, or was it only a trick of the light?

He didn't wait to find out. He gunned the engine and sped backwards, then spun around onto FM 203. He did not slow down until he reached Roy H. Laird Memorial Hospital in Kilgore. Throwing on the brakes, he jumped out of the car and ran into the emergency room, screaming to be protected from avenging dead women.

The emergency crew hooked him up to machines and wheeled him into intensive care, wondering how he had ever managed to drive in by himself and just where had he been, anyway.

But Reverend Mulhaney was unable to answer any of their questions, even about his insurance, for he was locked in a battle with the dead woman from the sludge pit, and they were both bathed in the light of a full moon.

13

'Second Woman Found Dead In Sludge Pit,'' Sunny read aloud from the headline of the *Longview News Journal*, then glanced at Billy Joe who was sitting at her kitchen table.

"I knew you'd want to read the article, so I brought the morning paper over." Billy Joe took a gulp of hot coffee.

"Doesn't it seem odd they didn't find the body when they dredged the pit?"

"Damned odd, but I suppose it could happen."

"And to think Reverend Mulhaney found a dead woman just the way I did." Sunny refilled her mug of coffee.

"Yes. It's strange, all right."

"How's he doing?"

"The paper says he's in 'stable condition,' whatever that means."

"Probably means he'll be all right, as long as he stays away from sludge pits." She grimaced at her attempt at humor.

"I keep wondering why he went out there alone in the middle of the night."

"What drew me out there?"

"I doubt if it was the same thing."

"Do you suppose Reverend Mulhaney saw the killer too?"

"I'd guess not, Sunny."

"Maybe not, but if he did, he isn't telling."

"Or he may have told the police more than the news media knows. In fact, the police still haven't given out the location of the sludge pit."

"But Reverend Mulhaney obviously knew."

"Maybe because he's a minister he got special information from the police." Billy Joe finished his coffee.

"Perhaps. Speaking of the police, have you heard any more from them?" She was surprised she could discuss the murders with Billy Joe so easily, but they were in it together and maybe that made all the difference, even though he was a man and normally she wouldn't have trusted him.

"They're pretty closemouthed about the whole thing."

"I figured they would be." She took a sip of coffee. "Nan Shubert is coming over today."

"What for? How'd you get mixed up with her?"

"You know they were questioning everyone in the area, and she saw some sketches I'd done of Miriam and decided she wanted me to draw a portrait of her."

"Is she being straight?"

"Who knows? I couldn't pass up the hundred dollars. It'll just be a few hours work, today and tomorrow."

"She's bound to ask more questions. Be careful, but find out what you can from her. Things are looking screwy. For instance, I don't understand how the Reverend found the body when the dredgers didn't."

"It doesn't make much sense, but nothing about this does, anyway."

"I agree." Billy Joe stood up. "I didn't mean to stay so long. I just wanted you to see the headline. I guess you've got to get ready for the portrait."

"No rush. Just pencil or charcoal, and paper. Have another cup of coffee."

"I don't want—"

139

"I'd be grateful for the company. I'm a little nervous about being with Nan Shubert. She's sharp."

He sat down again. "I know what you mean. Damned determined, too. Bet if anybody finds the killer fast, she's the one."

"At least it looks like she's trying hard, not that Sheriff Barker isn't. Still, I don't much want her nosing around me."

"Just be careful what you say, and—"

A rap on the front door interrupted them.

Sunny tensed, glancing in that direction.

"Time for her?"

"No. She's due at ten."

"About fifteen minutes early."

"I'd better let her in."

"Then I'll be going."

"No. Why don't you stay and have a cup of coffee with us first."

"You are nervous about her, aren't you?" He glanced at Sunny and noticed the heightened color in her cheeks.

"Yes."

"Okay, I'll stay awhile."

"Thanks."

Sunny answered the door. Nan stood on the porch, looking a little tentative in a pair of old jeans, tennis shoes, and a blue cotton shirt. She looked more friendly out of her business attire, but Sunny still didn't trust her.

"Morning," Nan said pleasantly. "Sorry I'm early, but it took less time to get here than I'd thought."

"No problem. Come on in. Billy Joe James is here. He just stopped by with the morning paper."

"Then you know about the second body?"

"Yes. Looks like Billy Joe was right."

"In a way," Nan qualified, then stepped inside.

"What do you mean?" Sunny closed the front door.

140

"Come on in the kitchen and have a cup of coffee with us before Billy Joe has to leave."

As they walked through the living room, Nan asked, "What's that on the wall?"

"Miriam made me a protective medicine wheel."

"Oh, it's nice."

"I appreciate her thoughtfulness."

They walked into the kitchen, where soft morning light warmed the room. Billy Joe stood up and smiled.

"I think you've met Nan Shubert," Sunny said, motioning for them to sit down at the table.

"Yes, I have." Billy Joe dropped back into his chair.

"At the sludge pit," Nan added, sitting down at the table.

Sunny poured Nan a cup of coffee and refilled Billy Joe's empty mug. "What did you mean about Billy Joe being partly right about the second body, Nan?"

Nan warmed her hands over the cup of coffee and sighed. "I've been up since about four, so I'm not sure how much sense I'm making right now. Anyway, since Billy Joe found the first body, I'm still hoping to pull more information out of him."

Billy Joe nodded, watching her closely.

"But please don't spread any of what I have to tell you around yet," Nan entreated, glancing at both of them.

"We won't," Billy Joe agreed.

Sunny nodded. "I guess the body was in pretty bad shape by the time you saw it."

"What do you mean?" Nan asked.

"I mean it had to have been in the water awhile," Sunny explained.

"Oh, you mean you thought it was the body Billy Joe thought he saw but they couldn't find?"

"Yes, of course," Sunny agreed.

"That's just the thing." Nan looked at each of them in turn. "Billy Joe must have had some sort of premonition.

141

I went down and saw the second body. It was another young woman, but she had been dead only a few hours, we think."

"What?" Sunny scalded her tongue on hot coffee. "But that can't be right."

"They dredged the pit," Nan explained, "and there wasn't another body in there. Someone put this woman in the sludge pit last night, actually early this morning about two, we're guessing. We don't have all the facts yet, of course."

Sunny felt sick to her stomach. Then this was the third woman to be killed. But what could have happened to the second, the woman with the long, blond hair? She caught Billy Joe's eye, and he raised a brow. He obviously was as confused as she.

"So we've got what I suspected from the first but couldn't prove until now." Nan took a sip of coffee. "We've got a murderer who has struck twice and will probably kill again if he gets the chance. We've got to stop him and soon."

"Have the police got any leads?" Billy Joe clutched his mug of coffee.

"And have they staked out the sludge pit?" Sunny asked.

Nan threw up her hands. "One question at a time, please. No, Sheriff Barker hasn't staked out the sludge pit. First he thought it was an isolated murder. Second, he's trying to deal with the second killing. Third, I doubt if he has the staff since it has been drastically cut these last few years. Also, do you really think the killer would trust his luck to use the pit a third time?"

"I don't know," Sunny replied thoughtfully.

"But have the police got any leads?" Billy Joe insisted.

"We have information on the first victim." Nan ran a hand through her hair. "She was a young woman from Shreveport, Louisiana, a computer programmer, going to pick up her children at her sister's place in the country. She had taken Interstate 20 across the state line into East Texas,

142

but never reached her sister in Tyler and never came home. It's a damned shame. The children are only three and five, and her husband's heartbroken.''

''That's horrible.'' Sunny lowered her head.

''They found her car,'' Nan explained, ''but it had been wiped clean. The murderer was smart. We've got little to go on. Sheriff Barker thinks the victim had car trouble or stopped to pick up a hitchhiker, who turned out to be the murderer. They also suspect the second woman was traveling on the interstate because no local woman has been reported missing.''

Sunny shuddered and wrapped her hand around her hot mug of coffee. But she knew nothing was going to warm the deep cold that had invaded her. ''Is there anything we can do?''

''Just try to remember anything or anybody unusual in the area.''

''I wish I could help more.'' Billy Joe gave Sunny a questioning look.

''Just keep your ears open. Any information you pick up could help.'' Nan opened her purse and took out a small, white business card. ''Here's my card with my business and home numbers. Call anytime. A lot of times the best clues come from people living and working in the area.'' She handed one to Billy Joe and another to Sunny.

''Okay,'' Billy Joe agreed, putting the card in his shirt pocket. ''I'll do what I can.'' He glanced at Sunny again, but she shook her head negatively.

''And, Sunny, do you suppose you could draw portraits of any strangers you've seen in the area?'' Nan asked.

''I haven't seen any strangers,'' Sunny replied, really sorry she couldn't be of more help.

''Well, if you do or know anyone who does, please sketch them for us. That would help a lot.''

"I will."

"That's it then," Nan said. "I just wish we had more to go on."

"So do I," Billy Joe agreed, finishing his coffee. "Maybe something will turn up soon." He stood up. "But for now, I'd better be going. You two've got work to do. See you around seven, Sunny."

"Okay. Thanks for stopping by."

After Billy Joe left, Sunny led Nan out to the back porch, then positioned her in a rocking chair in the yard so that the north light fell directly on her face. She hadn't been sketching long before Nan began to fidget.

"You can talk if it helps relieve the monotony," Sunny suggested.

"I didn't realize modeling would be such hard work."

Sunny laughed. "It is. I did a little of it for art classes to make extra money, and I quickly got to where I could hardly sit still."

"I see what you mean." Nan hesitated, closed her eyes against the brilliant sunlight, then looked thoughtfully at Sunny. "Billy Joe seems like a nice guy."

"He does, doesn't he?" But Sunny didn't say any more, determined not to let Nan trap her into any kind of confession.

"I sometimes wonder how there can be so much difference in men, with some like Billy Joe and some like the murderer. I also wonder how a woman can tell the difference when she meets a man."

Sunny stopped drawing and looked hard at Nan. "Do you think Billy Joe is the murderer?"

"No! That's not what I meant. Of course, I suppose technically he could be, but I don't think so."

"Are you trying to scare me?"

"No. I really do wonder how women tell the difference though, and if there really is a difference, or if men just move in separate directions from the same core, or if a Billy

144

Joe James-type is capable of being this murderer-type we're after."

"I don't know. Is there an answer?"

"Yes, there are a lot of answers, but the truth? All I know is what I see, and that version goes that men hurt women, much more than women hurt men. Men also hurt children and the earth, our natural resource that keeps us alive."

"But women do, too, don't they?"

"Sometimes." Nan hesitated. "If we could stop the men from hurting us, Sunny, think what a different world it would be."

Sunny nodded. Nan had no idea how close to home she had come in discussing this, and suddenly she wanted to pour out her burdens, all the pain and fear from Dan that still tormented her. But she couldn't, for Nan was involved with the police. She had to keep herself safe because Nan was certainly right that men hurt women, for whatever reasons, and Dan would kill her if he could.

"How's the drawing coming?" Nan asked, realizing Sunny wasn't going to talk, no matter how much she led.

"Good." She twisted her mind back to the simple task of reproducing Nan Shubert's face on paper. Fortunately, Nan was proving easy to draw because she had a strong facial bone structure. With a few lines she had the basic face outlined on the page. "Why don't you take a break, Nan?"

"Thanks. It's going to be a hot one again, isn't it?"

"Yes, it sure is."

"What you both need is some blackberry wine," Miriam interrupted, walking silently from the trees nearby. She carried a bottle of wine and wore an old, battered straw hat with a white owl feather sticking out of its faded red headband.

"Hi, Miriam. Come on over and sit in the shade," Sunny invited, not surprised at her friend's sudden appearance.

"Don't mind if I do. How's the portrait coming?"

145

"Very well."

"Good." Miriam went in the house and came back out with glasses. She poured the wine, handed it around, then looked over Sunny's shoulder. "Not bad," she commented, smiling, then sat down in a chair and began rocking.

"Miriam," Sunny explained, "the police found another woman's body in the sludge pit around two this morning."

Miriam stopped rocking. "Bad business." She looked at Nan. "You get the killer yet, girl?"

Nan knew the term "girl" referred to her, and although the word rankled, she replied calmly, "No, we haven't, but we're working hard on it."

"The police think this woman was killed last night," Sunny added.

"Last night?" Miriam looked puzzled, then took a long sip of blackberry wine.

"Yes," Nan agreed. "There's something else I wanted to tell you when Billy Joe wasn't here. I don't want this to get around, but I think you should both know. We know the killer is a man because he is strangling then raping them."

"What?" Sunny exclaimed, shuddering as she thought of Dan and how he had once raped her. She took a deep breath to calm herself, renewing her determination to stay out of the investigation.

"Evil." Miriam nodded. "You know I've felt it in my bones since that first night."

"Of course it's evil," Nan agreed, watching Miriam intently as she took a sip of wine.

"Not just human evil. Ancient, powerful evil. It's my feeling that there's a force out there stalking through our woods, waiting to catch us, destroy us. Women. It's more than murder, Nan Shubert, and the sooner we begin to confront that evil the better off we'll be."

"Miriam, it's bad enough that some man is killing women

146

around here, but ancient evil? I mean, he's raping the women! What kind of ancient evil is that?" Sunny threw down her charcoal pencil and paced toward the woods before turning back.

"I agree with Sunny," Nan insisted. "This is bad enough without involving some unseen, unknown, unheard of occult force. Unless, of course, you can take us right to it, and that'd be that."

"I can't do that, although I wish I could." Miriam took a sip of wine.

"Then why don't you do something helpful?" Nan asked.

"You young women are too skeptical. You haven't lived long enough, and you've lived away from nature too much. There is a cycle for all things, for the moon, for the earth, for animals, and for people, too."

"We understand that." Sunny sat down and picked up her charcoal pencil. She toyed with it while watching the emotions play across Miriam's face.

"But you don't feel it. That's the big difference." Miriam hesitated and glanced around. "What I'm trying to say is that the cycle has turned here. Why, I don't know. But I have enough feelings to know when things aren't right, when something ancient and evil has been stirred up, let loose, and it scares me."

"We're scared, too," Sunny agreed.

"But not scared enough." Miriam looked at each of them. "As women, it may be up to us to stop this evil. I don't think men and police procedures will be able to help much."

"All right," Nan said. "For argument's sake, we all agree that an ancient evil is stalking our part of East Texas. So what do we do?"

"I wish I knew." Miriam looked at the dark red liquid in her glass as if to find an answer.

"So we're back where we started," Nan insisted.

"Is there nothing you can do, Miriam?" Sunny asked,

still not wanting to believe her friend and yet almost beginning to trust her words.

"I'm trying to remember more of what my grandmother taught me. It could be vital, but I'm old, and it's been a long time."

"I'll listen to anything that'll help," Nan said, pushing a hand through her hair in agitation. "Who am I to turn down any help that's offered? And I apologize. Just because I don't think as you do doesn't mean I should automatically discount what you say."

Sunny smiled at Nan. "You're right. That's what I think too, although I'm awfully skeptical."

"I'm glad you're beginning to listen," Miriam replied. "We women have got to stick together until this evil is stopped. We may be all we have to rely on."

Suddenly a breeze rustled the pages of Sunny's sketch pad, and she cleared her throat nervously. "I guess I'd better get back to work. At least drawing a portrait is something I can handle."

"We'll make it through some way," Miriam said. "We've just got to work together."

"That's right," Nan agreed, taking a sip of wine. "We'll help each other."

"All right." Sunny smiled.

"Well, I'd better be going." Miriam stood up. "I've got a lot of remembering to do."

As Miriam walked away, silently as she had come, Nan looked at Sunny. "I could almost believe her. There's a strange feel about her, and I don't usually deal in feelings. I like cold, hard facts."

"So do I, but Miriam's special, and I don't think we should discount what she says."

"Neither do I, but I wish we could."

Sunny nodded, then looked at her sketch. "I guess I'd better do this, or it'll never get done."

Nan struck her pose again and began thinking. Surely

there was some clue she had overlooked, anything to help them.

"Don't frown, Nan. We'll be done soon."

Nan smoothed her brow, but continued to frown inside.

14

Return of the Killer Tomatoes was the first feature at the Gusher Drive-in Saturday night. Sunny and Billy Joe laughed through most of it, comparing it to the original classic, *Attack of the Killer Tomatoes*.

When the intermission lights came on, Billy Joe treked back to the concession stand, leaving Sunny to admire the waxing moon and watch the other moviegoers. They had parked in a good position, close to the front and near the center of the screen. Billy Joe had brought a blanket so they could sit on the hood of his pickup and watch the films. It was still hot, but there was a breeze now and then to cool them off.

Sunny was glad she had accepted Billy Joe's invitation, for she was enjoying being out of the house and away from her fears. Besides, she was discovering that she liked Billy Joe James. She had been suspicious of him at first, but he'd kept their relationship strictly on a friendship basis, and she had finally relaxed around him. She was also coming to realize she could have fun with a man again, and that surprised her.

Almost as an unspoken truce, they had avoided mentioning the sludge pit or the murders all evening, and she was glad they'd put it all away from them for at least a few hours.

She glanced around at the other cars, listening as an old-fashioned metal speaker blared a raspy version of Dolly Parton's "Jolene". She swung her foot in time with the music, feeling as if she had somehow reverted to her life before Dan.

"Having fun?" Billy Joe asked, placing a cardboard container with two huge Dr. Peppers and stacks of food on the center of the hood.

"How can we ever eat all that?" She laughed.

"Wait and see. You'll be hungrier once you start eating. Try this popcorn." He handed her a tub of buttered popcorn.

She dug in, crunched a mouthful, felt butter drip down her chin, but before she could stop it, he neatly wiped it up with several napkins.

"That'll teach you to be greedy."

"That's great popcorn."

"Didn't I tell you? Try some french fries. I don't know anywhere else you can buy them like this now."

"I'm going to put on five pounds."

"Wouldn't matter if you did. You'd still look great."

"Thanks. Then I won't have to diet after you fatten me up?"

"Not on my account." He bit off a third of a chili dog, then chewed and swallowed with gusto. "I even had them leave off the onions."

"Self protection?"

"Right. Got some Baby Ruths, too." He picked one up, tore open the wrapper and handed it to Sunny, who eagerly bit into it.

"Here comes the second feature," Billy Joe announced.

"What is it? I've forgotten."

"Something about dinosaurs."

"That's right. Look. *Dinosaur Revenge.*"

"Starring all your favorites. Have you ever heard of any of these people?" he asked.

"No. I think this is going to be awful."

"Great. That'll make it all the better."

"I mean really, really bad. Look at that dinosaur suit. And that island." She laughed.

"Yes, but look at the native women."

"Oh, no you don't. Don't think you get to ogle scantily clad lovelies while I—"

"Wait! Here come the native males."

"Where did they get these people?"

Billy Joe laughed. "You're right. This is really bad."

She joined his laughter, then took a drink of Dr. Pepper and glanced at him.

He wasn't watching the movie. He was watching her. "You know we can go if you hate this show."

"What! And miss *Dinosaur Revenge?* Not on your life. Have a french fry."

He smiled, then finished his hot dog, dividing his attention between the movie, the food, and Sunny. The evening was going pretty damn good. He'd been afraid since Sunny was a city girl she'd hate the drive-in, and worse yet, hate being with him. But she seemed to be having a good time. They shared the same sense of humor. He just wished they'd met under different circumstances. Then he remembered they'd originally met in Gusher when he'd plowed into her car. That hadn't been a good beginning, either.

"This is great Dr. Pepper, Billy Joe. I may have to come here for all my meals."

"I wouldn't blame you. Why don't we do it again next Saturday night?"

She hesitated. "Do you think we'll need to? I mean, maybe the murders will be solved by then, and we can get back to our normal lives."

"Damn. I don't know, Sunny, but I think we should

152

keep up our image unless you plan to tell somebody about what you saw."

"No. I'm still hoping they'll get some real clues. I'll talk to Nan again tomorrow. It's really awful."

"It sure is, and you're making me lose my appetite."

"Sorry. Okay, let's do it again next Saturday. But it'll be my treat. I've just made an easy hundred. I'll even drive. Remember, we live in a liberated age. I'll pick you up in my car, and—"

"That's going too far. It can be your treat if you insist, but I refuse to squeeze myself into a tiny car for hours, and we couldn't possibly sit on the hood."

"Okay. You get to drive, but I get to buy."

"Sounds good. Do you suppose this movie is ever going to end?"

"The dinosaurs are starting to eat the natives now. I don't think it can be long."

"All that crunching is making me hungry."

As Billy Joe tackled the food again, Sunny laughed and finished her hot dog, then squeezed in some more popcorn. "I'm not going to be able to move tomorrow. It's a good thing I'm not planning to do anything but sit and draw."

"What are those dinosaurs doing now?

"They've got the women."

"Well, it's obviously time for a rescue."

"And here it comes now." She chuckled, draining her soda.

"I can't read the credits," Billy Joe complained.

"You don't want to read the credits."

"Sure I do. I want to make sure I know the director so—"

"You can avoid him, or her, in the future."

He glanced at her. "You ready to go?"

"Yes." She gave him a warm smile. "And thanks, Billy Joe. I've really had a good time."

"So have I. Maybe we can top it next weekend."

They loaded everything back into the truck, then pulled

into line at the exit. Several people hollered at Billy Joe, obviously noticing he was with Sunny. He waved back.

"Our being here together will be all over Gusher tomorrow. Hope you don't mind." He glanced at her, looking worried.

"No. Like you said originally, it's a good way for us to get together about the murders and not look suspicious."

"Yes, a real good way." He glanced around, waiting to get out. "You know there was a popular drive-in down in Turnertown, an oil boomtown south of here. I guess its heyday was in the fifties and sixties, but it lasted a long time. It even had an inside seating area, plus a dance floor with a jukebox."

"Real fancy."

"Not so fancy, but it drew a big crowd from Wright City, Selman City, Joinerville, and that area. Plus, they'd come in from Gusher, Kilgore, London, Overton, Henderson, Troup, and Arp to check it out sometimes. I heard it was dubbed the Passion Pit."

Sunny laughed. "Oh, so that's why it was so popular."

Billy Joe joined her laughter. "You don't think it was the movies?"

"Well, maybe. But it'd be interesting to see that drive-in."

"I'd take you there, but it's closed now, like a lot of drive-ins."

"What a shame. Progress, I guess."

"It's more the problem that East Texas is a depressed area because of the oil slump and a lot of people have moved out of the oil boom areas."

"Well, at least the Gusher is still showing movies."

"Right. And we'll check it out again next weekend."

"If we ever get out tonight." Sunny laughed.

"Not to fear. Just a couple more cars and we're free."

Finally, they passed the exit sign, then Billy Joe headed toward Sunny's house, the pickup's headlights cutting a swath of light through the darkness. There was no music, for his radio had stopped working long ago. Instead, they were surrounded by the sound of the engine and the wind as it whipped through their hair, bringing the scent of wildflowers into the truck.

When he pulled off FM 203, he slowed the truck and glanced at her. "Don't invite me in. It'd be all over Gusher tomorrow, too."

"How?"

"Who knows? But I can guarantee the gossip would turn our ears red." He stopped in front of her house. "I'll walk you to the door. I don't think you should be out alone at night." He hurried around the front of the truck and caught the door just as she opened it. "Now, how can I be a gentleman if you open your own doors?"

"I thought that went out with women's liberation," she quipped, chuckling.

"Not in East Texas."

She stepped down to the running board, and he took her hand, helping her down.

"You are being gentlemanly tonight."

"I might as well." He wondered what the hell he thought he was doing. Damned fool. But he felt protective of Sunny, and he wanted badly to touch her. He reluctantly dropped her hand, then glanced around as they walked to the porch. He didn't see anything unusual, and the night was quiet, just the sound of pumping oil wells in the distance.

"Thanks again, Billy Joe."

"My pleasure. You'll be all right here alone, won't you, Sunny?"

"Sure. I've been all right by myself for a long time."

He hesitated, not believing her for a minute. "Okay, but call me if you need anything. I don't mind being awakened. And I'm not far away. Remember that."

"All right. And thanks for the concern, as well as the movies and food."

"Anytime. I'll call you tomorrow."

"Talk to you then."

She unlocked the front door and stepped inside, then watched as he walked back to his pickup. When he turned on the headlights, she shut the door and locked it. Suddenly, she felt uneasy.

She pressed the light switch by the door, and the room glowed softly in yellow light. Everything looked fine. But she wished she'd invited Billy Joe inside. With his strong, reassuring presence near her, she would have felt safe. Then she scoffed at that thought. She was safe on her own, and had been since she'd left Dan. She didn't need a man to reassure her.

Disgusted with herself for feeling afraid, she hurriedly went through the house flipping on lights and looking in closets until she was satisfied the house was just as empty as she had left it. Then she realized she hadn't needed a man to help her; she could take care of her fear all on her own.

Pleased with herself, she thought back to her evening with Billy Joe. She'd had fun with him, but it didn't mean she was suddenly going to become reliant on him. No, she had no intention of ever doing that with a man again, no matter what he seemed to be like.

Satisfied that all was safe, she hesitated in her studio. Maybe she should work on some Speedy Fix-It illustrations before going to sleep. But she felt so relaxed and contented, she just wanted to go to bed. She glanced at the drawing table, hesitated again, then turned out the light. She'd give herself the whole evening off for a change.

She switched out the lights as she made her way to the bedroom. It was another hot night, and the air-conditioner wasn't cooling the room again. She sighed. Maybe there was enough breeze outside to help.

She opened the curtains, pulled up the windows, and hoped for a breeze. The curtains moved a little and she was grateful for that, but she wished she had a small fan to stir the air in the bedroom. She also wished she hadn't eaten so many carbohydrates at the drive-in.

Quickly pulling off her clothes, she felt a little cooler. She'd sleep nude tonight for sure. Going into the bathroom, she took off her makeup, brushed her teeth, then snapped off the bathroom light.

When she returned to the bedroom, it hadn't gotten any cooler. But there was nothing to be done about it. The best way to deal with the situation was to go to sleep and forget the heat. She got into bed and pulled the sheet up. But sleep wouldn't come. Her mind was suddenly running in circles, thinking of the dead women, thinking of Dan.

For a long time she had believed in his love for her, even when he was hurting her, for he would always explain that he was doing it for love, to keep them together. He had been very good at twisting facts, and she had been very much in love and innocent. Perhaps he had even loved her in his way. Perhaps his fear of losing her had made him try to break her so she never could leave him. But now his love was very hard to believe in. Even if it had existed, it didn't make his actions right and never would.

One night he had demanded she become his total slave. He had forced a rope around her neck, then had led her about the house, shouting orders, whipping her with the end of the long rope. Finally he had pushed her to her knees and had demanded she admit to being his slave, a worthless woman, alive only to keep him happy.

She had cried, trying to reason with him, begging him to stop. She had even fought him. But nothing would stop his demands for power. When she wouldn't give in to him, he had tried to use sex to overpower her. She had refused him, unable to stand his touch or his brutality.

And he had raped her.

Just like the murderer was now raping women.

She shuddered, understanding the horror of rape all too well. It was one of the most degrading experiences she had

157

ever been through, and when it was over she had felt so out of control of her life that she could hardly go on. But the rape had had the opposite effect on Dan. He had used it to assert his power, to show her who was in control, and it had been an act of brutal force and violence, not one of passion or love.

Still, she had been lucky. He had not succeeded in breaking her, and she had escaped. The dead women hadn't.

But she didn't want to think of dead women or Dan. She wanted desperately to sleep. But it was so hot. She felt so claustrophobic. She pushed off the sheet, relishing the breeze that made its way in through the open windows. She thought of ice, of cold, of the frozen north, and finally fell into an uneasy sleep.

Much later she abruptly awoke. The room was stifling. Her body was bathed in sweat, and the sheets were wet under her. She pushed damp hair back from her face, and glanced at her alarm clock. 2:45 A.M. It was a long time till morning.

She looked at the window across from her, wondering why there was no breeze, and frowned. The window was closed. No wonder she wasn't getting any air. She must have forgotten to open it, and she felt too tired and sleepy to get up and do it now.

Suddenly she noticed that besides the heat there was a strange smell in the room. Flouncing over, she irritably flung out a hand, and struck something cold and clammy.

She screamed, and jumped out of bed. Snapping on the bedside light, she turned around, her heart beating fast. Lying in her bed was the dead woman with the long blond hair, her hands folded neatly across her breasts, her chest still. The smell in the room was the sweet, pungent scent of decay.

For a long moment Sunny was unable to move, terrified, horrified, and unable to look away. The dead woman was streaked with oil, her long hair matted with twigs and sludge. Her burgundy silk dress was oily and clung to her, revealing no stockings or panty line. She also wore no shoes. The lack of underclothes reminded Sunny that the murderer had raped the women after he killed them.

Suddenly she gagged and raced to the bathroom where she heaved up the contents of her stomach. The Dr. Pepper, popcorn, hot dog, and french fries, had tasted a lot better going down than coming up.

She wiped at her face with a cool, wet washcloth, and tried to slow her racing her heart. But nothing helped, because she was going to have to go back into her bedroom and confront the dead woman in her bed.

Or worse.

Had the killer placed the dead woman there, and was he still lurking about in the house just waiting to jump out and grab her, making her the next victim?

She began to shiver, her teeth chattering together as she glanced wildly around the bathroom, wondering if she should shut and lock the door and wait until someone came to find her. But, no, she couldn't do that. It was too similar to what she had done with Dan until it had almost been too late. No, she must confront whatever was out there.

And she had to do it now.

Slowly she began to stop shivering, slowly she squared her shoulders and walked out of the bathroom. The woman was still in her bed, and if she hadn't known better, the still form could have been sleeping. But it was the sleep of death that kept her so still, for Sunny had tried to breathe life back into her and it hadn't worked.

She walked to her closet and jerked open the door. Empty. She grabbed a T-shirt and a pair of jeans off a hook, then hurriedly pulled them on. She picked up her oak walking stick, deciding it would make a good weapon if the other person didn't have a gun.

Holding her fear wrapped tight inside her, she walked to the living room and switched on the light. Nothing. She ˙

went to the kitchen and turned on the light. Again nothing. She breathed a little easier, then went into her studio and flipped on the light. Nothing. She pulled open the closet door. Empty.

She collapsed in the chair in front of her drawing table, then lifted the receiver of the telephone. There were times to be practical and accept help, and this was one of them. She needed someone desperately. She couldn't call Miriam because she didn't have a phone, and Sunny had neither the courage nor the strength to set foot outside.

The number she wanted was inked on the edge of her drawing table. She dialed it with shaking fingers.

A deep, sleepy voice answered, "Hello."

"Billy Joe, it's Sunny. I need you. Would you get Miriam and come over?"

15

"Are you all right?" Miriam asked, taking Sunny in her arms and holding her close.

"I'm better now that you're here." Sunny held on tightly to Miriam, comforted by her friend's presence and the familiar scent of tobacco and blackberry wine.

"What's wrong?" Billy Joe asked, glancing around the living room, then back at Sunny. He should have been the one to hold and comfort her, not Miriam. But she hadn't turned to him, except for the phone call.

Sunny pulled back from Miriam. "I don't know any easy way of saying this, but there's a dead woman in my bed."

"What!" Billy Joe headed toward the bedroom.

"How did it happen? Who is it?" Miriam asked, setting her beaded leather bag on the coffee table.

"I don't know. It looks like the woman I tried to resuscitate."

"The one they couldn't find in the sludge pit?" Miriam put an arm around Sunny's waist, and they followed Billy Joe.

Sunny nodded.

"But that doesn't make any sense." Miriam suddenly stopped and looked confused.

"What is it?"

"I'm not sure. I mean, what you said reminded me of a legend my grandmother used to tell."

"And?"

"That's it. The memory just sort of teased my mind, then was gone."

"Maybe it doesn't matter."

"No. I think it's very important, and I'm sure it has to do with these murders."

"But how could an Indian legend have anything to do with the killer? I mean, I don't see how it all fits together."

"Neither do I . . . at least, not yet."

They stopped in the doorway of the bedroom. Billy Joe was looking down at the dead woman, a puzzled frown on his face.

He glanced up. "She doesn't look decayed, does she?"

"No," Sunny agreed, "but there's a smell."

"Death stench. I checked, and she's dead all right. But it's damned hot outside, and there're plenty of worms, bugs, and animals. So, how come she looks so perfect? And how the hell did she get in here? She damned well didn't walk in on her own, no matter how well-preserved she looks."

Sunny looked slightly green, and leaned against the door-jamb. "I don't know."

"There's a light coating of oil on her body," Billy Joe continued. "Maybe it preserved her in some way and kept the predators away. But that doesn't explain how she got in here."

"Did you see or hear anything?" Miriam asked, squeezing Sunny's hand before walking over to the bed for a closer look.

Sunny stayed by the door. "Everything was fine when I came home. I went to bed. It was hot. I woke up, rolled over, and found that body."

"Damn!" Billy Joe looked at her in concern. "Are you sure you're okay?"

"As okay as I'm going to be, I guess." She turned away and left the room.

Billy Joe exchanged a worried glance with Miriam, then threw a sheet over the dead woman.

"I'll make some coffee." Miriam patted Sunny's arm as she walked toward the kitchen.

Billy Joe shut the door to the bedroom and tentatively put an arm around Sunny's shoulders, expecting to be pushed away. Instead, she turned to him and put her face against his chest. He pulled her close, feeling his heart start to beat fast. Holding Sunny felt good, and he wanted to break the back of the person who had played such a nasty trick on her. She was trying hard to make it, and now she'd been almost spooked out of her mind. But she was being calm, maybe too calm, and that worried him.

"I'll be okay," she finally said and stepped back, but her gray eyes looked haunted.

They joined Miriam at the kitchen table. Three mugs had been set in front of three chairs, and coffee was perking in a pot on the counter. Billy Joe pulled out Sunny's chair, made sure she was seated comfortably, then sat down.

"What are you going to do, Sunny?" Miriam asked.

"Do?" She looked confused.

"About the body," Billy Joe explained, listening to the coffee perk, trying to make sense of the situation.

"I don't know. I don't know what to do. I mean, I don't want even to think about it."

"There's a dead woman in your bed, Sunny," Miriam replied gently. "You must think."

"Yes, I know, but it just leads to unanswered questions. Did the murderer put the body in my bed? If so, why? And why *my* bed? Is it a warning that I'm next? Or is it some horrible grisly joke by somebody who found the body in the sludge pit before the police dredged it? And if so, where has the dead woman been all this time? Why appear now?"

163

Billy Joe and Miriam glanced at each other, trying to think of something to say that would help.

"And how did the body get here? Could I really have slept through somebody pushing a body into my bedroom through a window, climbing inside, then putting a dead woman in my bed? Is that actually possible? And yet the body is there as proof."

Looking worried, Miriam held Sunny's hand.

"You want me to think? I'd like never to think again. As if I didn't have enough problems worrying about Dan, now I'm waking up with dead bodies in my bed. I almost wish I could believe it was Dan tormenting me, just so I'd know who it was. But he'd have no reason to do this, and he's in Dallas, anyway. It's also hard to believe some total stranger would go to this much trouble for a joke. So, I'm left with thinking that two men want to kill me, and one of them knows where I live."

"I know it looks bad," Miriam said, "but you mustn't give up hope."

"Hope's about all I've got," Sunny replied and shook her head.

"We need to get some facts," Billy Joe decided, "and then maybe things will start making sense. Did you notice anything unusual in your room besides the body when you woke up?"

"No. Well, the window was shut."

"Had it been open?"

"I don't know. I mean, I thought I'd opened all the windows, but maybe I didn't."

"Or maybe somebody shut it behind them," Billy Joe suggested.

Miriam nodded in agreement, then stood. She brought the coffeepot to the table and filled the mugs.

"Yes, that could have happened," Sunny agreed. "Of course, the first thing I thought after finding the body was that the killer might still be in the house." She stood up and paced. "I went through the house, but I didn't find anybody. That doesn't mean much though, because someone had to have gotten inside and left the dead woman."

"You'll keep all your windows and doors locked from now on," Billy Joe said, "and I'll check them first thing in the morning to make sure nobody can get in. I'll nail them shut if I have to."

"You're not alone, Sunny." Miriam took Sunny in her arms. "And we're not going to let anybody harm you."

Suddenly tears stung Sunny's eyes, and she hugged Miriam hard. Then she hesitated and stepped back. "I said I wouldn't cry again, that I'd be strong, that no man would ever hurt me again. Yet here I am, terrified."

"You are being strong," Miriam insisted, leading Sunny back to the table. "And you've got help this time. Now, drink some coffee while we come up with a plan of action." She sat down.

"That's right," Billy Joe agreed. "We're in this together."

"But what can we do?" Sunny asked, sitting down.

Billy Joe picked up his mug and looked hard at Sunny. "I think the first thing you should do is call the cops. This isn't like finding a body in the sludge pit. This one's in your own bed."

"But I'm terrified of Dan finding me if I go to the authorities."

"What choice have you got now, Sunny?" Billy Joe insisted.

"Well, maybe we could put the dead woman back in the sludge pit."

"You don't really mean that," Billy Joe objected. "You've got to get help, Sunny. Either the killer's after you or somebody's playing nasty jokes."

Sunny looked at Miriam. "What do you think?"

"I think you have no choice but to go to the police. I

165

know it's dangerous because of Dan, but I believe they'll do all they can to keep your anonymity.''

''But somehow my identity might leak out.''

''I know,'' Miriam agreed, ''but your life is now obviously in danger, Sunny. The murderer is close to you, for whatever reason.''

Sunny put her face in her hands, wanting to shut out everything. She didn't know how much more she could stand, and yet somehow she had to go on. Other women's lives were at stake, too, and she couldn't go on pretending the murders would go away if she just looked the other way. She glanced up. ''All right. I agree. Someone has to be told.''

''Good.'' Miriam nodded.

''We'll stand with you,'' Billy Joe agreed.

''But I'm worried about you, Billy Joe. What will Sheriff Barker say when he learns about your part in all this?''

''No matter what he says or does, it can't be as bad as women being murdered or you being hurt.''

''Okay then. But I don't want to tell the sheriff. I'll call Nan. She'll understand. I hope.''

Sunny stood up and walked quickly to her studio before she lost the courage. She dialed Nan's number and listened to the ringing on the other end. She hated to wake Nan this time of night, but they couldn't wait to catch the killer.

''Hello. Nan Shubert.''

''Nan, it's Sunny.''

''What's wrong?''

''You know that second woman they didn't find in the sludge pit when it was dredged?''

''The body Billy Joe thought he'd seen?''

''Yes.'' Sunny hesitated, toying with the telephone cord. ''Well, I found her in my bed tonight.''

''What!''

''Miriam and Billy Joe are here, and there's a lot we need to tell you.''

"Is this official?"

"Yes. I wanted to talk to you first so you could handle it."

"I'll be right over. Give me time to dress and get there. And, Sunny, are you all right?"

"Yes, or as right as I'm going to be."

"Just hang on. I'll be there as quickly as possible."

Sunny hung up, feeling as if a heavy weight had descended on her. She had thought she was safe hiding out in East Texas, but now it all seemed to be catching up with her again. Suddenly she was caught between two men who wanted to murder her.

She stood up and pushed her hair back from her face. Somehow she had to be strong and courageous, but she didn't feel that way. She felt scared, and even with Miriam and Billy Joe in the next room, she still felt alone. She had finally dealt with Dan by running and hiding. But how did she deal with this new danger? It had no face, no name, and yet it was very real. She felt as if she were being stalked. But why?

Flipping off the light in her studio, she hurried back into the kitchen. She didn't want to be alone. Billy Joe was sitting at the table by himself, drinking coffee, obviously deep in thought.

"Where's Miriam?"

"She's going to smudge the house?"

"What?" Sunny glanced around in concern.

"I guess you don't know what that is."

"No, and I'm not sure I want it."

"Go talk to Miriam then. But I'd let her do what she thinks is best. It won't hurt anything, and it might help."

"I don't know how you can be so casual about all this. First there was the medicine wheel, and now there's this smudging."

"I've know Miriam all my life, and she's one of the best.

167

There's a lot more to her than meets the eye, and I trust her."

"Well, I trust her too, but—"

"Go talk to her."

"Oh, all right."

Sunny was a little apprehensive as she walked into the living room. Miriam's shamanism bothered her. It gave her chills and made her want to run away. But where could she go? She was feeling more trapped by the moment. At least she had a few people to turn to for help.

"Miriam, I don't know about this smudging stuff."

"Let me explain it to you, then you can decide," Miriam replied, closing her leather bag and turning to look at Sunny. "Smudging is simply the word for an ancient Native American custom of using the smoke from herbs to cleanse a person or an area. In this case, I think you and your house need it."

"Wouldn't a bath be as good?"

"A bath is good, yes, and is similar to the old sweat lodges, but smudging is used to cleanse bad feelings, negative thoughts, bad spirits, or even negative energy. It works on the unseen part of us and our environment. In my grandmother's time, I've seen her change depressed people into positive, happy ones by smudging them and their surroundings. It works, Sunny. I've seen it. But you don't have to believe me. Just don't hinder me. Anyway, you've tasted the flavor and smelled the scent of herbs, haven't you?"

"Yes."

"Burning them is the same as cooking with them or healing with them, except we use the smoke, instead."

"Somehow you always give your beliefs a certain sort of sense."

"That's because they make sense from the right viewpoint. I haven't done a lot of this work, as you know, but

I still have my grandmother's medicine bag, and I brought it. Is it all right if I do it?"

"Yes. I suppose it can't hurt, and maybe it'll help. I don't know what to think anymore." She dropped onto the couch and watched Miriam, not wanting to think for a while.

"I'm going to explain what I'm doing, Sunny," Miriam said, showing her a cone-shaped object about six inches long and an inch in diameter and wrapped with red twine. "This is sage, and it is used to purify, drive out bad influences and keep them out."

She struck a match and lit the end of it. A thick white smoke began to pour from the sage wand, and she pointed it toward Sunny. "Now, I'm going to use this owl feather to move the smoke over and around you. It won't hurt, and I'll be sending positive thoughts and asking that you be protected from harm by the great spirit."

Sunny sat very still, watching Miriam and smelling the pungent scent of burning sage as it enveloped her. She coughed once, and Miriam smiled. Soon Miriam moved on, swirling sage smoke around the room before carrying the burning wand into the rest of the house.

Starting to get up and follow her friend, Sunny suddenly noticed she was feeling very relaxed, even sleepy, and there didn't seem to be a need to help. Miriam had it all under control. She leaned her head back against the couch and smiled. Strangely, she was feeling a renewed confidence in herself. There must be a way to win, and it was up to her to find it.

Then she frowned, surprised at the direction of her thoughts, and glanced around. She was definitely feeling better. Could the smudging really work? And if so, how? But she didn't want to question it now. She just wanted to relax and feel safe for a little longer.

Soon Miriam walked back into the living room, having completed the sage smudging. The sage wand was damp where she had extinguished it with water in the kitchen, and she rolled what was left in a red cloth. Putting it in her leather bag, she pulled out another object. She smiled at Sunny and held the new item up for her inspection. A foot long and about a half inch across, the herb looked like a braid of hair, though it was obviously grass.

"This is a sweet grass braid." Miriam lit the end of it, then waved the white plumes of smoke toward Sunny. "This attracts good spirits and good influences, and will carry my prayers into the spirit realm."

The scent and smoke tickled Sunny's nose, and she sneezed. "Sorry."

"That's good. We're driving out the bad influences. You'll be much better after this."

"Surprisingly, I am feeling more positive."

Miriam smiled, then continued smudging the living room before moving onto the rest of the house. Sunny noticed Miriam even entered the bedroom, carefully shutting the door behind her when she was done. When Miriam had smudged the entire house, she returned with only a small section of the sweet grass braid left over.

"What are you going to do with what's left?"

"I'll give the sage and sweet grass to the forest, and it'll be taken back into Mother Earth's embrace."

"I see. Well, do you think I'll be safe now?"

"No, Sunny. None of us are safe until we find that man."

Sunny shivered and glanced up as she heard a car stop in front of her house.

16

"Are you sure you're all right, Sunny?" Nan asked. She sat down at the kitchen table and glanced from Sunny to Miriam to Billy Joe.

"Yes. I guess so."

"She's going to be fine." Miriam poured a mug of coffee and handed it to Nan.

"All right then, Sunny," Nan said, taking a sip of coffee. "What is this about a dead woman in your bed?"

"It's hard to believe, but she's there."

"We've all seen the body," Billy Joe agree. "Do you want to?"

Nan hesitated. "No, I don't want to disturb anything. Sheriff Barker isn't too happy to be working with me as it is, and now that you've called me in first he's going to be even tougher to deal with."

"If this is going to cause you problems—" Sunny began.

"Don't worry about it. You just tell me what's going on, then we'll decide what to do."

"All right," Sunny agreed. 'I'd like to start at the beginning. We haven't been completely straight with you about the murders."

"I didn't think you had been."

Sunny took a quick sip of coffee, realizing Nan was just as sharp as she'd suspected. "I saw the bodies first."

Nan's eyes narrowed. "And Billy Joe?"

"He was helping out," Miriam explained. "Sunny has a problem, and she didn't want to get involved with the police."

"What's your problem, Sunny?" Nan asked.

"Let me tell you about the bodies first." Sunny took a deep breath. "The afternoon before Billy Joe called the police, I was taking a walk and thought I saw a face in the sludge pit. I couldn't, or didn't want to believe it, and went home. But I couldn't sleep for wondering about the face, so I went back. That's when I found the first body."

"You should have called the police immediately," Nan insisted.

"But I didn't," Sunny replied. "After I found the body, I was so scared I ran into the woods. Somebody drove up in a big car, stopped near the oil well, got out, and carried a woman with long, blond hair down to the sludge pit."

"You saw the murderer?" Nan stood up, her eyes wide with amazement and relief. "Then we can get him?" Suddenly she looked angry. "How could you not have come forward with this information sooner?"

"I knew you'd be mad, but I didn't see anything that night to really help," Sunny defended herself.

Nan sat down. "Of course I'm angry, and Sheriff Barker will be, too."

"Wait until you hear it all," Miriam said.

Nan nodded, and drank more coffee.

"I couldn't see the murderer's face. He was a big man, wearing an overcoat."

"An overcoat?" Nan looked confused. "In July?"

"I know," Sunny agreed. "Strange, isn't it? But let me continue. When he drove away, I ran down to the sludge pit and got the blond-haired woman out. She was still warm, so I tried to breathe life back into her. I couldn't, and then tonight I found her in my bed."

"You're sure it's the same one?" Nan asked.

"Yes. There was enough moonlight that I'll never forget her face."

Nan ran a hand through her hair in agitation. "My God, but that's grisly."

Sunny took a drink of coffee. "Anyway, after I couldn't save the blond-haired woman, I put her back in the pit and went to Miriam."

Nan looked hard at Miriam. "And you didn't send her to the police?"

"Nan, Sunny has an abusive husband," Miriam explained, glancing at Sunny. "He tried to kill her and she ran away. He threatened to finish the job if she ever left him, so she's hiding out here."

Nan inhaled sharply.

"Don't you see?" Sunny insisted. "I was terrified if I told the police, my name and possibly my photo might somehow get to the press and Dan would find me."

Nan clenched Sunny's hand hard, then finished her coffee. "Frankly, I could use something stronger right now."

"I think we all could." Sunny stood up. "I've got some of Miriam's blackberry wine." She got out the wine, four glasses, and set them all on the table.

As Sunny poured wine, Nan glanced around the table. "I respect your fear, Sunny, and you're not wrong in feeling it. My sister was killed by her husband. He had beaten her up for years, but she was terrified, and she hid what was going on until it was too late. I'll never forgive myself for not realizing it in time."

"And now you help women and children," Sunny said gently, handing Nan a glass of wine.

"Yes. I do what I can, always wishing I could have helped my own sister." She drank some wine, then glanced at everyone again. "But mine is an old problem. We can't

173

help it. Sunny and the women in this area can still be helped."

"I called you," Sunny explained, "because I thought you'd understand."

"I do."

"And you aren't angry now?"

"No. I understand only too well. But you're doing the right thing now by coming forward with this evidence."

"I want to help, but my name must be kept out of this."

"The police department will keep your name confidential if you request it."

"Good, but I'm worried it might still get out."

"There's nothing foolproof, but we'll do our best. Is there anything else you can tell me?"

"Nothing except about tonight. Billy Joe and I went to the drive-in. After he brought me home, I went to bed. It was hot, and I opened the windows because the air-conditioner wasn't cooling the room. I woke up later and touched something in my bed. It turned out to be the dead woman with the blond hair."

"You're sure it's the one you tried to revive?"

"Yes."

"Was there anything else unusual in the room?"

"No, except one window was closed."

"And had it been open before you went to sleep?"

"I'm not sure."

"Do you have any idea how the body got into your room?"

"It damned sure didn't walk in on its own," Billy Joe interrupted.

Sunny glanced at him, nodded in agreement, then looked back at Nan. "I guess somebody carried it in, put it on my bed, then left. But I don't know how I slept through that, and who would want to? Unless . . . unless the killer is stalking me now."

"It doesn't make any sense," Nan said. "I mean, this

174

doesn't fit into the pattern at all. And where has the body been all this time?''

"There's another thing," Miriam said. "The body hasn't decayed."

Nan ran a hand through her hair. "Then Sunny must be mistaken, and this is a new murder."

"No! I recognized the woman."

"Sunny, it'll just be your word against physical evidence."

"That woman has been in a sludge pit," Billy Joe said. "She's got oil all over her. You better come and see."

"No." Nan stood up. "I'm going to call Sheriff Barker and get him out here. I don't want any added trouble, especially on a case this important."

"But you'll tell him for me, won't you?" Sunny asked.

"I'll tell him, but he'll want to hear it from you, too."

Sunny groaned and slumped in her chair. "I knew it was going to get worse."

"You're all going to be lucky if he doesn't throw the book at you. Now, Sunny, where's your phone? We've got to get right on this."

"It's in my studio." She led Nan into her office, turned on the light, then left.

Nan hesitated, picked up the phone, and dialed Sheriff Barker at home. The phone rang twice and was picked up.

"Sheriff Barker here."

"This is Nan Shubert. I'm at Sunny Hansen's house. She's found another dead woman."

"What! In her house?"

"Yes."

"I'll get Price, an ambulance, and be right over."

"Okay. You know the location?"

"Price will. And Nan, don't touch anything."

"I haven't."

"Good."

Nan frowned as she heard the line go dead. So much for

trusting a co-worker. Suddenly she felt very tired. If she'd been a man, she knew he'd trust her professionalism and not doubt her every action. But that wasn't the kind of world she lived in. She walked back into the kitchen and sat down at the table.

"What happened?" Sunny asked.

"Sheriff Barker's getting Price and an ambulance. They'll be here soon."

"I wish I didn't feel so nervous," Sunny said, taking a sip of blackberry wine.

"It's all right," Nan replied. "We've got a lot more to fear from the killer than from Sheriff Barker."

"That's right," Billy Joe agreed. "The main thing is to stop any more murders."

Nan nodded, wishing she could drink enough blackberry wine to make her forget hurt and murdered women forever. But she knew there wasn't enough wine in the world to do that, so she took just a sip of Miriam's blackberry wine instead and was grateful for the warmth.

Not long after, they heard cars pull up in front of the house, then loud banging on the front door.

Sunny stood up. "Come on. We've got a killer to catch."

They walked into the living room. Sunny opened the front door and Sheriff Barker and Price hurried into the room, bringing the scent of outdoors and the power of authority with them.

"You must be Sunny Hansen," Sheriff Barker said. "I know everybody else."

"Yes, I am."

"And there's supposed to be a dead woman in your house?"

"Yes."

"Did you kill her?"

Sunny took a step back. "No, of course not."

"Now see here, Sheriff," Billy Joe interrupted, stepping

176

forward. "There's no need to badger Sunny like that. She needs help as much as every other woman around here."

"So what I've heard is true?"

"I'm a friend of Sunny's," Billy Joe insisted.

"So am I," Miriam added, "and I don't think gossip is what's important here."

"Maybe not, but I'm not overlooking anything." Sheriff Barker gave them all a hard stare, then focused on Nan. "So where's the body?"

"In the bedroom." Nan pointed toward the closed door.

"Okay, let's have a look."

As everyone started toward the bedroom, Price pulled Sunny aside.

"Listen," he whispered, "I talked with my wife about getting a drawing of the kids, and she's real excited."

"Good." Sunny watched the others as they opened the door to the bedroom.

"I want to get it done as soon as possible. The kids are out of school, and I can bring them by."

"All right. Call me," Sunny said, annoyed at the deputy for bringing up the portrait at this moment.

"Great."

They started toward the bedroom where everyone else had disappeared.

Suddenly Sheriff Barker shouted, "What the hell kind of a joke is this? There's no damned body in here."

Sunny hurried into the room, and pushed between Miriam and Nan to get a look at the bed. True enough, there was no body. Where the dead woman had lain, now there were only oil stains on the sheets and the indentation of a head on the pillow.

"I said," Sheriff Barker demanded, "is this a joke?"

"Of course not," Miriam replied, "we all saw the body."

"Nan, did you see it?" Sheriff Barker countered.

"No. I didn't look. I was waiting for you."

Silence descended on the room.

Sunny glanced around and noticed that all the windows were now open. She decided the body must have somehow left through the same window it'd entered, if that made any sense in the middle of something that was senseless.

"I don't know," Sunny said, "how somebody could have climbed back in the window, picked up the body, then gotten back out without us hearing something."

"Neither do I," Billy Joe agreed, "and I'm going to look outside."

"No you're not," Sheriff Barker commanded. "Price, get your flashlight and get out there and look around. If this is more than a hoax, there're going to be some prints or something."

"Yes, sir. Right away." Price shook his head in reproach at Sunny before leaving.

"You don't believe us?" Sunny asked.

"What's there to believe?" Sheriff Barker glanced around the room.

"But what about the oil on the sheets—and that indentation in the pillow?" Sunny pushed.

"It could have been staged."

"Barker, we've known each other all our lives. Do you really think we'd pull some fool stunt like that?" Miriam asked, glaring at him.

"You got a better explanation?"

"All we have is the truth," Sunny replied. "There was a dead woman in my bed. I'll never be able to forget it."

"There's no rational reason for that body to have disappeared," Billy Joe said. "I suppose the only sense to make of it is that the same person who put the body in the bed to frighten Sunny decided that to have it disappear would only feed her fear. But I don't see how it could have been done. We were in the house the whole time."

"Well, I don't know how it got in my bed in the first place," Sunny added, feeling as she did when Dan played psychological games with her. What was going on?

178

"Sheriff Barker needs to know all the facts," Nan interrupted, "and I think we'd better sit down and go over them together."

"What facts?" Sheriff Barker glanced around. Everybody looked guilty. "What the hell has been going on here?"

"Why don't we go in the living room," Nan suggested.

"Suits me," Billy Joe agreed and led the way.

"This had better be good, or I'm going to throw the book at all of you, and that includes you, Nan."

"Once you hear the whole story, I think you'll understand," Nan replied.

"And whether you understand or not, you're going to have to deal with it," Miriam concluded.

17

"We'll get the sheets analyzed," Sheriff Barker said as he left Sunny's house.

"But with no tracks around the place and no body, it's going to be hard to prove anything," Price added, carrying a plastic bag containing Sunny's sheets.

Billy Joe, Miriam, Sunny, and Nan followed them outside. The sun was just beginning to rise in the east. It was Sunday, and they were exhausted.

"Maybe so," Nan agreed, "but it's all we've got."

Sheriff Barker stopped and lit an unfiltered cigarette. He glanced from one to the other. "I'm not going to do anything about the three of you right now, but if you try to cover up anything else, I'm going to charge you with every law that'll stick."

"We won't do it again," Sunny replied, "and thanks, Sheriff, for understanding. I know what we did was wrong, but I honestly didn't know anything that would help the case."

"I wish to hell somebody did." Sheriff Barker glanced around. "And I wish I had more manpower, but I'm doing all I can do."

"But will it be enough, soon enough?" Miriam asked.

Sheriff Barker frowned. "Time will tell, I guess." He drew on his cigarette.

"About the sheets—" Nan began.

"I'll let you know when I know," Sheriff Barker replied. "In the meantime, why don't you get some rest. There's nothing else we can do for now, and if that body turns up anywhere, let me know."

Price chuckled. "You say this dead woman has long, blond hair?"

"Yes," Sunny responded, "and she's wearing a burgundy silk dress."

"Sounds like a woman I'd like to meet. If I see her out and around, I'll be sure to give her a ride to the office." He laughed long and hard.

"Young man," Miriam said, "your mother must have left you in the sun too long. I think your brains melted at an early age."

"Now see here," Price objected, "that's no way to talk to a law officer."

"Can it, Price," Sheriff Barker ordered. "Go ahead. Get those sheets to the lab."

Price gave Miriam a hard stare, then swaggered back to his car.

"You must have looked hard to find that one," Miriam remarked.

"Wife's cousin," Sheriff Barker said. "He's okay most of the time. He's just got this thing about women."

Billy Joe glanced at the police car backing out of the yard. Sheriff Barker was right. Deputy Price Simmons was a well-known womanizer, and he obviously wasn't particularly sympathetic about this case. From now on, he'd keep an eye on the deputy.

"Most men have 'a thing' about women," Miriam said, then added softly, "but they'd better watch out. When we've had enough, we've had enough. And Sunny's been

181

pushed too far. If I was a man, I'd tread lightly around her."

"If there really was a dead woman in her bed, I think she'd better be the one to watch out," Sheriff Barker replied, smoking his cigarette.

"Does that mean you're going to give Sunny extra protection, Sheriff?" Billy Joe asked.

"No. I've got no proof the killer's after her. Besides, I've got no one to spare. You women have all got to be careful till we catch this guy, but I don't think he'll be bothering local women."

"There's no proof of that," Nan objected.

"He got the first one on the freeway," Sheriff Barker explained. "Chances are he'll continue that, if he keeps on killing."

"What about the sludge pit?" Nan pushed. "Are you going to set up a stakeout there?"

"I'm having somebody drive by several times a day. Anyway, I don't expect the murderer to use it again. He's bound to know we're watching."

"Then we're pretty much on our own, aren't we, Sheriff?" Miriam asked, looking from Sunny to Nan.

"We'll give you all the protection we can, but there's just so much we can do. Besides, you and Sunny could stay together so you wouldn't be alone." Sheriff Barker nodded, pleased with his solution.

"Sunny is welcome to stay with me. She knows that," Miriam replied.

"Or with me," Nan added.

"And I wish she would." Billy Joe gave Sunny a hard stare. "I don't like the idea of her staying alone, not after last night."

"Thanks," Sunny replied. "But I won't be scared away from my own home. I've already been through that. I'll keep all my doors and windows locked from now on, and I'll be careful outdoors."

"And you're not going anywhere alone at night," Billy Joe insisted.

Sunny smiled. "I won't argue with that."

"All right then, it's settled." Sheriff Barker dropped his cigarette and ground it out under the toe of his cowboy boot. "Now, I've got to get back to the office."

"Thanks for coming, Sheriff Barker," Miriam said, then put an arm around Sunny and Nan. "Come on. Let's go inside. I'm hungry."

"And I've got a portrait to finish. Right, Nan?"

"Yes," Nan agreed as they walked into the house.

"I'll see you later," Billy Joe called. "I'm going to look around the area."

"Miriam watched the sheriff and Billy Joe leave, then turned back to Nan and Sunny. "They're gone."

"I'm glad that's over," Nan said.

"I'll set out some granola and milk." Sunny headed for the kitchen.

Miriam and Nan followed, and sat down at the table. Soon they were all eating, with coffee perking in the pot. The house was very quiet.

"I've been thinking, Sunny," Miriam remarked, getting up to pour coffee for everyone. "When you tried to save the blond-haired woman, maybe you somehow changed her life-force. Maybe you somehow willed her to live, giving her some of your own energy."

"So that explains it," Nan said sarcastically. "The dead woman has come back to life and is walking around on her own. Well, that certainly simplifies matters."

"It might be possible," Miriam persisted. "I'm trying to remember an old Comanche or Caddo legend, but I can't quite recall it. I know my grandmother had the power to do amazing things."

"Raise the dead?" Nan asked, finishing her granola and pushing the bowl aside.

"I never saw her do that. I don't even know if it's possible."

"Of course it's not possible!" Nan exclaimed. "Some man is out there killing women, and now he's after Sunny, trying to spook her for some reason. We've got to be rational if we're all going to come out of this alive."

"You're right," Miriam agreed, "but I'm still convinced there's a lot more going on here."

"Right." Nan stood up and paced. "It'd be real easy to say some man has been possessed and he's not responsible for his actions. Men go free all the time on excuses like being temporarily insane or not responsible. Well, damn it, whoever is doing this is responsible, no matter what, and he's going to pay for it."

"I wasn't implying the man doing the actual deeds wasn't responsible, Nan," Miriam replied gently. "Everyone is responsible for their own actions, for their own life, but I do know we can be influenced by unseen forces if we are attuned or susceptible to them."

"Of course we're influenced, but by the forces and conflicts all around us, not by something unseen. That's ridiculous, and a cop out, anyway." Nan sat down, picked up her cup of coffee, and glared at Miriam.

"Please," Sunny interrupted, "we need to work together. I'm beginning to believe we may be the only ones to save ourselves and other women from this murderer."

"Sheriff Barker is doing what he can," Nan defended.

"I know," Sunny replied, "but he's not getting very far. Besides, after last night, I don't think I can trust anybody to take care of me but myself."

"That's smart." Miriam nodded. "But you can depend on friends to help you."

"That's right," Nan agreed. "I have the experience to follow the clues, work with the police, and come up with a rational reason that will lead to the murderer."

"And I'll follow the clues I sense coming from the spirit realm," Miriam added.

"I'll help somehow," Sunny said, "but I'm not sure what that is exactly."

"It will come to you. Your role in this is becoming more important all the time." Miriam warmed her hands around her coffee mug, looking thoughtful. "The fact that you came here, the fact that you found the bodies first, and now the fact that one of them has appeared in your bed all points to your importance."

"But what does it mean?" Sunny asked.

"I don't know." Miriam shook her head.

"And neither do I," Nan agreed. "But if we think hard enough, maybe it will all begin to make some sense, and we can catch this man."

"What if it isn't a man?" Miriam asked.

"We know it is," Sunny objected, taking a sip of coffee. "He's raping the women and leaving semen."

"I mean, what if it's an ancient evil from the spirit world?"

"That's right," Nan replied. "It's some sort of sludge monster that kills and rapes women, then tosses them into beds."

"Girl, you think too much," Miriam said, tapping her mug with the tip of her fingernail. "And you don't listen enough. There's a lot going on around us that we don't know about, that we may never see or understand. I'm just trying to point out that you should keep an open mind."

"I'm sure Nan is trying to consider all the possibilities, Miriam," Sunny inserted, trying to keep the peace. "It's just that we're all confused and a little scared."

"We should be scared." Miriam looked fierce. "Our fear may keep us alive."

"I agree that fear can be healthy." Nan took a sip of coffee. "But what we're after is a man, a woman-hating man. Did you know there is a word in the dictionary for

185

woman-hater, but not one for man-hater? Interesting, isn't it?''

''No,'' Miriam replied.

''Men are always complaining about women-hating men, and yet there isn't even a word for it because it occurs so seldom. Yet, misogyny, which means hatred of women, especially by men, is a Greek word. It has been part of our language that long. Makes you think, doesn't it?''

''No,'' Miriam said.

''So, I believe we've got a mysogynist on our hands,'' Nan concluded.

''Your talking is starting to make my head hurt,'' Miriam complained. ''What we've got here are several dead women, and we don't want any more.''

''I certainly agree on that point.'' Nan nodded.

''Good,'' Miriam replied. ''That's the only thing that matters. We don't need fancy words or fancy thoughts cluttering up the problem here. We've got a killer out there, and he's being driven.''

''Driven?'' Sunny asked, looking confused.

''Sure he's driven,'' Nan agreed. ''Driven by his hatred of women.''

''Maybe,'' Miriam said, ''but I believe he's got himself in trouble, big trouble.''

''What sort of trouble, Miriam?'' Sunny asked.

''Old trouble. As I've been saying, I think something's been stirred awake.''

''Damn! This kind of talk is ridiculous,'' Nan interrupted. ''If we listen to you, Miriam, we'll soon be seeing big, black sludge monsters under our beds.''

''Or in them,'' Sunny said under her breath.

''Girl, you've been citified too long.'' Miriam glared at Nan. ''You had best move out here and walk in the woods, listen to the stories on the wind, hear the songs of the sparrows. It's about the only thing to save you now.''

''My lifestyle is not the point,'' Nan replied. ''We must

be practical, logical. We must gather information, sort through it, then analyze our findings, and proceed from there. It's the only right thing to do."

Miriam rolled her eyes. "Put you and Price Simmons in a nutshell, shake you up, and maybe—just maybe—we'd come out with one whole nut. I've decided both of you've been out in the sun too long."

"Is that an insult?" Nan asked stiffly.

"Look," Sunny intervened, "just because you two have a different point of view doesn't mean you can't work together. In fact, you do agree that we've got to find the killer and stop the murders. Miriam, why don't you go ahead and learn all you can from your end, and Nan can do the same from hers. You've both got to admit we can use all the input we can get."

"I'll agree to that," Miriam said.

"Fine," Nan added.

"Now we can get somewhere." Sunny glanced at her friends in relief.

"Well, I'd better be off," Miriam said, standing up. "The birds'll be wanting their breakfast." She smiled, then stepped outside, letting the screen door bang shut behind her.

"That woman!" Nan turned on Sunny. "I can't believe the way she talks to me. After all, I do know what I'm doing."

"Come on, Nan. She likes you. It's just her way of trying to get you to think in different ways."

"My thinking is just fine. It's hers that needs help. A nutshell. Really, Sunny, when I—"

"Let's go out on the back porch, Nan. I'd like to get some fresh air, and we can finish your portrait."

"All right, but I'm not going to put up with much more from that woman."

"Forget it for now. Let's finish your portrait, okay?"

They carried their coffee outside and sat down in the sun.

Sunny quickly picked up where she had left off the day before, sketching in the finishing touches of the charcoal portrait. She tried not to think of the horror of the previous night, instead concentrating on her work, the cheerful morning sunlight, the songs of the birds, and the gentle breeze ruffling her hair.

Finally, she stood up and handed Nan the finished portrait.

Nan looked at it silently for a long moment. "You're good, aren't you?"

"I try."

"Does my chin really jut forward like that, as if I'm constantly challenging the world?"

"Aren't you?"

"And do I look that defensive?"

"I just draw what I see. If you don't like it, I could try doing another."

"No. It's right. You captured me in a way I've never seen before. Thank you. You've taught me something about myself. Maybe Miriam's a little right."

"We've all had it rough, Nan. We learn to cope, we learn how to get things done. There's nothing wrong with that. I see strong character in your face, and you should be proud of it."

"You're strong, too, but in a different way."

"I've been hiding for a long time, but now the world's come for me. I guess I've got to face it, and I'm scared."

"You can count on me to help."

"Thanks. Just keep me posted on the case."

"I'll call as soon as I know anything, but I wish you'd stay with me in Longview until this is all settled."

"I appreciate the offer, but I'm determined to make it on my own this time."

"I understand, but don't be heroic. Call if you need anything."

"I will. Would you like some more coffee?"

"No, thanks. I should get back home. There's a lot to do."

"Do you want me to mat the portrait?"

"No. I'll get it framed in Longview. Something special. I really like it. And thanks again."

"I enjoyed doing it."

They walked into the house. In the living room, Nan picked up her purse, took out fifty dollars, and handed it to Sunny.

"I hate to charge you, Nan."

"Don't be ridiculous. I can afford it, and you may need the money. Besides, you should always charge for your work." Nan set the cash on the coffee table, then walked to the front door. Opening it, she looked back. "Remember to call if anything odd happens, anything at all."

"Okay, and thanks for buying the portrait."

"My privilege."

Sunny watched Nan drive away, then shut and locked the front screen and door. The house suddenly seemed quiet, too quiet. She could hear the wind in the trees and the pumping of oil wells in the distance, but it seemed too still out there, as if something were watching, waiting, ready to pounce.

A chill ran up her spine. She shook her head, trying to get rid of the thought, but the feeling persisted. She still felt watched, as if it were only a matter of time before she, too, succumbed to whatever was stalking women.

She wished Miriam hadn't talked about ancient evil and unseen forces. It was bad enough trying to handle a straight murder with a definite man doing the killing, but when the talk turned to sludge monsters and spirits, she got very uneasy.

To keep her mind off it, she decided to remake her bed. But as she began putting clean sheets on the mattress, she became more and more disturbed. How could she ever sleep in the bed now? She couldn't. Tonight she would sleep on the couch. In fact, she could hardly stand to be in the room. She finished making the bed, checked to make sure all the windows were still shut and locked, then left the bedroom, closing the door behind her.

She glanced around the living room. She was really all alone now. Everybody was gone. She had to face her life on her own. Dan. Somehow Dan had led her to all this fear. Even though he was far away in Dallas, he was still affecting her life, and now another man was doing the same thing. And she'd had enough of it. Somehow she had to fight back, but she didn't know how.

Walking into her studio, she sat down and looked at the drawing table. She wanted to run away again, but she didn't have the money. Besides, she couldn't desert her friends, not with the murderer still running loose. And most of all, she finally had to make a stand, or she would be running all her life.

Dan. Murders. Death in her own bed. How could she keep going? How could she deal with the fear?

She picked up her pen and began drawing absently on a piece of paper. It was time to start on her portfolio, a good, strong one.

She'd sketch several new illustrations, showing her technique, and add them to her work that had already sold and been printed. If a New York City art agency did decide to represent her, they could get her freelance jobs, and she might even be able to get work with advertising agencies and art studios in Dallas if she moved back there.

But Dan was in Dallas, so how could she move back? She stopped drawing and put away the pen. Maybe she could do it all through the mail, hiding until she had enough money to move farther away. Or maybe she could confront Dan with the law behind her. She couldn't imagine confronting him yet, just as much as she couldn't imagine facing the East Texas killer.

However, that wasn't going to stop her. She would work

up new illustrations for her portfolio and then send it to New York.

Using a piece of vellum and a 0.5 HB lead mechanical pencil, she began to work with ideas. Soon, she was caught up in a design and layout, and the horror and fear in her life melted into the background.

18

The phone rang loudly in Reverend Mulhaney's bedroom. He jerked awake and glanced at the alarm clock on his nightstand. 2:30 A.M. He put a hand to his heart. It was beating too fast. He should have turned off the telephone, but it was his duty to be available to his congregation.

He groaned, wishing for the relative quiet of the hospital, and picked up the phone. "Hello." He fumbled with the prescription bottle on the nightstand and took a nitroglycerine pill dry.

"Reverend, sorry to wake you, but I have a theological question."

"So, you called again. How are you?"

"Fine. But I'm troubled."

"Then you were right to call. What theological question troubles you?"

"You don't think women would take revenge, do you? I mean, they're bad. They must know they're bad and need to be punished, don't you think?"

"What makes you ask?"

"Women. All sin comes from them. They know that, don't they? I mean, they wouldn't seek revenge because they were punished for their sins, would they? They'd know you were doing it for their own good, wouldn't they?"

Reverend Mulhaney took a deep breath, suddenly worried. "You have not been . . . punishing women, have you?"

"That's not the question, Reverend. A man has to do what a man has to do. God's ordained that. The question is, do women realize it? What if they suddenly decided they weren't evil, that maybe you were evil, instead? What if they came after you? Revenge is wrong. You know that. I know that. It's right to turn the other cheek."

"That is correct. Christ taught that."

"But if women are evil and cursed, maybe they don't understand they have to be punished to show them the error of their ways. If that's true, what if they," and his voice suddenly lowered, "came after us?"

Reverend Mulhaney shuddered. This was, in fact, a theological question that he had wrestled with for some time, but he'd never voiced it. And he didn't now. "That is why we have the Bible. The good book explains to us our weaknesses, our faults, and how we can overcome them. Women must look to men, their natural superiors, and trust us to guide them to salvation."

"Yes, Reverend. But what about those women who might not agree, might not believe? I mean, what if a woman was a women's libber, man-hating, lesbian type? Would she think about revenge, if a man just tried to help her and show her the way to live God's word?"

Reverend Mulhaney was getting more and more worried, and his heart was pounding harder. Had this man done something, or was it truly a theological question? "Christianity has done its best to show the people of the world the light of Christ and give them the word of God through his holy book the Bible."

Pulling the receiver away from his ear, the reverend concentrated on slowing his heart. But his thoughts got in the way. He hated to admit it since the caller was a Christian man, but a pattern seemed to be emerging which might connect the dead women in the pit and the calls from the stranger. Of course, it could simply be coincidence. He was still weak from his heart attack and a little unclear.

But above all, if he was going to continue his ministry and carry it into television, he could not lose credibility in the community by appearing hysterical, especially after the way he had acted at the hospital upon seeing the dead woman in the sludge pit. It was probably best not to waste the police's time until he could get more information from the stranger, or decide that the man was more than a concerned Christian.

He put the phone back to his ear. "What was that you said?"

"What if women don't accept Christ's word? We don't want them all condemned for eternity!"

"Of course we do not, young man, but the church no longer sanctions some of the excesses that it practiced in former years."

"What do you mean?"

"The church no longer finds it wise to convert by the sword or the rack."

"That's right. Religious Crusades. The Inquisition. They knew what they were doing back then, didn't they?"

"Those were different times. Today, Christians prefer to spread God's word through persuasive speech, economic incentive, and Christ's love."

"But we wouldn't have these man-hating libbers running around hurting men if we had an inquisition, would we?"

"I think you should realize it is an established fact that women have an important place in the church. Now many even lead congregations. Women are trying to rise above their sin and help others. Some of these women are even feminists. We must not forget that women can help each other and should be encouraged to be useful, upstanding members of our communities. Remember, we want to save women's souls in any way possible."

"I understand what you're saying, Reverend. You're a pious, forgiving man, but women are starting to steal men's jobs like they had the right."

"Women have a right to jobs, too, if they must help support their families. Times are hard."

"That's right. Times are hard, and it calls for hard times. We've got to bring the word of Christ to women any way we can. But that's not why I called, Reverend. Like I said, do you think women might not understand that you had to hurt them to save them? Do you think they might get mad, call on the devil, and with his help, come back for revenge?"

Reverend Mulhaney felt a chill run up his spine. He had read in depth about the physical tortures of women and girls during the three-hundred years that the Inquisition reined Europe. It was estimated that nine million were tortured to death, even more than the Nazi extermination of Jews during World War II.

He had wondered if those women and girls had understood that they were heretics and had to be tortured and burned for their sake and the sake of the church? But what if they hadn't? The Jews had never accepted or forgotten what the Nazis did to them. Had the witches?

Fortunately, for his peace of mind, those millions of women burned as heretics were dead, and his Bible did not include reincarnation myths.

"Reverend? Do you think they might try to hurt us?"

"Women are docile creatures. They are raised to believe and trust in the supremacy of men. I don't believe, unless quite unbalanced, they would really want to harm a man."

"No matter what?"

"Well, of course, there are a few instances of women hurting men. But it is rare, and usually they are trying to protect or help their children. Also, women are normally severely punished when they hurt men, especially a wife her husband, so that discourages it."

"That makes me feel better. It's a load off my mind."

"Good. But remember, official servants of God, those trained in his ministry, should be the ones to help women overcome their natural obstacles."

"Sure, but you can't always be in the right place at the right time. Others hear the call of God, too."

"Yes, there have always been unordained men answering the call, but still—"

"Thanks, Reverend. You've helped a lot. Now I've got to go."

He hung up the phone and glanced around. It was a clear night and the moon was moving toward full so there was some light. He felt a lot better after talking with the good reverend. Funny, he'd almost felt like he was being followed recently, and he didn't like the sensation. He was the stalker, the predator, the man. It was his right.

He stepped out of the phone booth near the filling station on the north side of Gusher. A Buick Regency was parked nearby, the door on the driver's side stood open. He didn't like the car. He'd tried to clean it, but it was still dirty. He didn't want it. He slammed the door shut.

Anyway, he didn't need a car. He'd walk. He liked to walk through the woods. That's how he'd found his new home. It was as if the house had been waiting for him. After he'd unboarded the door, he'd found canned goods in the pantry, a comfortable bed, and all the room he could want. There was even running water from a well. It was a good place to live, and no women to bother him. Yes, God was watching out for him.

Glancing around, he started south on FM 203. It was a quiet night, punctuated by the sound of oil wells pumping, frogs croaking, and crickets chirping. He liked the night, liked to move through it unseen.

He took an oil road off FM 203 and entered the forest. He could smell the pines around him, and smiled as the darkness concealed his movements. He didn't know why he'd been so concerned over the theological question of female revenge, but it was a worry that had been growing in him. Of course, it was a joke to think a weak woman could hurt him in any way.

At that, he smiled again and trudged on down the oil road. He came to a sludge pit. He'd been watching it for a while. For some reason he was drawn to it. The oil-slick water was pretty in the pale moonlight, but he didn't go to the edge. He had to be careful and protect himself, for he had a mission from God to save sinful women.

He took a path that meandered deep in the woods and came to the spot where he had been spending his nights before he had found his house. He started to sit down, but heard a slight noise behind him.

Whirling, he saw a person not far away. His heart raced. Was he being watched? No, the person didn't seem to see him. Whoever it was had gone toward the sludge pit. Curious, he followed, keeping out of sight among the trees. But the person seemed unaware of the surroundings.

He drew closer, but stopped at the edge of the forest when the person walked out of the shadows of pines into the moonlit area around the sludge pit.

Suddenly, he could see the person was a woman. She had long, blond hair. His eyes narrowed, and he sniffed the wind, trying to get her scent. If she was evil, he had to know it. Evil could not be allowed in God's world.

She walked to the sludge pit and knelt. For a long moment she didn't move, then she dipped her hands into the oily water and bowed her head. After a while, she cupped her hands, filled them with sludge, raised them to her face, and drank deeply.

He felt sick to his stomach, and cold, really cold. What kind of disgusting woman was this? Certainly not produced from God, but devil spawn for sure. She needed cleansing if any woman ever did.

Then she stood abruptly and turned toward him, even

though she couldn't possibly see him. He shivered as she began walking slowly, determinedly toward him. Well, if she wanted to play games, he was willing. He'd be happy to teach her God's will.

When she was close, he suddenly recognized her, or thought he did. Her long, blond hair was familiar, although he didn't remember it being streaked with oil or matted with dead twigs. Her eyes were pale, maybe green or blue. No green. He remembered them being green, but how could he know that? It didn't matter. He didn't like the way she was looking at him, or through him, for her eyes were open wide and staring. He felt a chill run up his spine. Then he reminded himself that she was simply a helpless woman in need of salvation.

She wore a blood-red dress that clung to her curves and stopped just below her knees. She had good legs, but she was barefoot. He idly wondered about her shoes and if the pine needles hurt the soft soles of her feet. Maybe she wasn't the devil's helper, after all. Maybe she was an innocent, simply lost, thirsty, and in need of help.

He'd help her.

When she was close, he stepped out of hiding, smiled, and started to speak. But suddenly his stomach cramped, and he bent double in intense agony. Clutching his stomach, he looked back up. She was standing in front of him, and he caught her scent. Decay. He gagged, then tossed his head, trying to get rid of the smell, feeling confused. She must have been sleeping in the forest on a rotting tree to get that stench.

And her eyes. They never blinked. In fact, they were focused beyond him. Yet he still had her attention, for she suddenly smiled, showing teeth streaked with dark oil.

He had to remind himself that she was just a woman, lost, hurt, alone. "Can I help you?" he asked, finding it hard to speak over the pain in his stomach.

She nodded, then beckoned for him to follow her.

He hesitated, but the cramps were easing in his stomach and he was feeling a little better.

Beckoning again, she turned and started toward the sludge pit.

Maybe she needed help. Maybe she'd dropped something in the oily pond. Maybe she was lost in the woods. That was it. She needed a strong, intelligent man to help her. He could do that, and he would. And if she turned out to be devil spawn, he would still help her to reach God's side.

He hurried forward and caught up with her. "I guess you've had some problems," he said, walking beside her. "But don't worry, I'll be glad to help you. The woods can be confusing to a stranger. What did you say your name was?"

She stopped by the edge of the sludge pit, then looked in his direction.

He decided she might be blind.

She pointed at the water.

That was when he noticed her fingernails were strangely painted. The bright red neatly covered three-fourths of the nail, but from the cuticle to the polish it was natural. She must have been lost for a while, or it was a new style in nail polish.

Her right hand moved, the index finger pointing toward the sludge pit.

"Did you lose something in there? I can't help you with that. You'll have to get it dragged."

The hand pointed again, insistently this time.

"Sorry, but you'd better wait until light, anyway. If you want, I'll walk you to the main road."

She dropped her arm, looked at the sludge pit, then stepped back. Once more she pointed for him to stand beside her on the edge.

"Can't you talk?"

She turned her head toward him, her gaze going through him. Suddenly he could smell the strong stench of decomposition, and he could hardly breathe. His stomach cramped again, and he bent over, clasping his middle with both arms.

Dizzy with nausea, he looked up to see if she had noticed his weakness. She seemed to be more corpse than human, her flesh decaying, her jaw hanging open. Worms moved silently, sluggishly, in and out of her flesh. He gagged and turned aside to throw up, his stomach cramping, his head aching. But nothing would come up.

He glanced at her again. She looked normal, even pretty, and he didn't feel so sick anymore. Maybe it was something he had eaten.

She smiled and pointed at the sludge pit.

"All right," he said, his mind feeling fuzzy. "I'll stand by the edge of the pit for a minute."

He stepped close to the pit, shivering slightly as he looked down at the dark water. Suddenly he heard her step toward him. He started to glance around. The stench of decay was strong as she pushed him into the pit.

The water closed over his head. He choked, swallowed some of the vile-tasting sludge, and winced as slimy objects slid past his body. Horrified, he jerked his hands and feet as he tried to propel himself to the top. He was a good swimmer and wasn't really worried about drowning until his left foot snagged something and he couldn't get loose.

He pulled and pulled, but his foot wouldn't budge. There was no telling what had been thrown into the pit over the years, and he dreaded to reach down and feel whatever was holding him. But his lungs were burning, and he finally did.

Yelping in pain, he swallowed more sludge, choked, inhaled oily water, and thought he was going to die. But he called on God, found strength, and wrenched loose from what felt like barbed wire wrapped around his foot and embedded in his pants leg. But it had also felt a little like the ribs of a dead cow, or another animal that had gotten caught and died in the pit. Whatever it was cut his hands, and they stung as he broke the surface, gulping clean air.

He shook his head, tossing water from his face, and looked on the bank for the woman. She was gone. He was all alone. Now he could hardly believe she'd ever been there.

Striking out for the bank, he sliced through the sludge, batting objects away from his hands. He refused to think what he might be swimming through, refused in order to keep his sanity. For if there was one thing he abhorred, it was dirtiness, and he was now filthy.

The bank was slick with oil, but he clawed his way through the mud, embedding oil and dirt under his nails and in the cuts on his hand. Finally safe, he spit oily muck from his mouth, then crawled farther away from the pit and collapsed on the bank, breathing hard, shuddering. He had almost died at the hands of that woman, and only by calling on the aid of God had he lived. But he was filthy, and he didn't know if he could ever feel clean again.

As his breathing slowed, his mind raced. A woman had tried to kill him. Revenge. He shuddered. It was what he had feared. Women were rising against their masters. The reverend was wrong. Women were in league with the devil and they were trying to kill off all God's servants. They could not be trusted to understand their true nature.

He was in danger. The good reverend was in danger.

Then he remembered the old phrase learned early in God's worship. It went something like, "You mustn't suffer a witch to live." If women were in league with the devil, then they must be witches, and therefore, they must be killed in God's name.

He was not a violent man, but he knew his duty when he saw it. He pulled himself up from the foul ground and stumbled away from the sludge pit.

Something would have to be done. He'd have to warn the Reverend, protect him some way, and keep himself alive. He'd have to get cleaned up, too, but he was tired, so very tired. He'd have to get some sleep. But first he'd go to his secret house and prepare himself, for now he knew what he hadn't known before.

It was war.

19

"Nan. Nan, help me!" her sister cried as she darted around a kitchen table.

Behind her a tall, heavy man followed her, carrying a broken beer bottle. He threw it at her. It hit the middle of her forehead, then crashed to the floor. She stood stunned as blood ran down her face. "Nan, it hurts," she moaned, then crumpled to the floor. "Please help me."

The big man kicked her in the stomach. She tried to protect herself by drawing her knees up to her chest. He pulled her hands away, then kicked her chest until she curled into a tight ball, her ribs cracked and broken.

"Nan, help," she whimpered when the man picked her up. He held her upright while he viciously beat her face, then continued to beat her until she no longer moved. Finally, he dropped her to the floor like a broken doll. And walked away.

Nan thrashed in her sleep, clutched at her pillow, and groaned.

"He wouldn't let me buy any shoes," the tall woman with the bruised face said softly. "That way I couldn't go anywhere. He said wives should be interested only in the home and their husband and kids. So I stayed home, but I guess I must have talked about going out too much. So he beat me."

"If I'd had his dinner on the table when he came home from work every night, he wouldn't have beat me," the dark-haired woman said as she rubbed the cast on her right arm. "It was my fault. I'm sure it was. I just couldn't please him, and I should have."

"He said he loved me," the small woman explained, carefully picking lint off the white sweater she had draped around her shoulders. "But I was never good enough for him. He told me so. I couldn't keep the house clean enough, or the kids disciplined, or prepare the food right. It was my fault. Yes, I'm sure it was. In fact, when he gets the money, he's going to replace my teeth—the ones he knocked out. That proves he loves me, doesn't it?"

Nan flounced and desperately reached out, trying to help. She woke up and glanced around. No battered women in sight. But she was bathed in sweat, her emotions in turmoil. She could feel all the horror and pain of the women she'd helped and those she'd tried to help and had failed. Some of them were still alive, but too many were dead, like her sister, killed by a brutal husband or boyfriend.

She hadn't dreamed like this in a long time, and it always meant a job was going badly. But these dreams had been worse, more real, than any before. She ran a hand through her hair and got up. She went into the bathroom and turned on the shower. She stepped in, and let the hot spray hit the back of her neck. She tried to relax, but couldn't. She felt afraid, as if she was being stalked.

She hated the feeling. She must have been working too hard, too long. She obviously needed a vacation to get away from the pain and anguish she had dealt with for so many years, but she couldn't take one now. There was a man out there preying on women, and she had to stop him.

Or he might kill again.

Turning the shower massage to a higher setting, she felt

her muscles finally begin to relax. Relieved, she turned off the shower and stepped out. As she dried off, she reminded herself that she had been dreaming about old cases. She couldn't help those women, so she had to put them out of her mind. Instead, she needed to concentrate on helping Sunny and the other women in the area.

She had to solve this case as quickly as possible. But she couldn't be emotional about it, or try to follow Miriam into some occult world where they could all wind up lost and dead. No, she had to sort through the facts until they made some sort of rational sense. That was the way to catch the killer.

She pulled on a gray, terry robe, and walked back into her bedroom. She wondered how Sunny was doing. Despite Sunny's braveness and the fact that she had managed to extract herself from an unhealthy marriage, she was still an abused woman.

And Nan knew the statistics on that profile by heart. In the United States a woman was abused every eighteen seconds. One-eighth of all murders involved one spouse killing another. According to a 1979 FDI uniform crime report, forty percent of all female homicide victims were killed by family members or boyfriends. And in Texas, a study conducted by Sam Houston University revealed that fifteen percent of Texas women had been severely and repeatedly beaten.

Nan ran a hand through her hair in agitation. All of those statistics broke down to individual women, like Sunny, who lived in fear and pain. And now, Sunny was dealing not only with Dan's abuse, but she was dealing with a nameless, faceless murderer stalking her neighborhood and her home.

Suddenly Nan was very concerned about Sunny. Sitting down on the edge of her bed, she dialed Sunny's number.

"Hello."

"Sunny, it's Nan."

"Oh, hi, Nan. How are you?"

"I'm all right. But I'm concerned about you."

"There haven't been any more dead bodies in my bed, if that's what you mean. And I slept on the couch last night. But the best news is that I'm working on a new illustration. It's good, too." She tucked the phone under her chin and kept drawing.

"For a hardware catalog?"

"No. This is for my personal portfolio. I haven't felt like doing anything but hardware art for a long time. But I've decided if I'm ever going to straighten out the mess of my life I should try to get an artists' agency in New York City to handle my work. So I'm working up some new illustrations for my portfolio."

"Sunny, that's wonderful news. And it's a really positive step." Nan smiled, feeling much better about Sunny. "I have a friend in New York who might know of a good agency that could handle your work. Would you like me to contact her and find out?"

"Yes, that would be great. It'd help a lot not to have to send my work in cold."

"I know what you mean. Well, give me some time to get in touch with her, and I'll let you know."

"Thanks."

"Sunny, there's something else."

"Yes?"

"Sheriff Barker called me. They got the analysis back on the sheets from your bed. There was definitely sludge on them, and long blond hair."

"Well, that proves we weren't making the whole thing up, doesn't it?"

"I wish it did. But from Sheriff Barker's viewpoint, the three of you still could have done it."

"But why would we do that?"

"It doesn't matter. What matters is that there's no absolute evidence of anything."

"But that's ridiculous. He's known Miriam and Billy Joe all his life."

"We're talking law here, Sunny, and that makes all the difference. Besides, now that he knows about Dan, he's not so sure of your mental stability."

"Oh, no!"

"I'm afraid so. But don't worry, I believe you, and I'm in there fighting for you."

Sunny suddenly felt down. "I wonder if there's any point in trying. It seems like I'll never be free of Dan."

"Sunny, you can't let this depress you. First, they did find something on your sheets and it'll help solve this case. Second, you're going to get a New York agency to handle your work. Eventually, you'll be able to make enough money to live anywhere you want. Remember, you've got to have faith in yourself. You're going to come out of this stronger and smarter."

"Maybe, but I don't much feel that way right now."

"Don't let Sheriff Barker bother you. He doesn't trust me much, either, but we can't let that stop you."

"No, I guess you're right."

"Okay. And don't worry about Dan. He's far away. He can't hurt you. And we're going to catch this murderer."

Sunny smiled. "Thanks for the pep talk."

"Anytime." Nan stood up, paced several steps, then sat back down. "Now I've got some other news."

"It's better, I hope."

"No. But it's going to make us work that much harder to catch this killer. Sheriff Barker got a report on the second woman."

"And?"

"She was white, twenty, a college student at Stephen F. Austin in Nacogdoches, and lived with her parents in Henderson, a town not far south of here. The last her parents saw of her was when she left Friday evening to visit friends in Longview."

"And she never arrived?"

"Nor returned. Her friends thought she'd changed her mind, and her parents thought she was with them until Sunday."

"But the murderer had her, didn't he?" Sunny felt sick to her stomach. Another woman's life ruined, and she'd come so close to having the same thing happen to her. No, she couldn't give in, not now, not ever. She had to fight back.

"Yes, he had her, and like the first woman, she was strangled and raped."

"It makes me sick. I wish we could have prevented it."

"Me, too. But we can't look back now. We've got to catch this killer before he hurts anybody else."

"I'll help any way I can, but I don't know what to do."

"Sunny, the most important thing for you to do is stay safe. I don't know what to say about that dead woman being in your bed, except we have to think the worst. Are your doors and windows locked?"

"Yes."

"Keep them that way."

"I will, and I've been staying inside working. It helps to keep my mind off everything."

"Good. And you're sure you're all right? You know you're welcome to stay with me."

"Thanks, but I'm fine."

"Okay, then I've got to get to work."

"Thanks for calling."

"Be careful. Bye."

Sunny hung up and glanced around her studio. Lately, it had begun to feel like a prison. After finding the dead woman in her bed, she was afraid to go outside and take long walks through the woods. She felt trapped, and she knew she was hiding, not only from Dan, but from the murderer, too.

But it was Monday, and at least she was alive. Plus, Dan

208

hadn't found her yet. However, she couldn't help wondering how long her luck would hold and how much longer she would be safe. She had thought about leaving the area, just packing her stuff in her Volkswagen and getting out, but what about Nan, Miriam, and Billy Joe? And what about money to finance her trip? Besides, would Sheriff Barker even let her go?

And now that she was working on her portfolio again, she hated to disrupt the process by moving, either into Longview, which she didn't think she could afford, or staying with Miriam or Nan. Also, if she ran again, she was afraid she would never stop.

So, she was going to ride it out, at least for a while yet. But if she found any more dead bodies in her bed, she didn't know if she could cope. As it was, she still didn't understand how or why the killer would have put the woman in her bed. It just didn't make sense, and she wanted to solve that mystery almost as much as she wanted to stop the killer.

She sighed and looked at her illustration. It was good. The best work she had done in a long time. Maybe fear was driving her to create something so special there would be no way she could get turned down by an artists' rep. Whatever the reason, at least something was going right in her life, and she wasn't going to let anything stop it.

The phone rang.

She hesitated, and set aside her pencil. It rang again. She didn't want to hear any more bad news. But in the middle of the third ring, she picked it up. "Hello."

"Sunny. Billy Joe here."

"Hi." She was relieved. "How are you?"

"Okay, other than tired. You're the one I'm worried about."

"I'm doing fine. In fact, I'm working, and it helps to keep my mind occupied."

"Good idea."

"Why are you tired?"

"I'm on a building site in Longview. I got called in today, and it looks like I'll be working for a while."

"Great. Are you phoning from work?"

"Yes. A pay phone. I'm on a break. Feels like I've already put in a day's work. You know, we start at dawn in the summer, trying to beat the heat. But it doesn't help much in hundred-degree weather."

"I can imagine, since my house is always so warm."

"You need bigger air-conditioners."

"I know, but it's rented so—"

"You need to get out and forget your troubles for a while. How about I stop by later and take you to the best burger and shake place in East Texas."

"Sounds wonderful. Is it far away?"

"No. The Purple Cow Shake and Burger Barn is in Gusher."

"The Purple Cow? You're kidding, right?"

"No, it's been called that for two generations. Rosey and her daughter Beth run it, and it's a hell of a place. They make shakes so thick you have to eat them with a spoon, and great old-fashioned Texas hamburgers."

"It sounds good, although I'm beginning to wonder if Gusher is the place that time forgot."

Billy Joe laughed. "So how about I pick you up at six?"

"Fine. My house is beginning to feel like a prison."

"So I can't take your wanting to go out with me as a compliment?"

"That's right, Billy Joe," she teased. "I'm desperate to get out, so the first one to call and tempt me, gets me."

"I knew it couldn't be my Texas charm that was luring you away from your work."

"It's the Texas burger."

They both laughed.

"But it'll be my treat," Sunny insisted.

"No. I'm getting a fat paycheck, and it's my idea."

"But you took us to the drive-in."

"And we agreed it's your turn at the drive-in next time, but Rosey's place is all mine."

"All right, you win. I can't argue with your logic."

"Good. Then I'll see you at six."

Sunny hung up, picked up her pencil, and started back to work. She was surprised, but she was looking forward to going out with Billy Joe. They seemed to get along well, and the Purple Cow sounded great. Besides, she really would enjoy getting out of the house.

She liked having someone to go out with, and she was surprised she could enjoy a man's company again. But she had enjoyed Dan's company before she had learned how violent he truly was. Perhaps she shouldn't allow herself to trust Billy Joe too much. That thought saddened her. But she had to be careful. She was no longer naive, and she couldn't afford to be vulnerable.

Would she ever be able to trust a man again? Maybe. But it would take awhile.

20

Billy Joe pulled into Sunny's yard and cut the engine. He glanced around. Her place looked normal, but so did the damned sludge pit, for that matter.

He'd driven around Sunday, trying to find some sort of clue that would explain how and why a dead woman had ended up in Sunny's bed. Hell, he'd even gotten out and walked around, but he hadn't seen anything strange. And it wasn't like he didn't know his way around. His dad had taught him to hunt in the piney woods of East Texas, and he was no amateur. But he hadn't found anything, and had gone home. He'd been so frustrated he'd wanted to get drunk, but he hadn't. There was Sunny to think about.

Sunny. Pretty woman. If he didn't get his hands on her soon, he was going to go a little crazy. Maybe he already had, and was just hanging on for the ride. But he knew better. There was something special in the way he felt about her, and at thirty-three he knew it didn't come along often. That's why he also knew he'd take it easy with her, if he had to tie his hands behind his back.

It was getting bad, but he wasn't backing off. He couldn't. There was her damned husband to think about. Dan could come waltzing in any day if he found out where she was. Besides, there was the murderer, the dead woman in her bed, and the murders. No, he wasn't backing off Sunny Hansen. She might think she could take care of herself, but it was a man's world, and she was wounded, signaling herself as prey.

Sunny needed him whether she realized it or not. It was funny how that affected a man. When he'd gotten the call to work in Longview, he'd normally have told them to shove it. Who the hell with more than air between their ears worked on Mondays, anyway? But he'd needed the money to take Sunny out, and she might need more if she had to get away.

Maybe he was being stupid, wanting to help her. Maybe it was all an act on her part. Maybe there wasn't a Dan back in Dallas. Maybe she was just using him. He'd been the target for plenty of jock-groupies, and he'd been through a marriage gone bad, so he could believe it. But he didn't think so. Miriam didn't think so. And Sunny Hansen damned sure hadn't dreamed up the murders, or her fear, or the dead woman in her bed. No, she needed help, and he wanted to be there for her. Stupid as that might seem, especially since he didn't trust women.

As a young football star, he'd decided that girls were out for the status they could get from being seen with him, from having him spend money on them, so he'd taken what he'd wanted and moved on. He'd been a macho man, and he'd liked it. They'd liked it, too. But then he'd gotten his knee busted. Kicked out of college and flat on his ass back at his parents' house, he'd become a fallen hero.

So he'd been trying to prove his manhood ever since, while drinking to forget he'd lost it. Now he was beginning to think he'd never lost a damn thing, except a football career. He was born a man. Who the hell could ever take that away from him?

For the first time, he realized he didn't care so much about his image, even if Sunny was trying to use him. He'd gotten caught up in something bigger than himself, something a hell of a lot more important than being the biggest stud on campus, or in East Texas, or wherever. For the first time he was seeing just what could happen to women when they trusted and depended on men. It was scary.

Maybe after all he'd seen, he wanted to help even the odds in the man-woman game. And that meant helping Sunny, Miriam, and Nan win, because it looked like they were down to the last few minutes in the fourth quarter and somebody needed to throw a Hail Mary pass to Sunny for the touchdown that could save their lives. He was still the best quarterback in East Texas, and probably the only one Sunny knew. Anyway, he was sure as hell the only man he was going to let throw her a pass.

So he'd just have to throw the best Hail Mary of his career and hope Sunny caught it and went in for the touchdown. If she didn't, they might all wind up dead. Or maybe she'd catch it and walk off with the Superbowl ring and leave him in the dust. If she did? Well, he'd live with it. He'd already lived through worse.

For the first time in a long while, maybe ever, he wanted to do something for somebody else, and in the process he was beginning to see that it might help himself. And for some damned reason this woman made him feel like a real man, like he was worth something, and not just some macho man wound up to fit everybody's expectations.

He glanced at Sunny's front door. It was no time to be holding up the show. She was waiting, and he was anxious to see her. Besides, he wanted to know if she was being brave and putting up a front, or if she was really doing okay.

Stepping down from the pickup, he heard the front door open. He glanced up. Pretty woman. Sunny looked good in a pair of tight jeans and a yellow knit top. It was going to be hard to keep his hands off her. He might have to get the rope out yet.

"Hi!" she called, then locked the front door. "Did you have a hard day?" She walked up to him and smiled.

"Not too bad." He could smell her perfume. It was something tangy. He wanted to taste it. Instead, he opened the pickup door for her, and she stepped inside. Slamming the door shut, he walked around to his side and got in. He started the engine and gunned it.

"Quite a hot rod." Sunny laughed.

"I wish I had the Porsche I drove in college."

"So do I, but I'm not complaining about this Chevy, as long as it gets us to the Purple Cow."

Billy Joe laughed, too, then backed out and headed for FM 203. "We'll get to Rosey's place if we have to walk."

A hot breeze blew in through the open windows of the truck, and the scent of pine, grass, and wildflowers filled the air. Sunny sniffed, then smiled, relishing being out of the house and feeling safe with Billy Joe. He glanced at her and grinned.

"I can't tell you how good it feels to be out riding, free from . . . well, you know."

"Yes, I do. Are you really doing okay?"

"I don't know. I guess. The main thing is that I'm working on my portfolio again, doing new illustrations which I'll get slides of, then send them off to a New York art agency and see if they'll handle me."

"And if they will?"

"Then they'll show my work and maybe sell me to all kinds of markets I'd never find on my own, and hopefully I'd get paid very well."

"That sounds good, Sunny."

"In theory, yes. And Nan is going to call a friend of hers in New York who may know of an agency that'll look at my work."

"Good. I'm happy for you."

"Thanks. Of course, I've got to keep up the hardware art because that's how I eat, but I can do both kinds of

215

work, especially since I haven't been sleeping too much lately.''

"You know you can call me anytime you want to talk."

"I know, but somebody's got to get some sleep."

"Right. I don't want to be dropping bricks on anybody's head at work." He chuckled.

"Do you like construction work?"

"It's hard, but it's outdoors, and I like that. Still, I don't want to do it the rest of my life."

"What had you planned to do before the injury to your knee?" She held her fingers out of the window and felt the wind whip through them.

"Pro football. And when I wasn't quick enough anymore, I thought I'd probably coach."

"Why didn't you go ahead and coach after the injury?"

"They like degrees. I was less that two years into one, so I came home and got my doctorate in drinking beer."

"You weren't interested in Kilgore College?"

"Sure. The Rangerettes are great."

"I'm serious. Stephen F. Austin's only about an hour's drive south, isn't it?"

"Yes. But after being the community hero, I was suddenly a loser. It'd been hard to be plain Billy Joe James down in Nacogdoches around the kids I'd grown up with. Besides, there was no more college scholarship, my knee was healing, and my parents didn't have the money to send me."

"I'm sorry."

"Don't be. I could have done something, but I was too macho to accept any less than I'd had. Soon afterwards my parents died and left me the house, so I've just gotten by ever since."

"My parents are dead, too."

"How'd it happen?"

"They were killed in a car crash near Dallas about two

years ago. They'd never had much either, but they always gave me love and support.''

"You're lucky. A lot of people don't get that.''

"I know. Are you an only child, too?''

"Yes.''

"It's lonely sometimes, isn't it?''

"Yes, but it's got its benefits, too.''

"I know. I spent a lot of time drawing when I was growing up since I didn't have a brother or sister to play with.''

"And I was always throwing a pigskin.''

"It's a shame you can't use that ability, Billy Joe. I bet there are a lot of boys who would give a great deal to know half of what you do about the game.''

"It's changed some since I played.''

"Surely not that much.''

"Maybe not.'' He laughed suddenly. "You know, I still dream about completing Hail Mary passes. And I've been thinking lately about going back to college and finishing my degree. Then I could coach.''

"That'd be great. I want to complete mine, too, but with Dan and the murderer, well—''

"Don't think about it now. First things first. What we both need is a burger and shake at Rosey's. See that small building up ahead with all the cars around it?''

"The one with the purple cow on top?''

"Right. That's Rosey's.''

"I had in mind a bigger place. I bet you can't even go inside there.''

"You guessed it. We'll eat in the car. There's plenty of room.''

As Billy Joe pulled up in front of the Purple Cow Burger and Shake Barn, Sunny got a better look. It was a small, square, white building with two sliding windows in front for orders. Straddling its roof was a faded purple cow. Inside two women were cooking and taking orders as fast as they could.

And scattered over the roof, on the purple cow and around the building were sparrows, small brown and gray birds who obviously made their home at the Purple Cow. They chirped happily as they gathered leftovers from Rosey's diners, chittered angrily as they fought over the best pieces, and flew back and forth to the roof as cars drove in and out.

Billy Joe turned off the engine of his pickup. "What do you want?"

"I'm so hungry I could eat anything, or everything. What's best?"

"Let me order for you." He smiled, and got out of the pickup.

Sunny watched him approach a woman who must be Rosey. She smiled at Billy Joe, talked with him some, then took down his order. Billy Joe walked back to the car and got inside.

While she turned to stare at all the other cars, Billy Joe watched her, listening to the confusion of music coming from the car radios around them.

He'd changed lately, and knew it. He was working more and drinking less. Since he'd gotten involved with the murders, he'd begun to value his own life more and knowing Sunny had made him realize he could have a good future. He wondered if she'd noticed the difference in him and hoped she had.

Hell, he really was thinking about going back to college. He wasn't that old or out of shape yet, and maybe Billy Joe James still meant something in the athletic world. But it'd be taking a chance to find out, putting his self-worth on the line. He could get rejected in a big way, just like when his knee had gotten busted. Besides, maybe he was afraid of success. It carried a lot of responsibility, and he'd avoided that for a long time.

But he wasn't twenty anymore, and his dreams were more realistic. Besides, if Sunny Hansen could find the courage to fight back, stalked by a violent husband and a murderer, could he do any less? Her life was at stake if she lost, but pride was all he had to lose. No, he couldn't do any less than Sunny, or how could he ever respect himself again?

"Is that Rosey motioning for you, Billy Joe?" Sunny asked, interrupting his thoughts.

"Looks like that's our order."

He got out of the car, walked over to Rosey, and picked up their food. When he came back to the Chevy, he motioned for Sunny to roll the window on her side up halfway so he could set the tray against it. Then he hurried around and got inside.

She began distributing the cheeseburgers, french fries, onion rings, and two huge chocolate malts with spoons as well as straws. Handing him salt, catsup, and lots of napkins, she began eating, the tantalizing aroma making her feel like she could eat all the food he'd bought.

After she'd taken the edge off her hunger, she smiled at him. "You're right. This is really great."

"As good as the drive-in?"

"Yes, but different." She spooned up a big mound of the shake. "I guess we're lucky to be living in such an underdeveloped area."

Billy Joe laughed. "That's what I keep telling myself."

Finally, when they were down to empty wrappers, Sunny groaned. "I ate too much. And it's all your fault."

"What about a sundae?"

"No! I can't possibly!"

"I thought you were more of a sport than that."

She laughed. "Not when I'm this full."

"We'll see."

He got out, tossed a few french fries to the sparrows, then walked around the car and picked up the tray. He threw away the crumpled wrappers in the white trash container in front, then handed Rosey the tray. He talked with her again, then hung around the window, watching the other cars. He waved at a few people, then turned back to the window.

When he came back to the pickup, he was carrying a huge hot fudge sundae with whipped cream, nuts, and a candied cherry on top. He got in the pickup and offered the sundae to Sunny.

She groaned and shook her head in denial. He grinned and handed her a spoon. After he'd taken several bites and looked ecstatic, she gave in, deciding she could hold a few more mouthfuls, after all. Soon they were both digging into soft white ice cream and thick dark fudge, murmuring their appreciation all the while.

Finally, when the sundae was gone, Sunny groaned, rubbed her stomach, and leaned back against the seat. "That was wonderful, but I already regret it."

Billy Joe laughed, and dropped the sundae dish under his feet. "Everybody needs a feast like that once in a while."

He started the engine of his pickup and backed out. Sparrows flew up to the back of the Purple Cow, and Rosey waved good-bye from the window. Sunny waved back, then shut her eyes as Billy Joe pulled out onto FM 203. For the moment she felt full, safe, and contented.

She glanced over at Billy Joe. "Thanks."

Reaching over, he squeezed her hand.

21

"I'm going to take a walk while you draw the kids," Price said, standing in Sunny's back yard. "I may even solve the case this afternoon."

"I'd be glad if you did," Sunny replied, smiling at Cory and Randy, who sat on a blanket, turning the pages of a comic book.

"Now, kids, do what the lady tells you and don't move till she's done."

Sunny laughed, shaking her head. "Do you really think it's possible for them to sit still that long?"

"If I tell them to, yes."

"I think we'll be better off if we take several breaks. I might even read them that Wonder Woman comic they brought."

"Comics are for kids. You'd get bored," Price said.

Sunny laughed. "Comics are for anyone who likes them! As an artist I always enjoy looking at the art. Besides Wonder Woman is a favorite of mine."

"Well, do what you want."

"Maybe we'll even have some lemonade later."

"Now that's a good idea," Price agreed. "Cory and Randy, if you're good and sit still, you'll get lemonade later."

"I'd rather have ice cream," Cory replied.

"Me, too," Randy agreed.

Sunny laughed harder.

"You'll get what she gives you," Price said, then glanced at Sunny in exasperation. "There's no pleasing them."

"Maybe you can get them ice cream on the way home. The Purple Cow is a good place."

"Purple Cow. Purple Cow. Purple Cow," Randy began chanting, and Cory quickly joined him.

"Enough of that," Price commanded.

"Purple Cow. Purple Cow. Purple Cow," they continued.

"I'm leaving," Price said. "Kids, mind your manners while I'm gone."

He quickly walked into the woods, leaving the sound of Purple Cow behind. Purple Cow! That just went to show you Sunny Hansen knew nothing about kids. You couldn't make a suggestion like that or you'd never hear the end of it till you actually went there. He loved his kids, but sometimes he was damned glad he was away a lot, and his wife took care of them most of the time.

It was hot in the woods, even with the shade. Damned hot. There was no way to get away from this humidity, and soon he was sweating in his crisp uniform. "Hell and damnation," he cursed, glancing at the spreading stains. He'd be a mess when he got back to the office. He only hoped the cockeyed portrait would be worth the money and time. His wife had been crazy about the idea, so here he was.

But he was hoping he could find a clue, something to break the case. His career would be set if he could catch the murderer single-handedly.

He felt the revolver in his belt and smiled grimly. He wouldn't even mind shooting the bastard if he got the chance. Or fight him. Yes, he'd like to feel his fists punching in the guy's face, breaking his nose, blood spurting out. Then he'd handcuff him, drag him from the woods, and surprise the hell out of everybody. He'd get a raise, a promotion, and he'd be the biggest man in this part of East Texas. The girls would love it, and him.

Smiling to himself, he walked on, thinking of long legs and hot thighs. Suddenly, he stopped and cursed. He'd been so busy thinking about promotions, money, and girls, he'd forgotten to look for clues. Well, there probably weren't any in this part of the woods, anyway. If there was something to find, it'd be nearer the sludge pit.

He hit the oil road that led to the pit and examined the land on either side as he walked. Everything looked all right. He stopped by the pumping oil well and patted the black metal. He'd give a lot to own it. Just one little old well could make a big difference in a man's life.

Girls. He would really get the girls if he could take them to Vegas or New York or Hawaii on a regular basis. And he'd like to visit those places, too. First he'd get a big girl, maybe one six feet tall with blond hair and long legs that wouldn't stop. He got hotter just thinking about her. Yes, a big girl, about a head taller than him. The other men would look at him with envy, and he'd drop piles of cash on green casino tables.

Yes, what he needed out of life was one producing oil well, or maybe several. In fact, he ought to be real rich, and not just in oil but in real estate, too. He'd be so rich his wife'd have to stay with him no matter how many affairs he had on the side. Yes, that was the way life should work. He'd be a stud bull, but not just in East Texas. Across the United States, too. Hell, he could screw women all over the world.

He was really sweating now. Cool, blond Scandinavian girls. Hot, dark Mediterranean babes. Sophisticated French. Black Amazons. Orientals. Yes, maybe one of those beautiful girls from Thailand he'd heard about. And Indian women with voluptuous bodies, huge dark eyes, and thick black hair. You could get lost in a woman like that. He was so hard now, he thought he'd step into the trees and . . . who the hell was that near the sludge pit?

It was a tall man in an overcoat.

"Hey, stop!" Price called, reaching for his gun.

The man glanced up, then ran into the woods.

Price shot twice after him, missed, and followed, running as fast as he could. He stopped at the edge of the woods and listened. But all was quiet. It was as if the man had simply disappeared into thin air, but that wasn't possible.

"Come out!" Price shouted. "I've got you covered. You can't get away."

Silence followed.

"Damn," Price muttered to himself, wishing he had backup, anybody to help him search the area.

Clenching his gun with two hands, he began making a sweep of the area around the sludge pit, but it was soon evident the man had gotten away. Finally, he dropped his arms, put his revolver in its holster, and walked back to the sludge pit.

He felt defeated, robbed. The girls had disappeared. He was still plain Deputy Price Simmons, with his kids being drawn by a crazy artist. Then he felt terror race through him. What if the murderer ran toward Sunny Hansen's house? What if the strangler took his kids as hostages? What if he just killed them all and kept going?

Horrified, he ran down the oil road as fast as he could. He didn't even notice the oil well as he concentrated on reaching his children before the murderer. He ran through the woods, knocking branches out of his way, losing his balance as he slipped on slick pine needles, then racing the final few feet into Sunny's back yard.

His children were sitting happily in the sunlight, drinking lemonade. Sunny Hansen was drawing them. It was such a happy, peaceful scene that for a moment he couldn't believe it was real. Then they glanced up and looked shocked.

"What happened to you?" Sunny asked, setting aside her sketch pad and rising.

"Daddy's got tree in his hair," Cory singsonged.

"And dirty clothes," Randy joined in.

Price looked down at himself. He was a wreck. He'd have to shower and change before going to the office. He ran a hand through his hair and pulled out pine needles. He threw those on the ground and stalked toward Sunny.

"Have you seen a man in an overcoat here?" he asked.

"You saw the killer?" Sunny froze, then glanced around apprehensively.

"I think so. Let me use your phone. I'm going to get Sheriff Barker out here."

"There's one in my studio. First door on the left. But what happened?" Sunny persisted.

"I'll tell you later. Watch the kids. As soon as I get the sheriff, I'm taking them home."

"Good idea," Sunny agreed. "You can take the portrait too. It's finished."

"Great. I'm just glad they didn't get killed getting their faces drawn."

"We've been fine here," Sunny explained, but turned back toward Cory and Randy. She wouldn't leave them outside a moment longer.

As she shepherded Cory and Randy into the house, Price stepped out of her studio. "Okay, the sheriff's on his way, but I don't think he'll find anything. That guy disappeared superhuman-like. Real spooky. I'd have shot him if I could. Anyway, I'm taking these kids home, getting cleaned up, and I'll be back on the job. We've got to catch this guy."

"At least somebody's seen him besides me," Sunny replied.

"If it was him," Price said. "But I don't know who else'd be around the sludge pit wearing an overcoat in this kind of weather. I mean, it's got to be over a hundred degrees out there."

"I know."

"Well, I'm going to get these kids home."

"Here's the portrait." Sunny handed him the large drawing.

He took it, then whistled. "I'll be damned. That's good. It may even be worth one hundred fifty bucks."

"If you want to wait, I can mat it for you. That'll protect it."

"No. I don't have time. My wife'll know what to do with it."

"I'll roll it then. It'll be easier to carry." Sunny quickly rolled the piece of art, then carefully put a rubber band around it. Hesitantly, she gave it to Price, hoping he didn't ruin it on the way home.

"Okay, thanks. And here's your money. I thought you'd like cash."

"Thanks." She smiled at Cory and Randy. "Be careful going home."

"Purple Cow," Cory began to chant.

"Purple Cow," Randy chimed in.

"Oh, no!" Price exclaimed, ushering his children out the front door. "See what you've done, Sunny Hansen."

She couldn't help laughing as she watched him struggle to get them in the car as the Purple Cow chanting got louder. He didn't stand a chance against them, and she knew, despite his worry and fear about the murderer, they'd get their ice cream at the Purple Cow. Seeing him with his children made her feel better about the deputy sheriff.

As he pulled out of her drive, he honked, then headed fast toward FM 203.

Alone, Sunny locked the door and turned back into the

house. She glanced around. So the murderer was still in the area. But was he getting careless or arrogant? Maybe. If so, it might give the police a better chance of catching him. She certainly hoped so.

22

That night Sunny sat at her drawing table, working. She'd been jumpy ever since learning Price had seen a man in an overcoat near the sludge pit.

She was playing the radio, switching stations as she tried to find something she liked—a difficult task here in East Texas. She was used to the wide selection of music on the stations in Dallas. However, tonight she didn't want to hear the howling of the wind outside or tree limbs scraping against the roof, so she was listening to whatever she could get.

Nan had called earlier, concerned. She'd heard about Price spotting the man in the overcoat, and she didn't want Sunny staying alone. Even though Sunny was frightened, she'd refused Nan's repeated offer of refuge in Longview, for she was determined to remain in her own home.

Also, Nan had told her Sheriff Barker and Price had been unable to find any further sign of the murderer around the sludge pit that afternoon. Sunny hadn't been too surprised, for the killer was obviously clever.

She stopped her thoughts. Her doors and windows were locked. She was safe, and she was not going to be spooked.

Turning her thoughts to Billy Joe, she smiled. He'd

called, too. But when she'd told him the news of the day, he had wanted her to stay with Nan, or Miriam. Again, she had explained that she couldn't run anymore.

But she had cheered them both by telling him Nan's exciting news. Nan had called her friend in New York City, and now Sunny had a person's name at an art agency to whom she could send her portfolio slides as soon as she completed the new illustrations. Billy Joe had been thrilled for her, and they had talked awhile about his work that day and little things of interest.

After he'd hung up, she had felt terribly alone again, and she'd been fighting her fears ever since. But she wasn't going to give in. She was determined to stay home.

Switching stations on the radio, she selected a drawing pen, then began to ink in a new piece of art for her portfolio.

Suddenly there was a knock at the back door. She froze. She screwed the cap back on the pen, but didn't move from her drawing table. Perhaps she had been mistaken. It might only be the wind.

The knock came again.

Getting up, she walked into the kitchen without turning on any lights, so whoever it was wouldn't know she was there. She hesitated by the door, her breath coming fast.

Another knock. "Sunny! It's Miriam."

Relief flooded her. But what was Miriam doing out this time of night, especially when she knew the killer was in the woods? She quickly unlocked the door, then pushed open the screen.

"Miriam, hurry inside."

"Evening, Sunny." Miriam stepped across the threshold.

Sunny glanced around outside, didn't see anything suspicious, and quickly shut and locked the door.

"What happened to your lights?" Miriam asked.

"Sorry." Sunny turned on the kitchen lights. "I didn't

know who it was, so I was being careful. I never dreamed you'd be out walking in the woods. Really, Miriam, you must be more careful. And you're not walking home alone. I'll drive you, or you can spend the night here."

"Did something spook you?" Miriam glanced around.

"Price brought his children over for me to draw this afternoon. While he waited, he went for a walk in the woods. He saw a man in an overcoat by the sludge pit."

"Was it the killer?"

"I don't know, but who else is running around in the middle of summer wearing a coat?"

"Good point."

"Price and the sheriff went back later, but couldn't find any evidence."

"You should have come over and stayed with me, Sunny."

"There's no need to, really. I've got all the doors and windows shut and locked, despite the heat, so I'm as safe as I can be. But what are you doing out?"

"I need to talk to you, Sunny."

"Okay. Let's have some of your blackberry wine and peanuts."

"Are you sure I'm not interrupting anything?"

"I've been working, but I need a break." Sunny opened a cabinet, glancing back over her shoulder. "You look worried."

Miriam sat down at the table. "I am. Have you heard anything unusual tonight?"

"No, but it's only about one in the morning. There's still plenty of night left." She set two glasses, a bottle of wine, and a can of red peanuts on the table.

"It's not a joking matter, Sunny."

"I know. I was just trying to make you feel better."

"Until this is all settled, I don't think you can."

"What did you hear?"

"I live closer to the sludge pit than you do, and tonight, for the first time, I heard women wailing, howling winds, and rushing water. The sounds all came from the pit.''

"And you went to check on it? Alone?"

"Yes."

Sunny stood up. "Miriam, don't you ever do anything like that again. You come to me if you want to go exploring at night, and I'll call Billy Joe. The three of us can go together, but don't you dare go out there alone again."

Miriam smiled, shaking her head.

"Now promise me?"

"But Sunny—"

"I'm serious."

"All right."

Sunny sat down. "Price just saw that man this afternoon, and tonight you go out there alone."

"When I got to the pit, the sludge was boiling, dust devils were whirling all over the top of it, and I could hear women wailing, so pitifully it almost broke my heart."

"What did you do?"

"I looked around. I couldn't see any women to help. There wasn't anything I could do, so I came here."

Sunny poured two glasses of wine and handed one to Miriam. "You need something to drink, and so do I." She took a sip, then looked hard at Miriam. "I believe you, but who else will?"

Miriam nodded. "I've been having trouble with that all my life. It doesn't matter, but Billy Joe probably will."

"You realize that the women's voices could have been the wind in the trees, or maybe owls, and gusts of wind could have stirred up the water and dust."

"I know." Miriam nodded. "But it has to do with the murderer."

"Oh, Miriam, not again."

"I know you don't want to hear that. This world we call

reality has come so far from accepting the existence of any other reality. When another world influences ours, nobody wants to admit the truth.''

"And what is the truth?'' Sunny took a long drink of wine, wishing Miriam wouldn't talk this way.

"Those dead women I heard wailing and Mother Earth are crying out to be avenged and warning us that the evil is growing, and it must be stopped before it consumes us all.''

"Miriam, I can understand that is what you think, but there is no proof.''

"I thought you'd understand.''

"I'm trying to, but this is so far out of my realm of experience or belief, it's just too much. Besides, the police are getting closer to the killer. Price saw him today. They'll catch him soon.''

"You don't really believe that anymore, do you, Sunny? You're just spouting what you think should be true, but you're refusing to look at reality.''

Sunny stood up again and paced.

"There's more, Sunny. And you're not going to want to hear this, either. I'm having dreams, waking visions. I'm even hearing voices, and it all has to do with you.''

"Me?'' Sunny sat back down and clutched her wineglass.

Miriam took a drink and got out her pipe. She filled it with tobacco, packed it down, then lit it.

"I'll get you an ashtray.'' Sunny got up, wanting to put off hearing what Miriam was going to say as long as possible. She felt nervous and afraid. She got an ashtray out of a drawer and set it on the table. Too soon, she had to sit back down again.

"I'm not the medicine woman my grandmother was, but I've been trying hard. It's working, too. I'm remembering more and more. Maybe my grandmother is even helping me from the Good Black Road.''

"What?'' Sunny looked at her in disbelief.

"There is the Good Red Road that Native Americans travel in this life, then they pass over to the Good Black Road."

"I don't believe in any life except this one."

"I know, but you may have to change your mind. From everything I'm learning, it all points to one fact. You, Sunny Hansen, have been sent to lead the forces of good against the evil that has awakened to prey upon women."

"That is ridiculous!" Sunny shouted.

"No matter what you think or say, for here and now you are the savior."

"I can't imagine how in the world you could have come up with such a crazy idea. Savior! What we need is some damn good police investigation, not some mumbo jumbo."

"I thought you had come to trust me, Sunny."

"This isn't trust, this is—"

"The truth."

"All right. Prove it to me. Show me something tangible. And just what evil is it, anyway?"

"I don't know, Sunny, and I can give you no physical proof, yet."

"And why me?"

"I don't know that, either. But, believe me, I am desperately trying to remember that Comanche-Caddo legend my grandmother told me so long ago, and I'm determined to find out why you are so important. It's vital to all our lives."

Sunny put her elbows on the table and buried her face in her hands. Miriam was not going to back down. She could see that now. She was determined to push this savior and ancient evil theory as far as it would go. But what could she do? If she denied Miriam her right to believe as she wanted, she would lose their friendship and abandon Miriam when she was struggling to come to terms with something from her heritage. She couldn't do that, didn't want to, either.

But if she didn't stop it right now, she would have to go along with it. And where would that get her? Did it matter? The important thing was Miriam. She was obviously working through something personal right now. Miriam had helped her when she was down and out, without a friend to stand by her, and could she do any less for Miriam?

She raised her head and smiled at Miriam. "Well, I can't believe in or agree with what you've been saying, Miriam, but I certainly support your right to think it."

Miriam grinned, then took a long draw on her pipe. "You sound like Nan."

Sunny laughed. "Maybe I've been spending so much time around her I'm picking up her rhetoric. But it's the truth. You have the right to believe whatever you want."

"Thanks. And do I have the right to try and change your mind?"

"Oh, no! I was afraid you'd say that."

Miriam laughed, too. "Friends?"

"Yes. What was that in *The Three Musketeers*, 'All for one and one for all?' You and Nan and me."

"I don't know, but that sounds about right if we're going to come out of this alive."

Sunny shook her head and popped some peanuts in her mouth. "You have to be the most tenacious person I ever met."

"We've got to protect ourselves, Mother Earth, and helpless women."

"That's kind of what Nan does, doesn't she?"

"Yes. She just gives it another name."

"Nan mentioned the term Ecofeminist the other day, and it seems to be a growing movement of feminists and ecologists combined, women and men helping women and the earth survive."

"Ecofeminist." Miriam exhaled and smoked curled around her head. "That's as good a label as any. But a word won't keep you safe, and above all, I'm going to make

234

sure Dan and that murderer don't get you. You're too important, Sunny. Never forget that."

"Thanks, but—"

"No buts! Now, I want to talk to you about Comanche and Caddo medicine, because you're bound to start having unusual, maybe frightening dreams, at the very least."

"Tonight, Miriam?"

"Yes. This can't wait. It's all starting to move fast, and we must be as prepared as we can."

"All right."

Miriam relit her pipe, took several puffs, then concentrated on Sunny. "I want to mention herbs first. Before all the pharmaceutical companies, prescriptions, and drugs, people were healed by nature. Herbs, grasses, roots, trees, animals, medicine springs all had different and powerful healing properties. Then you didn't go to a doctor and get a prescription for a pill, you—"

"Went to a medicine woman?"

"Right. Or a medicine man. And, more likely, he or she came to you. Medicine people were also shamans, for they dealt not only with physical illnesses or disorders, but with spiritual ones as well. For they believed the two usually went together, one influencing the other."

"That's why you believe there's more than just murder involved with their deaths?"

"Yes, partly. From the first I felt a powerful, ancient, evil force at work, and that feeling has grown as more women have been killed. I think now the evil is killing to increase its power."

Sunny shivered and poured them more wine.

"But to get back to the herbs. My grandmother used to take me into the woods and point out plants and tell me how they healed. Of course, too much of any plant could hurt, so you had to know how to use it."

"Do you think plants will help us?"

"Yes. I used some in your medicine wheel. And I want

235

us to make a medicine bag, filled with herbs and other protections, for you to wear all the time. I'm going to make one for myself and Nan, too."

"Do you really think it's necessary?"

"Anything that might help us can't be overlooked." Miriam set aside her pipe and took several sips of wine. "Of course, there are different names for plants, depending on the language. My grandmother tried to teach me both, but I haven't used the Comanche and Caddo languages in so long, they're almost impossible to remember. But I do know the English words."

"Do you feel you've lost a lot by not using your medicine skills sooner?" Sunny decided to try and help Miriam try to remember her heritage's ways and teachings.

"No. I've used bits and pieces of it before, but I honestly didn't realize my own latent power and strength until I began calling on my shaman legacy."

"And how do you feel about it now?"

"Good. But also uncertain if I'll be able to remember enough in time."

"I have confidence in you, Miriam."

"Good, then, I'd like for us to walk in the woods tomorrow so you can pick out some special plants for your medicine bag."

"I don't know if that's such a good idea." Sunny took a sip of wine.

"We'll stay away from the sludge pit."

"Okay then."

"Another thing my grandmother taught me was about vision quests. You can go on one for various reasons. For instance, if you feel you need help or a strong totem to get through some coming ordeal or problem, you could go on a vision quest and come back with strong medicine."

"What type of medicine?" Sunny found herself interested despite her disbelief. "And how do you go on a vision quest?"

"You can go in your night dreams or in a waking dream state. Sometimes people go into the hills or mountains alone and fast until their vision comes to them, or if it isn't as difficult a problem they might stay at home." Miriam relit her pipe and began smoking again. "As for the type of medicine found, it's often animal totem medicine."

"How could animals help someone?"

"My grandmother explained to me that all animals have their own personal power, which varies in strength and type depending on the animal. For example, bear is a powerful totem, representing strength and healing. Eagle is a protective power, which explains the eagle war bonnet. Coyote medicine is for knowing the future. Do you see?"

"Yes, but how does an animal totem help you in a time of crisis?"

"If an animal comes to you in a vision quest, you realize the strengths of that totem can be yours if you study it. In learning about the animal, you also learn about yourself and how to deal with your problem. Also you feel strengthened, knowing you're protected by the animal totem spirit, the spirit that connects all the animals of that species. The great bear spirit, for example, would be watching over and protecting you."

"That's fascinating. And you really believe this?"

"Yes. Lots of my people do."

"I can see a certain sense in it, if you knew the animals and their powers."

"Right. Have you dreamed of an animal lately?"

Sunny hesitated. "I doubt if it means anything, but I dreamed last night of a white owl."

"Do you remember the dream?"

"No."

"In Comanche and Caddo lore, owl is feared and respected. It's a night bird, and for creatures of the day that's frightening and mystical. Owl also has 'deceiver feathers'

237

so it can fly without sound and catch prey off guard. It's a wise hunter. Owl also brings messages in the night through dreams. Maybe that's what happened to you."

"But I don't remember the dream," Sunny said.

"Then it will come again."

"Maybe not. I don't usually dream."

"Everyone dreams, but you must train yourself to remember." Miriam pointed a finger at Sunny. "You are now on a vision quest, and I want you to remember your dreams and tell me about them. And that means anything at all that comes to you about a dream."

"Oh, Miriam, please—"

"I'm serious, Sunny. I'm determined to help you, and this is the best way I know how. And, don't forget, it'll protect you from Dan, too."

"All right. I'll tell you my dreams, if I have any." Sunny was trying to remain skeptical, but everything Miriam taught her made a certain sense. And the more she learned, the more she wanted to know, even though she still couldn't believe it was any more than mind games.

"Good. And I'll take you up on your offer. I'll stay the night, then we'll hunt for plants early tomorrow morning."

"Do you want the couch or the bed?"

"Where have you been sleeping, Sunny?"

"The couch."

"Then I'll take the bed, and you won't have to make up something extra."

"Are you sure you won't mind sleeping there?"

"No. Maybe the dead woman will send me dreams to help catch her killer."

Sunny felt a shiver run up her spine. She was glad she wasn't going to be sleeping in the bed waiting for that kind of dream. "There's a clean nightgown in the nightstand. Do you want to go to sleep now?"

"Yes. I'm tired. And we have a lot to do tomorrow."

They rinsed out their wineglasses, then left them drying

on the kitchen cabinet. Miriam left her pipe in the ashtray and followed Sunny into the living room.

"Don't hesitate to wake me if you dream, and I'll be nearby if you need me," Miriam said as she walked into the bedroom.

"Good night," Sunny called, then pulled off her jeans and laid down on the couch. It was lumpy, but anything was better than the bedroom. She glanced at the medicine wheel on the wall, heard Miriam get into bed and saw her light go out, then switched off the lamp beside the couch. She immediately felt sleepy. With Miriam in the house, she felt safe and knew she wouldn't have trouble going to sleep.

Soon she descended into darkness. She was walking through the woods. A bright moon lit the path she followed. She could smell the clean scent of pine. Wind moaned through the trees. It was warm but not hot.

Suddenly there was movement behind one of the trees ahead, and Dan's head popped to one side then the other of the tree. He grinned.

Terrified, she tried to stop, but instead she kept moving toward him, even though she wasn't walking. He ran to a closer tree and looked at her from one side then the other, as if playing a childhood game. Her fear was growing. Her breath was short and her heart raced. Again, she tried to stop and turn back. But she moved relentlessly forward.

Suddenly, Dan leaped from behind the tree into the middle of the path. He was wearing an overcoat and held up a butcher knife. He grinned again. Once more she tried to run away, but she couldn't move, could only look in horror as he ran toward her, brandishing the knife.

Then the dead woman with the long, blond hair rushed out of the woods toward Dan, only now she was wearing a beautiful white owl mask. She held up a hand toward Dan, and he stopped. Then she motioned for Sunny to get behind

239

her. Sunny could suddenly move. She started toward the dead woman.

And woke up.

"Miriam," she called, shivering all over. "I'm dreaming of that dead woman!"

23

Reverend Mulhaney was having trouble sleeping after he went to bed Thursday night. He kept waking up with his chest tight, and since the heart attack, that sensation made him tense. He was not frightened, of course. God was with him, and he could not believe that his benevolent protector meant to call him home anytime soon. After all, he had yet to expand his ministry into television.

But there was the matter of the phone calls. Being abruptly awakened around two in the morning was not good for his heart. It made him have to take his heart medication, and after the conversations, he had trouble getting back to sleep. Now he had started waking at two, whether the phone rang or not.

And he was worried about the man who called him. The stranger was obviously too preoccupied with women, maybe even dangerously so. He wanted the man to attend church or come in for guidance, but so far he had stayed away. That bothered the Reverend, too, for he liked everything in his life to be neat and orderly. And the phone calls were not.

He glanced at the digital alarm clock on the night table. 2:07. Would the stranger call soon?

The phone rang.

241

Taking the cap off the prescription bottle, he took a pill, then picked up the phone.

"Hello."

"Reverend, how are you?"

"Better. But you have yet to join us at church."

"I know. Sometime soon. Tonight I wanted to ask you something. You know those strangled women they've been talking about in the newspapers?"

"Yes."

"Do you think it's God's punishment being dealt to bad women?"

"I don't know. What makes you think they were bad?"

"Women are born bad, and only salvation can bring them to God. Maybe those women were saved and sent to God. What do you think?"

"I have prayed their souls went to heaven. But perhaps you would like to come to the parsonage and discuss this in more detail?"

"No, I can't. I have too much work to do. There's so much evil in the world. It must be cleansed."

"I think you should come to see me."

"Soon, when I've done enough work and am worthy of you."

"You can come in right now. I'll wait for you."

"No. I've got to go."

The phone went dead, and Reverend Mulhaney clenched the receiver before carefully setting it down. The man needed help. He was not quite balanced where women were concerned, but he obviously would not accept guidance. Therefore, Sheriff Barker should be alerted. It might be meaningless, but at this point he did not want to take a chance on any more women being killed. It was his duty to help and protect the weaker sex.

He punched in the sheriff's home number.

"Sheriff Barker here."

"Sheriff, this is Reverend Mulhaney. I am sorry to disturb you this time of night, but I feel there is something you should know about right now.''

''Yes?''

''Ever since you found the first woman's body in the sludge pit, I have been receiving phone calls about two in the morning from a man. He talks about women and how they must be cleansed.''

''So?'' It sounded like a sex phone call to the sheriff, but he didn't say so.

''I think maybe there is a connection between this man and the murdered women.''

''You think he killed them?''

''Maybe.''

''What makes you think so?''

''It is the way he talks about women.''

''Who is he?'' the sheriff asked, his voice low.

''I do not know.''

''Where is he?''

''Again, I have no idea.''

''Well, that's not much to go on.'' Sheriff Barker quickly decided the Reverend must have been seeing dead women in sludge pits since his heart attack and was now trying to attach every unusual event to their deaths.

''I know, but I thought I should warn you. I want to be of help. Maybe the next time he calls, I could get more information from him, or perhaps you could bug my phone and trace the call.''

''This isn't a cop show, Reverend. I'm short of staff and money, so I'd need more to go on than an anonymous phone caller talking about women.'' He was desperate to catch the killer, but he was doing all he could.

''I see. Well, maybe you could have somebody drive by the parsonage more often. They might notice somebody watching the place or something and could pick him up.''

''All right. I can do that. I'll keep what you said in mind, and if he calls again, let me know.'' Sheriff Barker was disappointed. He'd hoped the Reverend might have something he could really follow up on. He was beginning to suspect the killer was an outsider, somehow staying hidden in the area.

"Thanks, Sheriff. We must catch this man and soon."

"I agree. Bye."

The Reverend hung up, but he felt dissatisfied with the sheriff's bland reaction. He lay down, but the uneasiness persisted. There should be something he could do to help.

He tried to sleep, but could not. His chest felt heavy. Thinking of dead women was making him think of the woman who had funded his ministry. She had been ninety-one, old by anyone's standards, alone, and sick. She was going to die. Mostly ignored in the community, with no living children, husband, or relatives, she had been thrilled and grateful when he had begun to visit, taking a special interest in her.

She had loved to discuss the Bible, and she had known it well. She particularly had liked to point out the discrepancies and frequently had bested him on quotations and interpretations. But he had not minded. She was sick, lonely, and she had owned a small house in the woods and two producing oil wells. He had helped her change her will, leaving it all to him.

After her funeral, he had boarded up the house where she had breathed her last breath and had never returned. With the income from her oil wells, he had built his church.

But he did not know why he was thinking about her. She was now sitting happily at the right hand of God. She needed no help. It was the women still alive who needed him, and he would find some way to help them, as he always had.

24

Miriam was sitting on her back porch late Friday night, rocking, smoking her pipe, and drinking blackberry wine. A kerosene lantern lit the area, and insects buzzed around it. She could still hear the sound of wailing women, howling winds, and rushing water coming from the sludge pit. But it didn't frighten her now. She looked on it as a message from Mother Earth.

And that message was that the murdered women were crying out for vengeance and their cry appeared to be centered at the pit. Even the earth seemed to be demanding revenge, calling for the return of its black blood. She was still desperately trying to remember the old Comanche or Caddo legend told by her grandmother which might explain the murders and how to catch the killer, thereby exacting revenge.

But until she could remember the legend or figure out another way to stop the murderer, they had to protect themselves as best they could. Yesterday she and Sunny had gathered herbs and made three medicine bags. She touched the soft leather one she now wore on a thong around her neck next to her skin. It was strong protection, but she doubted if it would be enough to stop the murderer in a direct confrontation.

She took a sip of wine, thinking of Sunny. Her young friend learned just as easily and quickly as she had thought she would, for it was more remembrance of medicine knowledge than learning for the first time. And Sunny had to learn quickly, for there was no time for anything else.

As she rocked, thinking, she glanced up and gasped. A woman with long, blond hair was walking from the woods into her back yard. As the woman got closer, Miriam could see that oily water dripped from her, and she smelled of sludge and decay.

Miriam fought her fear. She wanted to get up and run in the house, slamming and locking the door. But she knew she mustn't do that. Her hand shook and she set down her jar of wine. The woman came closer, and Miriam could see that she was decomposing, maggots crawling through her flesh, insects buzzing around her. This had to be the woman that had lain in Sunny's bed. And she was dead, very dead.

But Sunny had somehow breathed life back into her.

The woman beckoned, then turned back toward the woods. Miriam didn't move. The woman looked over her shoulder, beckoned again, then walked to the edge of the forest. Miriam realized the woman wanted to be followed. She was frightened, and yet she couldn't pass up any opportunity to learn something to help catch the killer. And she firmly believed the woman, just like in Sunny's dream, was there to help them.

Miriam stood up and stepped off the porch. The woman nodded and waited. When Miriam was near, she began to walk through the woods. Miriam followed, soon realizing the woman could see as well in the dark as an owl. But how? She had no idea, any more than she knew how the dead woman could still be walking the earth.

Soon they arrived at the sludge pit. Once more the waters boiled, dust devils swirled over the pit, and women wailed. Miriam put her hands to her ears, hardly able to stand the pitiful sound.

246

Then the dead woman began to dance around the sludge pit, slowly at first then faster. But the dance was nothing of beauty, instead it was of death struggles, a woman fighting for her life, fighting to breathe, fighting to live, then finally succumbing and disappearing into the sludge pit.

Miriam felt it all with the dead woman, reliving the disbelief, the terror, the horror, and finally surrendering to blackness.

The sound of birds chirping woke her the next morning. She felt stiff and damp. Confused, she sat up and gasped. She was lying near the sludge pit, but it was quiet and still this morning. What was she doing here?

She glanced around in confusion, then remembered the night before. Could she have been dreaming? Surely, she hadn't really followed the dead woman with long, blond hair to the pit? Surely, she hadn't experienced the woman's death with her? But what else could it have been? How else could she have come to be at the pit?

She felt afraid and old, almost too old to go on, and she didn't want to be alone. Taking one last glance around, she hurried into the woods, wanting to put as much distance as possible between herself and the pit. She took a path that led to Sunny's house and hurried up to the back door.

Knocking, she glanced behind herself. What if the killer had seen her? What if he had followed?

She knocked again. "Sunny! It's Miriam."

Sunny unlocked the door and let her inside. "What happened to you, Miriam? I thought we agreed you wouldn't go walking alone again."

"Please get me a cup of coffee."

Looking at Miriam in concern, Sunny quickly poured a cup of coffee and handed it to her. "Sit down." Sunny pulled out a chair and helped Miriam into it. Then she sat down near her. "Can you tell me about it?"

Miriam took several sips, holding the cup for warmth, and nodded. "In a moment."

"You need to get out of those damp clothes."

"I want to talk first. Just bring me a towel."

"All right. Sit still." Sunny hurried into the bathroom, got a towel, and brought it back to Miriam.

Miriam dried her face and hair, then put the towel in her lap, pleating it nervously with her fingers.

"Now, what is going on?"

"I don't think the killer put the dead woman in your bed, Sunny. She's walking around on her own."

Sunny stood up. "I'm going to call an ambulance. You're sick or something."

"Sit down. I've never been better. This is all finally starting to make sense."

"If a walking dead woman makes sense to you, then we're in trouble." But Sunny sat down.

"I think when you tried to breathe life back into that woman, it brought a spirit into her body."

"Maybe she's really alive and I saved her, after all."

"No, she's dead, Sunny. Her body is decaying."

"Then you saw her?"

"Yes. She came into my yard last night and led me to the sludge pit. Somehow she caused me to experience her final moments of life."

"And death." Sunny shuddered. "Miriam are you sure it wasn't a dream? I'm still dreaming of her wearing that white owl mask."

"I woke up near the sludge pit." Miriam took a sip of coffee, then clutched the towel.

"You could have sleepwalked."

"Maybe. I have no proof, other than my word, that it actually happened."

Sunny stood up and poured herself a cup of coffee. "This is getting weirder and scarier all the time."

"She's returned to life to help us, I think."

"A lot of good a walking, decaying corpse is going to do

us. Really, Miriam, you must have been dreaming. It just doesn't make any sense, but then none of this does.''

"No, it's starting to make more sense. In fact, this woman is triggering something about the legend I've been trying to remember. I'm getting bits and pieces, but I can't quite grasp it yet. I'm going home. Maybe it'll come to me there."

"Miriam, you're going to stay right here. Besides, it's not safe." Sunny sat down and took Miriam's hand. "Look at you. We'll get you cleaned up, then you can take a nap. I'll fix us some lunch later."

"No, I've got to go. Time is running out. Anyway, if the killer didn't get me out by the sludge pit last night, he's not going to get me now."

"You're not immune. And I don't think you should stay alone anymore if you're going to be sleepwalking."

"I've been living alone for a long time. I need to be alone to think, to remember, and a walk in the woods will help. I'm feeling much better now. Thanks for the coffee." Miriam stood up.

"But you can't just go. Maybe you should see a doctor or something. At least, let me drive you home."

"No. Sunny, I need to do this on my own. You understand, surely."

Sunny hesitated. "If anything happens to you, I'll never forgive myself."

"I'll be all right. But before I go, I want to tell you something else."

"Something I won't want to hear, no doubt."

Miriam smiled, looking more like her old self all the time. "I had more visions of you. Now I know why you've been chosen to lead the battle against this evil."

"Chosen?"

"Yes, or agreed to before you returned to this life. You have been a priestess, a shaman or medicine woman, in many other lives before this one. And you always worked

249

for the good of the earth and women. I saw you as a priestess in Atlantis, Egypt, Celtic Ireland, and as a Native American shaman. You are simply once more doing the work you have long been trained to do.''

''Thanks, Miriam. Now you've eased my mind and simplified the entire situation.'' Sunny bit her lower lip. ''Of course, that is ridiculous, and I don't believe it.''

''I thought that's what you'd say. But can you explain in any other way why you're so quickly learning and grasping the ideas, concepts, and information I've been teaching you about shamanism?''

''I've always been a fast study.''

Miriam simply smiled. ''I'll stop by later this afternoon.'' She walked to the door.

''You'll be careful, won't you?''

''Yes. Take care.'' Miriam stepped outside and shut the door behind her.

Sunny locked it, then turned back toward the kitchen. She felt uneasy, confused, yet excited. Priestess? Atlantis? Could that be possible?

She did know she was feeling better than she had in a long while. It was as if Miriam was peeling layers off her psyche as she taught her about shamanism. In fact, she was feeling more in control, more sure of herself, as if she didn't have to be afraid anymore. Also, for the first time she no longer felt guilty, no longer wondered if Dan's hurting her had been her own fault.

And she wanted to learn more. She wanted to have power over herself, so that no one could ever manipulate or hurt her again. Miriam's teachings gave her that personal strength in a way she had never felt before.

A priestess who helped women and the earth. She liked the sound of it, even though she had never heard of it. But maybe Nan and Miriam were already like the priestess, and maybe she was becoming that, too. As far as other lives,

250

could it be possible? She didn't know, but she did know she wasn't quite the atheist she had been.

Walking into her studio, she sat down at the drawing table. She had a lot of hardware illustrations to do if she was going to spend time with Miriam this afternoon. Her portfolio was coming along well, and she hoped to have it finished soon. But with Miriam teaching her, she hardly had enough time for everything. Nevertheless, being with Miriam suddenly seemed more important than anything else.

Checking her list of illustrations, she decided faucets would be next.

25

When Sunny and Billy Joe got back from the drive-in Saturday night, they were still laughing about *Macho Men on Mars* and *Bimbos From Venus*.

"And they had the nerve to bill them both as science fiction classics," Billy Joe said, turning off the truck.

"Maybe they meant classy." Sunny laughed.

"Classless!"

The both laughed harder, until finally their laughter died away.

"I had a good time." Billy Joe looked at Sunny with moonlight glinting through the windshield. "I always do."

"So did I. Thanks."

"I should thank you. You paid."

"But you drove."

"Do you want to argue?"

"No."

"Is this where we say good night?"

"Yes, I guess so." Sunny suddenly realized she was coming to care for Billy Joe, and it surprised her. More than that she wanted him to touch her, kiss her. But how could she trust a man that far again? She couldn't.

Billy Joe put his hand on the seat between them, then clenched his fist. He cleared his throat. "I wish you'd move in with Miriam or Nan. You're not safe, and I worry about you."

"I'm all right."

"Sunny, I wish I had some rights with you, then maybe I could get you to take better care of yourself. Besides, you're working too hard."

She smiled and touched his hand. He quickly grasped her fingers and held on tightly. She could feel his heat and strength, and wanted him, but she pushed the feeling down and withdrew her hand. He wrapped his fingers around the steering wheel and held on hard.

"I know you're not ready for a man, not after Dan, but I—"

"No. Please don't say anything. You're right. I like you, but I'm not ready to get involved with anyone right now." I can't afford that, not when I'm just getting my strength and courage back."

"I understand, but I wish I didn't. Then I'd say to hell with everything and just hold you."

She smiled. "I wish I could say to hell with everything and let you. But it's not that way, at least not right now."

"Is there any chance for me?"

"Maybe."

"What the hell does that mean?"

"It means I don't know."

"Thanks." He looked at her. "You know I'm working steady now, and I've sent off for some college catalogs. I going to get on with my life, Sunny. I was something once. I know I can do it again."

"I know you can, too. It's not that."

"It's Dan then."

"Yes, and all he represents and all he made me feel and think about myself. I've got to get over that, and I've got to deal with him. I'm still married, and I'll have to get out of that when I have the strength to face it."

"I'll help you."

253

"I need to do this on my own. But if I didn't have our friendship, I'd miss it."

"I want to be more than your friend, and I just want you to know where I stand."

"Thanks." She leaned over and kissed his cheek, surprising both of them.

"Now you've got me for life." He chuckled. "Sunny, if you could do anything you wanted, what would you do?"

She hesitated. "I guess I'd go back to Dallas, face up to Dan, and get a divorce. Hopefully, the New York agency would represent me and begin to get me some work. While I was doing that, I'd go back to college and finish my degree. After that, who knows? Maybe New York City." She smiled at him. "What would you do?"

"I'd like to get my degree, then teach and coach. I might even get to be the best there is. But I'd also want to be with you, and help you get over Dan. You know, I could go with you to Dallas. You aren't going to be safe for a while, and I could make him back off."

"I have to do this on my own. I can't run from one man to another."

"You wouldn't be. We wouldn't have to live together. I would live near you, so I could be there for you. Maybe we could even go to school together."

She smiled. "That'd be nice."

"Good. And maybe Miriam'd even come."

"And leave her East Texas?"

"To keep you safe, I think she'd do a lot."

"Maybe so. I know I'd hate to leave her."

"Dallas isn't so far away."

"No." She looked out at the night around them. "But this is all just dreaming, anyway. First, we've got a killer to catch."

"I know. But somewhere down the line we've got a future to plan, and I hope it's together."

"I almost wish I didn't like you so much."

254

He laughed and let go of the steering wheel.

"You want a beer?" She smiled.

"I wouldn't pass it up."

"Good. Let's go inside."

Billy Joe got out and walked around to her side of the pickup. He opened the door, then took her hand and helped her down. As they walked to the front door, he held on to her hand and she didn't pull away. He was making progress, but he didn't know how much longer he could keep his hands off her. The kiss had almost undone him.

But he was worried about her. She wasn't safe, and now that he'd found her, he couldn't stand the idea of losing her. There was no way he was going to let the murderer get her. When he could, he would spend his nights keeping vigil outside her house, and he'd try to keep it up till the killer was caught. But he'd never let her know he was doing it.

As they walked up to the porch, Miriam stepped out of the shadows. "I've been waiting for you two."

Sunny yelped and clutched Billy Joe.

"Damn, Miriam!" Billy Joe exclaimed. "You just scared a year's growth out of both of us."

"Sorry. I didn't know how else to let you know I was here."

"Why didn't you come on up to the pickup?" Sunny dropped Billy Joe's hand and squeezed Miriam's.

"I didn't want to disturb you."

"We were just talking about the silly movies we saw." Sunny glanced at Billy Joe, feeling slightly embarrassed.

"That's right," he agreed.

Miriam smiled.

"And what are you doing here?" Sunny asked. "You weren't supposed to go wandering around in the woods."

"Nan brought me over."

"I'm sorry I missed her," Sunny replied. "Why was she here?"

"She was in the area talking with people, trying to get

255

some clues, so she had some blackberry wine with me. She's not sleeping well, and it shows."

"Is she still dreaming about her dead sister?"

"Yes. I told her what we'd been learning and discovering, but she still doesn't put much faith in it."

"That's Nan." Sunny took out her keys. "Why don't we all go inside and have something to drink?"

"I came over so we could go look at the sludge pit," Miriam explained. "I want to know if you two see or hear anything unusual."

"All right," Billy Joe agreed. "We'll drive over there. Sunny's been keeping me up on what you two are doing, and I'm ready to help out."

"I'm glad you waited for us," Sunny added.

"I promised I wouldn't go alone," Miriam replied. "Besides, I need the two of you."

"Come on." Billy Joe started back toward the truck. "Let's get it over with. I don't want to spend any more time at that pit than necessary."

He held open the pickup's door. Sunny got inside, then Miriam. Finally, he slid behind the wheel and started the engine. As he backed out, the movement threw Sunny against him, their bodies touching for the first time. He glanced down at her in surprise and pleasure. She smiled, realizing it wasn't nearly as frightening as she had imagined, then edged away from him. They were both very aware of their nearness as he drove them to the sludge pit.

Parking near the pumping oil well, Billy Joe left the lights on so they could see better. They walked down to the sludge pit and looked around.

"Do you hear anything?" Miriam asked.

"No." Billy Joe glanced at the trees. "And it all looks normal."

"I don't hear anything, either," Sunny agreed.

"It's quiet tonight," Miriam said, walking closer to the

256

sludge pit. "I feel almost as if it's gathering strength, drawing in power. Do you feel that, Sunny?"

"I don't know. It all seems about the same. Except maybe I feel something like the electricity in the air just before a storm."

"That's what I mean." Miriam smiled and squeezed Sunny's hand. "You're a good student."

"I have a good teacher." Sunny glanced up. "What's that?"

"Where?" Billy Joe pulled Sunny and Miriam toward him protectively.

"I thought I saw the woman with the long, blond hair at the edge of the forest, but I guess I was mistaken." Sunny frowned, still watching the woods.

"I've believed a lot of things you've said, Miriam," Billy Joe said, "but the walking dead is too much. We're not making a horror movie here."

Suddenly a white owl flew from the woods across the sludge pit from the direction Sunny had thought she'd seen the dead woman.

"Good medicine." Miriam smiled.

Sunny felt a chill run up her spine, and her skepticism began to wane. She had been dreaming of the dead woman wearing a white owl mask, and now she suddenly saw a real owl fly from where she thought she'd seen the dead woman standing. Could Miriam be right that the dead woman was actually watching over them?

She shivered and clutched Billy Joe's arm. He put a warm hand over hers and pulled her closer.

"You're starting to believe, aren't you, Sunny?" Miriam glanced around the area. "Come on, it's time to go home. We're getting closer to the killer, and we're gaining power. Now, I've just got to remember that legend."

26

Reverend Mulhaney jerked awake. It was late Sunday night. He looked at the clock beside his bed. 2:05. No, it was already Monday morning. His heart raced. He looked at the phone, thinking of dead women.

It rang. He took a pill and picked up the receiver.

"Hello. Reverend Mulhaney."

"Reverend, I need your help."

"I have been waiting for you to come to church."

"I've been busy cleansing the world of dirt."

The Reverend shuddered. "Perhaps you need the church to guide you in this. I could help."

"Yes, I need help. I'm afraid the dirt of women is beginning to rub off on me. I don't feel clean anymore. I can't get clean. What can I do?"

"You can come in for spiritual guidance. We will discuss the way you feel."

"I know how I feel."

"And you can get a hot bath here. That would cleanse you." The Reverend was more convinced than ever that the stranger was the murderer. But he was not worried for his personal safety because he did not believe the man would harm a minister. If he could lure the man to the parsonage, he could have the police waiting to catch him. Then they would find out if he was the killer or not.

"Thanks for the offer, Reverend. But I've got a good home with plenty of water."

"What kind of a house is it?" Perhaps he could get some information that would help the police locate the killer, if the man would not come to the parsonage.

"A good house back in the woods with its own well, plenty of food, and nice furniture."

"Is it near my church?"

'Yes, but why are you asking all these questions, Reverend? I'm the one supposed to ask questions."

"I was just wondering if the place was good enough for you." The Reverend felt his heart speed. The place the stranger described sounded very similar to the house he had been willed along with the oil wells. Could that be possible? Although he had left the house boarded up, he supposed someone could be living in it.

"Oh, it's a good house."

"But you could still come to see me."

"I will. I'm planning on that, but I've got to go now."

"Wait—"

The phone went dead.

Reverend Mulhaney took a deep breath and dialed Sheriff Barker at home.

"Sheriff Barker here."

"This is Reverend Mulhaney."

"More dead women, Reverend?"

"This is not an amusing matter, Sheriff. In fact, the stranger called me again. Because of the call, I think he has killed another woman and put her in the sludge pit. In fact, there may be several more dead women in it by now, if he calls me after every kill. Would you please check the pit this time."

"Reverend, it's the middle of the night, and—"

"Do you have any other leads?"

"I'm not at liberty to say."

"Please check the pit and put a constant watch on it. These killings have got to be stopped." Reverend Mulhaney decided not to mention the boarded-up house because he believed the murderer could be caught at the sludge pit. That way there would be no need to involve the house which he never wanted to enter again. Besides, he had to keep everyone away from the place. He did not want the secret buried there ever to see the light of day.

"All right, Reverend, I'll check the pit again, but only because of your position in the community. It makes no sense for the man to keep returning to the pit. He has to know it's being watched."

"But is it watched constantly?"

"No, but—"

"I believe a twenty-four-hour watch would reward you, Sheriff."

"I'm short of staff, but I'll check the pit again."

"And you will call and let me know what you learn?"

"Yes, I'll talk to you later."

"Thank you."

"Good night, Reverend." Sheriff Barker hung up, cursed, then dialed Nan Shubert. Maybe the Reverend was right. At least it was something to follow up, and all his other leads had been dead ends. He'd have Price stake out the pit at night, and maybe they'd catch something.

"Hello. Nan Shubert."

"Nan, it's Sheriff Barker."

"Yes?"

"Reverend Mulhaney called me again, complaining about crank calls. He's sure his calls and the murders are connected. He wants me to check the pit again. I'm going to get a team out there at dawn, dredge the thing again, and put an end to this nonsense once and for all. You want to help?"

"I'll meet you there."

"Thanks. I doubt if we'll find anything, but we've got to try. And, Nan, I wanted to say your work and commitment to this case have helped a lot."

"Thanks. I'm skeptical about the pit, too, Sheriff, but I'm as anxious as you are to catch this murderer. I'll see you there."

"Right. Bye."

27

Sunny awoke bathed in sweat. She'd just had another horrible dream. In this one Dan had been strangling her, with rotting female corpses standing in a circle around them. He had worn an overcoat, and she had clutched at it, trying to pull him off. The fabric had felt greasy, sludge-coated.

She sat up and switched on the light beside the couch. Clutching the medicine bag around her neck, she looked at the medicine wheel. Surprisingly, she felt comforted by it and thought of Miriam. She wanted to talk to her friend about her dreams, for she was still seeing the dead woman in the white owl mask, and she didn't want to be alone a moment longer.

Getting up, she hurriedly dressed, then grabbed her car keys off the dresser. Turning on the front porch light, she looked around to make sure she was safe, then unlocked the door and stepped outside.

The night was quiet, except she seemed to hear women crying in the distance. She shook her head to dispel the sensation and hurried to her car. The VW didn't want to start. She pumped the pedal several times, and it backfired. She kept at it, grinding the starter and pumping the pedal. It backfired again, then kept running. She hoped it wasn't a sign of needing an expensive tune-up.

She drove quickly but carefully to Miriam's house, feeling a strong need to be with her friend. What if something had happened? What if the murderer had found her? What if she was hurt?

But she stopped the thoughts as she pulled up in front of Miriam's house. A soft yellow light shone from the back porch, and she breathed a sigh of relief. Getting out, she slammed the door. But as she started to lock it, she noticed the sound of wailing women, rushing water, and howling wind. It was just as Miriam had described.

She shivered, then quickly locked the car door. She didn't want to admit it, but now she was hearing things, too. She walked hurriedly around the house, knowing Miriam would have heard her drive up and not be startled.

Miriam was sitting on her back porch, rocking, smoking, and drinking blackberry wine.

"You okay, Miriam?" Sunny walked up the steps and sat down in a rocker, which creaked under her weight.

"Evening, Sunny. Yes. Glad you could make it."

"You sound like I had an invitation."

"You did."

"But we hadn't made any plans. I just suddenly woke up from a bad dream and wanted to talk with you."

"I was thinking about you, wanting you to come over."

"You make it sound like I picked up your thoughts or something."

"I imagine you did."

"Oh, Miriam."

Miriam chuckled.

"Well, maybe I did. What do I know? Anyway, now *I* can hear sounds coming from the sludge pit. It's scary."

"Don't be frightened. It's a message from Mother Earth. You're getting sensitive very quickly, Sunny." She took a sip of wine. "Did you dream about Dan?"

"Yes. And the murderer and the dead woman wearing the white owl mask."

"Why don't you have some blackberry wine?" Miriam puffed on her pipe, then sent smoke spiraling upward.

"I'll get a glass."

"There's already one beside the bottle of wine."

Sunny froze. "You really did expect me, didn't you?"

"Yes. Your psychic powers are much stronger than you realize, Sunny."

"I think I do need some wine." She picked up a small jelly jar and poured a generous amount of wine into it.

"There's a good reason I wanted you to come tonight. I have an old legend to tell you."

"You remembered?" Sunny leaned toward Miriam expectantly, suddenly realizing she no longer discounted Miriam's visions, dreams, or tales from her grandmother. Now she, too, was hearing sounds from the sludge pit, noise only she and Miriam could hear. Besides, she had learned too much from Miriam, experienced too much herself, ever to go back to the way she'd been.

"Once long ago when the white man first came to Caddo and Comanche land, he brought with him an ancient evil that had long caused men to hunt, rape, and kill women, treating them as creatures without spirits, just as they treated the earth.

"Soon women were murdered and raped, as was the land. The Comanche and Caddo warriors fought back, but could not stop the spread of these terrible deeds. Until, under the light of a full moon in the late summer, powerful medicine women called upon Spider Grandmother for help.

"She sent a spirit to breathe life into one of the murdered women who rose and walked the earth until she could carry the killer to the Land of Spirits, imprisoning the evil force in the arms of Mother Earth.

"They called this evil the Spirit Stalker, for he stole women's spirits and power to use for himself."

"And you think that's what has happened again?" Sunny frowned, thinking. It was certainly true the police couldn't seem to catch the murderer. Maybe Miriam was right and the killer was protected by a powerful evil force.

"Yes. Sunny, because you tried to breathe life back into one of the dead women, I believe you unknowingly called upon Spider Grandmother, who sent a spirit to animate the body of the blond-haired woman."

Sunny quickly took a sip of wine. "If that's true, Miriam, why has the Spirit Stalker returned now? How did the force get free?"

"A long time ago the sludge pit was a medicine spring used by the Caddos and Comanches for healing. It's a natural place of power, and the Spirit Stalker was imprisoned there by the medicine women with the help of Spider Grandmother. Since then the land has been polluted and drained, robbed of its strength, until it could no longer contain the Spirit Stalker."

"And the murderer?"

"He must be a man weak of will, or one attuned to the Spirit Stalker in his hate and use of women."

"Can all this be true? It's so fantastic. It's hard to believe."

"You must believe, Sunny, if we and many others are to come out of this alive. You are the savior, so you must win the battle." She relit her sea horse pipe, taking several puffs.

"If you're right, I'd have no idea how to fight something of this magnitude. I'm not strong or wise enough."

"You're growing stronger and wiser all the time."

"Only because you're helping me."

"That's why I'm here, but the power you feel is your own, not mine. Since I made the medicine wheel, my personal power is growing, too. I'm tapping into my memory, becoming stronger and stronger. I'm getting back to my roots, and it's empowering me like nothing else in my life ever has."

"I'm glad for you, Miriam." Whatever was happening, she felt as if Miriam was working through her own crisis, and coming out a stronger person. She was going to have to accept the fact that shamanism was part of Miriam's life, and maybe hers, too, at least for now.

"You know, I'm old, but I'm finding out that no matter how old you are, the spirit is ageless." Miriam smiled and raised her glass of blackberry wine to Sunny.

Sunny raised hers, too, and they both drank. "I'm beginning to agree. With all you've taught me and all I'm seeing and experiencing, how could life be as simple as I'd thought?"

"Youth wears blinders, but age grinds them down until there are so many options you feel you can never learn it all, know it all, or experience it all. Not in one lifetime, anyway. My grandmother and her people believed there was life after death, and I have never doubted it. Now she walks the Good Black Road, and eventually I'll join her there."

"But not soon?"

"No, it's not my time yet."

"I'm walking the Good Red Road, with you, Miriam, and I'd like to walk the Good Black Road with you, too."

"Then so it will be." Miriam took her hand and poured her more blackberry wine.

"We're in this together." Sunny took a long drink.

"That's right. And now that I've remembered the legend, I must push even harder to build our psychic power so we can fight the Spirit Stalker, for with each woman he kills, he gains power. But it's you he wants, Sunny."

"Me!"

"You have great power. As I told you, you've been a priestess, a leader, in many lives, working for the good of women and Mother Earth. You have great psychic power to tap into. You have connections with the spirit world. The Spirit Stalker wants that, needs that. He must complete himself here and now, gain the female power he lacks so he can complete his destiny. If he devoured your power, there

266

would be no stopping him, and he would spread his death and destruction over the earth.''

"But why does he need female power?''

"It is the creative force. All is born of the female. There is no more powerful force on earth than the power to create life, for without life, including all forms of existence, there is nothing. And think, there are only two types of people on earth—mothers and children.''

Sunny hesitated, then said, "You're right. There are only mothers and children.''

"The Spirit Stalker wants to kill you and eat your spirit. Then he will be able to devour the earth. We must stop him.''

Deeply shaken, Sunny asked, "But can this be true? I mean, I was only trying to have a career as an illustrator and build a good marriage. I got away from Dan and started my career again. All I ever wanted was love and security. What is all this? How can this intrude into my life? I don't understand.'' She stood up, and paced. "I don't want it. I want to run away.''

"You can't run, Sunny. The Spirit Stalker will follow you. He is attracted by the smell of your blood. It's rich with all that he needs. He must feed on your power.''

"But I have no power. I'm just trying to survive from day to day, and I've almost finished my new portfolio. I don't have time to fight the Spirit Stalker or catch a murderer. I want to go home.''

"Where is home, Sunny?'' Miriam asked pointedly.

"I don't know. I guess I don't have one anymore.''

"Of course you do. Think! You are your home. Feel your strength and security inside yourself. As long as you don't give up your own strength and self, you have your home. But if you give up yourself to another, or to something that isn't right for you, then you'll feel homeless. And empty. Then others will be able to fill you with themselves, using you to their ends.''

"Is that what happened with Dan?"

"Yes. He tried to devour you."

Sunny shuddered and paced, then walked back up the steps. She looked down at Miriam. "I think you've always been home."

"I owe that to my grandmother. You must be yourself, Sunny. You must accept yourself. You must love yourself. Only then will you be at peace."

Sunny sat down and put her head in her hands. Her chest constricted. She wanted to cry, to scream, to run, but there was no point. She was dealing with something she couldn't run away from, as she had from Dan. It would follow her wherever she went, for it was inside her. "How do I know what's me?"

"That's what we've been working on." Miriam took a puff on her pipe and blew smoke into the air. "When you can truly feel yourself, know yourself, then you'll know when another, or even society, is trying to turn you into something you aren't."

"And when that happens?"

"Then you draw back into yourself and center, feeling your connection to the earth, to life, and most of all to your innermost self."

"How did you learn all this, Miriam?"

"I've lived a long time, but mostly I've been desperate lately and I've been thinking and pushing and exploring. The Spirit Stalker has forced me to face myself and my beliefs. It hasn't been easy, but it's been worth it, for I've gotten back parts of myself I thought I'd left behind forever."

"Maybe that's what I'm doing, too."

"Yes, you are. But you're also drawing from other lives, other memories, bringing them together here and now so you can fight the Spirit Stalker. And win."

"You know, there's no proof of any of this, and if we told anybody else they wouldn't believe us or they'd laugh."

"Billy Joe will accept what we say, and Nan will eventually come around. She's wearing her medicine bag, isn't she?"

Sunny laughed. "You have a way with her, Miriam."

"I just want her to be a whole person. She needs to explore light and laughter to balance her concentration on the dark."

"What do we do now?"

"Why don't you spend the night here? You'll be safer, and we need to discuss how to deal with the Spirit Stalker."

"I don't suppose the legend told you how to catch him."

"No."

"I hope we have the power to stop him."

"So do I. In any case, I believe the power of the Spirit Stalker, if he doesn't devour you, will reach its peak on the next full moon, eve of the first of August, a powerful medicine day."

"But that's only a few days away."

"No, it's tomorrow night."

"What! You must be mistaken. I can't be ready by then." Sunny frowned. "Besides, I've got to get my portfolio finished. I'm going home early tomorrow morning to work on it. I'm going to get a good night's sleep, and when I wake up maybe it'll all look different."

Miriam smiled, rocking and smoking. "Like a bad dream, perhaps it'll be gone when you wake up?"

"That's right. It's only talk, you know."

"And are dreams, visions, ideas, talk any less real than physical events?"

"I always thought they were."

"You'd better think again, Sunny."

Quivering, Sunny sipped her blackberry wine. Miriam's words were turning her world upside down, so maybe she was right in this, too. But she simply was not ready to face the Spirit Stalker tomorrow night.

"You realize," Miriam said, "it's now a contest between

you and the Spirit Stalker. Tomorrow I want us to make four medicine shields, one each for the spirit of the east, south, west and north, invoking their protection and power to draw the murderer to the sludge pit on the full moon. We'll perform a ritual to cleanse the sludge pit so the land will be strong again, and call on Spider Grandmother to help us and give us strength.''

''Miriam, I need to work tomorrow.''

''If we don't do this, you may have no need of your work ever again.''

Sunny looked at her fearfully. ''Why do you want to draw the Spirit Stalker to the sludge pit?''

''To try to catch him. As I said, I don't know how, but we'll ask Billy Joe to help us. Nan, too. And the police. Although it will mainly be up to you.'' Miriam gave Sunny a hard stare. ''Let's plan to meet at my house around dusk tomorrow night and invite Billy Joe. All right?''

''I'm getting scared, Miriam.''

''You have every reason to be frightened. I don't know if we can win, but we have to try.''

''Even if we all end up dead?''

''There isn't a choice.''

Sunny frowned. Maybe none of this was true. Maybe the police would catch the killer tomorrow, and it would all be over. Then she wouldn't have to be involved. She had come so close to death at Dan's hands that she didn't know if she could ever face a killer again, for she was truly terrified.

28

Sheriff Barker, Price, and Nan stood by the sludge pit, watching as three stretchers, each with a woman's body sealed in plastic, were taken to an ambulance.

"I just can't believe three more women have been killed," Nan said, then suddenly gagged and rushed toward the woods.

Price started after her, but Sheriff Barker pulled him back. "Give her some privacy, Price. I think she's going to be sick."

"I know. I feel sick, too. But what about the killer?"

"He's not going to show his face with all this activity." The sheriff pulled out a pack of cigarettes and lit one. Inhaling deeply, he watched the spot where Nan had disappeared into the woods.

"No, I guess not, but I don't like her being out of sight."

"Neither do I. But this has been hard on her. She had to watch them dredge out three partially decomposed women. And she's a woman." He hesitated. "Did you know her sister was murdered by her husband?"

"No. That's awful."

"It's why she's so determined to help women."

"No wonder."

"I blame myself for these bodies." Sheriff Barker took a

long draw on his cigarette. "If I'd listened to the Reverend before, or if I'd put a constant watch on the pit, we might have saved one or two of those women."

"Or none. You did what you thought was best. Who'd have thought the nut'd keep coming back? It makes no sense."

"But nothing about this case does. Remember, there's supposed to be another dead woman with long, blond hair we haven't found yet."

"You think Sunny Hansen was making it up?"

"No. Billy Joe and Miriam swore they saw the body, too, and the lab report confirmed their story."

"It could have been staged."

"I know. But why? That makes no sense, either."

"Okay, then where's the body?"

"I don't know. We've searched the area."

"And why was it in Sunny Hansen's bed?"

Sheriff Barker threw down his butt in disgust, then stamped it out. "We've got no answers. Few clues. And five, maybe six dead women."

"Hell and damnation! This can't go on."

"I know. I want you to watch the pit dusk to dawn, Price."

"I'm your man."

"Reverend Mulhaney says the stranger usually calls about two in the morning. If we believe the Reverend, that means the murderer must be dumping the bodies in the pit around that time."

"So we're looking at one more dead woman before we can catch him." Price rubbed the butt of his revolver, wishing he could shoot the killer full of holes that very minute.

"Yes, if he comes back to the pit."

"That's cold."

"I know. You got a better idea?"

"No. But if he comes back here, I'll get him."

"Park back in the trees so you can't be seen when you

272

stake out the place. And don't be brave. Radio in as soon as you see him, then follow his car."

"No problem." But Price was already thinking ahead. It was going to be lonely and boring on stakeout. He'd have a hell of a time staying awake. Maybe he could find a thrill-hungry woman to accompany him. Suddenly he was glad he'd given his wife the portrait of their kids. It'd ease his conscience, and keep her content for a while.

"Here comes Nan. Don't say anything."

"Right."

"How're you feeling, Nan?" Sheriff Barker looked at her in concern.

"Better. I'm sorry. This is one rough case."

"I know. Price is going to start staking out the pit dusk to dawn."

"Good." Nan fingered the medicine bag she was wearing under her navy suit. For some reason, it made her feel better. If she and the police couldn't do anything, maybe Miriam and Sunny could. At this point, she was willing to try anything so long as the murderer was stopped.

"Nan, I'm going over to Reverend Mulhaney's place to question him some more. You want to help?"

"Sure, thanks."

"Price." The sheriff lit another cigarette. "Take care of the paper work on these bodies, then get back out here."

"Okay."

"And, Nan, I've got to check on a couple of thing, so why don't you get something to eat, then meet me at the the Reverend's parsonage."

"I don't know if I can handle any food," Nan replied, still feeling slightly sick.

"You've got to get hold of yourself. Women need you strong and smart." Sheriff Barker gave her a hard stare.

"Right." She ran a hand through her hair. "Okay, I'll try to get something down."

"Good. The Purple Cow's near here."

"Okay. See you at Reverend Mulhaney's."

Nan hurried to her car and sat down behind the wheel. She took a deep breath, tried to calm herself, then turned on the engine. She needed to get away from the sludge pit, but she knew the memories of the dead women would haunt her forever.

She backed out, popped through the gears as fast as she could, then floored it on FM 203. When she'd left the sludge pit behind, she eased off the accelerator and snapped in a classical tape. She let the music run through her head, driving out the sound of pumping oil wells and dredging machines.

Heading for the Purple Cow, she tried to think of pleasant things, but couldn't remember any. All she could see were the lifeless faces of the three dead women. She was finding it more difficult to cope with death than she ever had before.

She glanced up and saw the faded purple cow astride the small, white building and smiled. There were some good things in life. She'd learned that after Rosey's husband had deserted her and her infant daughter twenty years before, Rosey had been left with nothing but an unshakable determination to make it on her own. Now, the Purple Cow was famous all over East Texas, and Rosey and Beth were entrepreneurs.

An hour later, Nan was feeling better on a full stomach, and was more determined than ever to catch the killer. She hoped the Reverend was right, for it would be the first real break they'd had.

She pulled into the parking lot in front of Reverend Mulhaney's parsonage and parked beside Sheriff Barker. She nodded to him as they both stepped out of their cars. He smiled, and she realized he was actually beginning to accept her as a colleague. She was glad, for she respected him and it had been a small battle worth winning.

They walked up the sidewalk to the Reverend's front door.

Sheriff Barker rang the doorbell. Nan glanced around, noticing how quiet it was, except for the wind in the trees and the sound of pumping oil wells. She suddenly felt anxious. Running a hand through her hair, she reminded herself to be totally professional and not let her emotions get in the way of the job. But it was easier said than done. Sheriff Barker rang the doorbell again.

Inside the house, Reverend Mulhaney struggled to sit up in his easy chair. He had not gotten much sleep the night before, so he had been napping. The doorbell had startled him awake. Now his heart was hammering and he felt queasy. He reached for his prescription bottle.

Tossing back a pill, he held a hand over his heart. The doorbell rang again, but he did not care. He was thinking about the dream he had just had. It was a nightmare, and he never had those, for he lived his life according to God's laws so there should be nothing to haunt him.

But in his dream he had been haunted by the woman who had made his church possible. She had accused him of murdering her for her money. But he had not done that. God had sent him a vision, and he had stopped her pain, sending her quickly to heaven. She had wanted to be at the right hand of God, and he had helped her attain her goal.

Why would his conscience suddenly bother him? He had done the right thing. Hadn't he?

But he had also dreamed of her house. It might now be giving refuge to a murderer, a serial killer. He dreaded the thought of entering the house again, but it was his Christian duty, if it was within his power, to see that no more women were killed.

And that meant telling the police about the house. The pain in his heart began to ease. Yes, he would call Sheriff Barker and tell him about the boarded-up house in the woods.

No, he had a better idea. He would tell the sheriff the killer had said he was staying in a house nearby, but he would not mention the boarded-up house. Then he would have time to get there first. If the killer was in the house, he would confront the murderer, save his soul, then present him to the police. He was sure the man would not harm a minister. If he was wrong about the house, then the police would search the area until they found the right house and caught the murderer. Either way, soon there would be no more bad dreams or dead women.

The doorbell rang again.

Before he could do anything, he had to receive company. He got up, suddenly feeling old and tired, though he must not let physical problems stop him. He had a mission to accomplish, and nothing must get in his way.

He opened the front door. He was surprised to see Sheriff Barker and Nan Shubert. "Please come in." He stepped back. "You are just the people I wanted to see."

Nan walked into the house, and the sheriff followed. They glanced around, noted the neat, Early-American furniture, and took a seat on a plaid couch.

Reverend Mulhaney sat down across from them. "Can I get you something to drink?"

"No, thanks." Sheriff Barker noticed the Reverend didn't look well, but figured it had to do with his heart attack. "We won't take up much of your time, but I wanted you to know we found three dead women in the sludge pit."

The Reverend paled, rubbed his chest, and leaned back in his chair. "I'm sorry I was right."

"So are we," Nan agreed.

"Is there anything else you can tell us?" Sheriff Barker asked.

"I have been thinking about it, and I was going to call you. When I last spoke with the stranger, he mentioned he was staying in a house with running water, food, and furniture. He said it was near here."

"That's vital information. You should have told me sooner." Sheriff Barker frowned.

"Only today did I realize its importance."

"But it's still not a lot to go on. Did he tell you anything else?" The sheriff pulled out his cigarettes, glanced around, didn't see an ashtray, and put them back. "What did he mean by 'near here'?"

"It could cover a lot of area," Nan agreed. "Do you suppose it's an abandoned house, or could he be holding a family hostage in the basement or something?"

"That is all he told me," Reverend Mulhaney replied, looking from one to the other.

"It would explain how the killer comes and goes with nobody seeing or hearing him." Nan nodded, her mind running through the possibilities of a hidden house.

"I am sorry if this is not enough help." The Reverend looked apologetic.

"Thanks. It helps," the sheriff replied. "We'll go back to the office and study a map that shows the houses in this area. Then we'll check out every abandoned shack and occupied house, if it takes us the rest of the day."

"Or all week," Nan added.

"Good." Reverend Mulhaney was pleased. He would have plenty of time to get to the house first.

"I'm glad you told us." Sheriff Barker glanced at Nan. "Let's get back to the office. Maybe there'll be partial lab reports on those three bodies."

Nan nodded in agreement.

"I hope you catch him soon," Reverend Mulhaney said, thinking that the road to the house was probably overgrown, but he would drive as close as he could, then walk the rest of the way. He would take it easy. He could not afford to strain his heart.

"We'd better go." Sheriff Barker stood up, and Nan joined him. "Thanks for the information. We'll let ourselves out."

"Let me know what happens." The Reverend remained in his chair and watched them leave.

Outside, they walked quickly toward their cars.

"Nan, you've been in on this case from the first," Sheriff Barker said. "And if you want to help me search the houses, I'd like to have you."

"Thanks. You'd trust me to watch your back?"

"You can shoot straight, can't you?"

"Yes. I'm trained."

"Okay, then let's check that map."

"If there's time, I'd like to stop and see Sunny Hansen while I'm this close. I want to see how she's doing and find out if she knows anything about this house."

"Okay, but don't take long. I'll be at the office."

"Fine. I'll see you there."

They parted at their cars. Nan quickly got into hers and took off. She wanted Sunny, Miriam, and Billy Joe to know about this latest development. Also, if Miriam'd had any more visions, especially about a house, she wanted to know about it.

Soon she pulled into Sunny's front drive, cut the engine, and glanced around. How could an area that looked so peaceful be menaced by something so dreadful? She shook her head and got out.

"Nan, come on in!" Sunny called, opening the front door.

"Hi. I hope I'm not disturbing you." Nan stepped into the living room.

"Never. What've you been up to?" Sunny shut and locked the front door, then followed Nan over to the couch and sat down across from her.

"I've got some bad news. We found three more dead women in the sludge pit this morning."

Sunny paled and clutched the arms of her chair. "Three!"

"Yes. Reverend Mulhaney thinks the killer has been calling him every time he murders one. And I guess he's right."

"But why?"

"I don't know. Something religious, I guess."

Sunny stood up and paced across the room. She looked

at the medicine wheel. She couldn't fight Miriam anymore. Something had to be done, and as quickly as possible. The murderer had to be stopped before another woman was killed.

"There's more." Nan touched the medicine bag under her clothes. "The killer told the Reverend that he was staying in a house in the area. Sheriff Barker and I are going to try to find it today. It won't get dark until late, so by dusk I'm hoping we'll have the murderer in handcuffs."

"Nan, you've all got to be especially careful. Miriam remembered the legend, and she thinks this murderer has been possessed by something called the Spirit Stalker, an ancient evil that gains power from killing women and devouring their spirits. She says there's a full moon tonight, and it's the eve of August second, a powerful day. She thinks the Spirit Stalker's power will reach its peak tonight."

Nan ran a hand through her hair. "What are you going to do?"

"We're going to make medicine shields later, then take them to the sludge pit and perform some kind of a ritual to cleanse the place and draw the killer there."

"And then what?"

"I'm not sure. We're going to catch him somehow, I hope."

"Sunny, really! You don't know what you're doing."

"I know, but Miriam will."

Nan shook her head, knowing she couldn't stop them. "At least Price will be there on stakeout, and we'll have some backup. Hopefully, we'll catch the murderer, and he'll never reach the pit. So maybe you don't have too much to worry about."

"Billy Joe is going with us, too. We'll be all right, Nan. Anyway, I'm glad to know you'll probably have arrested him by the time we arrive at the pit. Then we can perform some kind of Comanche ritual, and it'll all be done. And when it's over, I'm thinking of going back to Dallas and pressing charges against Dan. You know, there was a witness when he almost killed me.''

"Well, it won't be easy. It may mean going to trial. You should be very sure you want to go through with it before you get the process started."

"I know. But how do I keep Dan away from me once I report his violence?"

Nan shook her head. "With a protective court order. They're usually tailored to each situation and would restrict his access to you, say to within a hundred feet."

"But what is that worth if he finds me and decides to kill me?"

"Not much, if you consider that if he's willing to kill, then the penalty for violating a court order wouldn't matter much."

"Can I expect police protection?"

"Probably not. They just don't have enough staff."

Sunny took a deep breath. "Then I'd be pretty much on my own."

"There are battered women's shelters in most cities now, and you can get their hotline numbers from the police. If there's room, a woman and her children can usually stay in a shelter for up to four weeks while she tries to get her life together. Plus, the shelters offer a battered woman a court advocate, someone who will go with her to court so she won't be alone. That's especially important if her husband is going to be there." Nan ran a hand through her hair in agitation. "The main problem is there aren't nearly enough shelters."

"I think I could make it on my own."

"So do I, but I wanted you to know there is help. I know it will be difficult to go back and press charges, Sunny, but there are benefits, too. For one thing, if you win your case Dan'll be off the streets for a while. For another, every case like this that goes to court and is won helps and encourages other women to get out of similar situations. Also, every man who is punished for this type of crime is a signal to other men that they will be held accountable for similar actions."

"I see what you mean. Maybe I can do it."

"Just remember, I'll help you, and we'll get you a good attorney. There are women who donate legal time to help win cases like this, and court-appointed attorneys are available, too."

"I'm glad to know that, because I don't have the money for a lawyer."

"Well, you're in control now, and you have help." Nan stood up. "I'm sorry, but I've got to go. Sheriff Barker is waiting for me."

Sunny stood up, too.

"By the way, my parents loved the portrait. They thought it was the best anniversary present I'd ever given them." Nan smiled.

"I'm so glad."

"And how's the portfolio coming along?"

"Great. When this is all over, I'll be sending it off to New York."

"Good." Nan walked to the door. "Now, be careful tonight."

"I will. You, too."

They hugged, then Nan stepped outside.

29

Sunny was wearing all black—jeans, T-shirt, and boots. Miriam had told her to wear it for psychic protection. She had also explained that black was the color of spirit, and since they were going to be working with the land of spirit, black would help focus her. But she felt more like she was dressed for a funeral. Her own.

At least black would make her less visible at night. She looked out her kitchen window. The sun was setting. Dusk. She shivered. She was getting more nervous all the time.

And she shouldn't be. She and Miriam had made the medicine shields and taken them to the sludge pit, where they were now hanging in trees to the east, south, west, and north. Then they had circled the pit, chanting, tossing dried herbs, plants, and roots into the dark, stagnant waters. Miriam had said it helped, but Sunny didn't know.

Walking into her studio, she checked to make sure the windows were shut and locked. There was no art on her drawing table for the first time in a long while. She had even cleaned out her drawing pens. Her art was carefully placed in a black portfolio and hidden in the closet. If she never came back, all her work would be meaningless, and if she did, she wanted it to be safe.

She took a deep breath and walked into the bedroom.

Again, she checked all the windows. They were closed and locked. She went into living room. Those windows were closed and locked, too, as was the front door. She stopped in front of the medicine wheel and clutched the medicine bag around her neck.

Her heart began to pound. How could she possibly confront the Spirit Stalker, or even a plain, ordinary murderer? She was just Sunny Hansen, not Wonder Woman, Supergirl, or the She-Hulk. She wasn't a comic book superhero who could battle a sludge monster and win. She didn't work out with the X-Men or the New Mutants in their danger rooms. She didn't have spider powers like Spider-Woman. No, she was just simply Sunny Hansen, who had run and hidden when her husband had almost killed her.

And now Miriam Winchester expected her to fight and capture some ancient, powerful, evil force called the Spirit Stalker. How could she possibly do that?

She glanced around the room, feeling threatened and frightened and trapped. She felt light-headed and nauseous. She might throw up at any moment.

Sitting down, she put both arms over her stomach and pressed. She was not going to be sick. Wonder Woman never threw up.

She began to shake all over. She couldn't do it. She couldn't leave the house. She might die. She might be hurt. No, she could not make her legs move.

And then she thought of Dan, for that was how she had felt when he had been beating her that last time. She had been breathing blood, the scent of iron strong in her nostrils. She had tasted blood, and blood had run into her eyes, so that she had looked out through a red haze.

And she had cried, salty tears mixing in with the blood. She had pleaded, her voice strange, not hers at all, and still he had hit her. Her stomach had cramped, and she had doubled over. But he had simply held her upright, taunting her, hitting her, wanting her dead.

She had tried to fight him, but the anger had turned to fright. Her strength had turned to weakness with the pain and then his hands had been around her neck. She couldn't breathe. She couldn't cry out. She could see only his eyes, huge and wild and angry—and filled with murder.

At that moment she had seen and smelled and sensed her own death, and she hadn't been ready to die. Then she had felt something else, something she hadn't experienced since that moment when Dan was chocking her. Anger. She had been consumed with blazing, righteous anger.

Now she felt it again, pounding through her veins, suddenly giving her strength, energy, and determination. Something broke in her, and she stood up, clenching her fists. She would never again let any woman be hurt like she had been, if it was in her power to stop it, no matter the price to herself. She was a survivor, not a victim.

She paced the room. After that moment of intense anger in Dan's arms, she had passed out. Maybe she had died, for she remembered walking down—and suddenly her heart beat fast with surprise—a long black road. Could it have been Miriam's Good Black Road? And at the end of it a woman in a long, white gown had stood waiting for her. She had been anxious to embrace the woman, but before she could reach her, she was suddenly pulled back.

And Dan was gone. She was being cradled in the arms of her apartment manager, a good friend. Her friend's husband stood nearby. They quickly explained that they had heard her screams and used their passkey to get inside. Overpowered, Dan had left.

Then the fear had taken her. She had quivered and sobbed and thrown up. With all the strength she had left, she had thanked them and insisted on packing a few clothes, getting her hidden money, and leaving. She had told her friends she would call them when it was safe, but she had doubted if that time would ever come. And she had been running and hiding ever since.

But suddenly the fear had been burned out of her. She was no longer afraid of Dan. He was just a bully, and one who deserved to be punished. She would go back to Dallas and do what she could to see that he never hurt another woman again.

But first she had a killer to catch, whether he was the Spirit Stalker or just another brutal man like Dan. It didn't matter anymore. She'd had enough.

Then she smiled. Miriam's teachings had worked, for now she had the self-confidence to meet life and all it threw at her. She would never let anything overcome her again. She might have to rest and heal from time to time, but she would still be her own person, with her dreams and hopes and loves to make reality.

Yes, after they'd dealt with the East Texas murderer, she would go back to Dallas and get a divorce. She'd report Dan's abuse and attempt to kill her, so that it would go on record. And maybe Billy Joe would want to go with her. She knew she could use his support, and it didn't mean she was leaving Nan and Miriam forever. They were her friends, and that would never change.

But for now, Miriam and Billy Joe waited for her, and she didn't want to keep them waiting any longer. If they were lucky, Nan and Sheriff Barker had arrested the killer at that very moment. But if they weren't lucky, the killer still had to be caught.

Picking up her keys, she stepped outside, then locked the front door behind her. The sunset was beautiful, but the air was hot and muggy. She walked to her car, got inside, and took a deep breath.

She turned the ignition, and the engine ground. She pumped the gas pedal and tried again. The motor turned over, but wouldn't catch. Then she remembered the last time she had started the Bug it had backfired a lot. Tonight it wasn't doing anything. She tried pumping the pedal and grinding the starter. Nothing. After several more tries, she realized her car wasn't going to move.

What could she do? Billy Joe would already be at Miriam's house because she was so late getting started. And Miriam had no phone. She couldn't call Nan because she was with Sheriff Barker hunting the killer. Anyway, she couldn't wait for somebody to come and get her. She needed to be at Miriam's place right now.

But she didn't want to walk alone in the woods. She took a deep breath. What had she just decided about not being afraid anymore? She got out of the car, locked the door, then pulled the house key off the ring. She put it in her boot and hid the key ring in the bushes by her front porch. Taking a good grip on her emotions, she started for Miriam's house, night descending rapidly around her.

30

Reverend Mulhaney stopped in front of a fallen tree on a one-lane blacktop back in the woods. He turned off the car, then sat still. He did not want to carry out his mission. But God was watching, and he could not be weak. He must always live his life as an example to others.

Just as he had suspected, the road to the boarded-up house was overgrown. He would have to push past waist-high weeds to get there. Touching his chest, he thought of his heart. He did not want to do anything to overly exert it, and hated to leave the comfort and safety of his big New Yorker.

But duty called, for there was a soul to save. He pulled a prescription bottle out of his pocket, popped a heart pill, and waited for it to take effect. When he felt more stable, he picked up his flashlight and got out.

Locking the car door, he glanced around. It would be dark soon, and he felt uneasy. He had planned to come to the house earlier, but he had wanted to rest first and had fallen into a heavy sleep, awakening much later. Now he could not let darkness daunt him. He had a mission.

He stepped over a fallen log, and began pushing tree branches out of his way as he walked own the oil road. Pine needles were thick under his feet, and their fragrance filled the air. Suddenly he jerked to a stop, his breath coming fast. He had almost walked into a huge spider web stretched from one limb to another across the road. A black spider, probably a black widow, crouched in its lair; dead insects were trapped here and there, waiting to be eaten.

Disgusted, he carefully pushed his way through heavy brush around the web, feeling much like those insects, drawn to a black widow's web to be eaten. Then he forced the fanciful thought from his mind. He was one of God's chosen, so he was in no way connected to a spider. In fact, he should have killed it just to prove who was in control. No devil spawn could ever frighten him.

He continued on until he came to the edge of the forest and stopped. The house was just as he remembered, except grass and shrubs had overgrown the lawn and vines now entwined the house, covering most of the boarded-up windows. Then he noticed how quiet it was, no sound of birds, insects, or any living creature.

He took a deep breath and looked behind him. If he had been a man who scared easily, he would have been panic-stricken now, for there was something eerie about the house. He supposed it was because the building had been vacant so long. He should have sold it ages ago. Now it looked so deserted, he could hardly believe the murderer was living there. Maybe he should turn around and go home, letting the sheriff find the killer.

Turning back, he took a few steps, then stopped. No, he could not give up this close to accomplishing his mission. Besides, the nightmare was still vivid in his mind, and it seemed to be driving him. He turned back and walked quietly through the woods.

Pushing his way through high grass and wildflowers, he reached the house. He stepped onto the front porch. It creaked, cracked, and he jumped back in alarm. He took a good look at the wooden porch and realized it was rotten.

A huge, yellow sunflower had poked its head through the soft wood and moved back and forth in the breeze.

Besides that, the front door was still boarded up. There had to be a better way of entering the house. He decided to try the back door. He pushed his way through more grass that was a high as his knees, wound around shrubs that were taller than his head, and came to the back yard.

A board nailed across the back door had been wrenched free and was now dangling loose. Somebody had been in the house.

He glanced around. Now that his way was clear, he wanted more than ever not to enter the house. He had sworn never to do it again all those years ago. There were too many memories inside, too much water under the bridge. But God was watching and waiting, and his servant must not be found wanting.

He fit his key in the lock, but there was no need for it. The door swung open, squeaking on its hinges. He stepped into the kitchen, carefully shutting the door behind him. He glanced around. Empty cans of food filled the sink, littered the cabinet top, and covered the table. The stench of rotting food was strong in the muggy air.

He rubbed his chest. Yes, someone had definitely been here, but it could have been teenagers, a vagrant, or the murderer. The main thing was to remain calm, and not surprise or frighten anyone who might be in the house.

The place was dim, with only diffused light coming in through the cracks of the boarded-up windows. He turned on his flashlight and cast the beam around. The kitchen was in a bigger mess than he had at first realized. And it was hot, unbelievably hot. He was sweating, and his face felt flushed. But he would not be afraid. God was with him. He would call out as he searched the house to make sure that if anybody was there, they would know he was a minister.

"Hello. Is anybody here? I'm Reverend Mulhaney."

He walked into the living room. Following the flashlight's

289

beam, he noticed all the furniture was covered with thick dust. It didn't look as if anyone had been there, except footprints had been left in the dust on the floor. As he walked, he stirred the dust and sneezed.

"Hello! I'm Reverend Mulhaney."

He moved on toward the bedroom. The door was shut. He dreaded opening it, for in that room the old woman had breathed her last breath.

Turning the knob, he pushed the door open. It creaked. He aimed the flashlight's beam on the bed. For an instant he thought a man was lying on the bed, then realized it was the woman he had sent to God. She clutched the pillow he had used to smother her. He gasped, unable to move. He could only stare in horror at her, his flashlight spotlighting her face.

She smiled. "Good Reverend Mulhaney."

He screamed in terror; she had always called him that. He dropped the flashlight as he grabbed at his chest, feeling pain shoot down his left arm. Then he slammed the door shut and staggered into the living room. But he heard the bedroom door creak open. She was coming after him. He hurried to the kitchen, his breath loud in his ears, the pain in his heart getting worse. He headed for the back door.

"Good Reverend Mulhaney."

He whirled around. She was almost upon him. He jerked open a cabinet drawer, spilling its contents to the floor. He knelt, grabbed a butcher knife and jumped to his feet, brandishing it in front of him.

She smiled and held out her hands for him.

He slashed at her with the knife and missed, then stopped, confused. She was suddenly decaying, her flesh rotting, melting away to expose white bones. He gagged at the stench, the horror, and felt the knife jerked from his hands.

Crying out in terror, he felt his heart spasm. He reached for his pills as he crumpled to the floor. He pulled out the bottle, but as he started to open it, the pain in his chest spread and his left arm went numb. The bottle rolled away, and he collapsed on the floor.

Helpless, he looked upward, waiting for his death. The woman's face wavered, blurred, and became the face of a concerned man wearing an overcoat.

"Reverend Mulhaney, can I help you? What happened?"

The Reverend recognized the voice of the man who had repeatedly called him on the phone, but he could barely breathe, much less speak for the terrible pain in his chest. Still, he was determined. "Atone . . . women."

Then he died.

The man bending over him threw back his head and screamed in rage. The good Reverend had been attacked by vengeful women, wild witches, and now he was dead. He was the first casuality in their war with the weaker sex. But they would pay! The dirty, lying bitches would suffer! Reverend Mulhaney's death would be avenged this very night.

Furious, he clutched the butcher knife and ran from the house.

31

For the first time since coming of age, Deputy Sheriff Price Simmons was deciding there was a time and place where having a woman was not a good idea. And that time and place was at a sludge pit with a vicious killer on the loose. Not only was Price endangering the girl he'd brought with him, but his job, as well. His future in the department depended on nabbing this killer. Was he willing to let the guy get away while he was rolling around in the back seat with Sally Ann?

The whole damned mess was making him think, which was always a bad idea, and it was making him feel more like a grasshopper than a stud bull. At this rate, he wouldn't be able to get it up again the rest of his life.

Maybe if he drove Sally Ann home, he'd feel better. In fact, he knew he would, but he hated to leave the pit for even a minute. Things could break loose when you lease expected them. Hell and damnation! Maybe he could call her a cab. Sure, and it'd arrive next December. He couldn't call another patrol car to come get her, for then his job would be shot to hell and back.

When he thought about it, the best thing to do was to go ahead and enjoy her. But the problem was, he suddenly had a gut feeling that something bad was going to happen, and he needed to be alert, not half in the saddle.

From where he had parked the patrol car, he could see the sludge pit, but nobody there could see him. It was a good position, but he was having trouble keeping an eye on the pit and satisfying Sally Ann at the same. And now he didn't even want to. He just wanted to get her away, but she was a wild thing. Danger excited her, and she wanted him bad.

She had his shirt unbuttoned and was heading for his pants when she discovered the revolver at his waist. That seemed to excite her even more, and she pulled it out of the holster, kissed it, stroked her face with it, then tossed it on the floor. Frowning, he reached for it, but she pulled him back and began kissing him until he started to forget all about sludge pits and murderers.

Suddenly she pulled away, opened the door and jumped out. She looked back, grinning. "Hide and seek!" Then she headed away from the sludge pit into the woods, dropping pieces of clothing as a trail.

His gut wrenched, and he jumped out of the car, realizing she must have forgotten the murderer was lurking about, or maybe the extra danger added to the thrill. Either way, she hadn't seen the dead bodies and didn't know what she was getting into.

"Sally Ann! Come back here!" He ran after her, but she simply laughed and ran harder, deep into the woods. Now he could no longer even see her. "It's not safe. Come back!"

A few moments later, he heard her begin to laugh again, but from behind him, from the direction of the sludge pit. She had doubled back to trick him.

Suddenly her laughter changed to screams.

He froze. The murderer!

He changed directions and pushed through underbrush, stumbled over fallen limbs, and tore away vines. Finally, he struggled into the open area around the sludge pit. Sally

Ann was running from a tall man in an overcoat carrying a huge knife.

"Police! Stop!" He reached for his revolver. It wasn't in his holster. Shocked, he remembered Sally Ann had taken it off him. It was in the car. "Police. You're under arrest."

The man ignored him, closing in on Sally Ann.

Bellowing in rage, Price ran. He grabbed the man and tried to throw him to the ground. But the murderer was incredibly strong. He overpowered Price, slashing across his face several times as he tried to reach Price's jugular vein.

Price defended himself as best he could, hoping to buy Sally Ann time to get away, then the man sliced through Price's neck. Blood spurted out, pumping in time with Price's heart as he fell on his face, a hand splashing into the sludge pit. His blood spread along the muddy bank, running to mix with the oily sludge.

The man dropped his knife, satisfied, then looked around for the woman. Dirty witch! Now he'd avenge the good Reverend.

She was still running, but it didn't matter. He was feeling powerful and strong, like the man he was always meant to be. He could catch her. And he did. She struggled, but he backhanded her, leaving her stunned. Then he dragged her to the sludge pit and dumped her on her back on the oily bank.

He smiled, knelt, and encircled her neck with his hands. He squeezed, and felt himself start to harden.

32

Sheriff Barker parked his patrol car behind Reverend Mulhaney's car and glanced at Nan. "What do you suppose the reverend's doing out here? He looked fairly sick at the parsonage."

"I know. Maybe he didn't tell us all he knew." Nan glanced at the woods around them. It was almost dark, and there was something oppressive about the area. The gloomy feeling had increased with each house they'd searched that afternoon.

"He looked shifty-eyed, but I thought it was because of his heart." Sheriff Barker pulled out a cigarette and lit one.

"Maybe we should have come here first." Looking at the overgrown road, Nan was once more glad she had decided to wear boots, jeans, and a shirt. If she had worn her usual suit, hose, and pumps, they'd have been ruined in no time. She also wore a revolver in a holster at her waist, but the last thing she wanted to do was use it.

"Did you know a woman died and left him this house we're going to look at?" The sheriff took a long drag, then exhaled.

"Yes. But he obviously hasn't been here in years. Look at this road."

"I wonder why he never rented or sold the house?"

"I guess we can ask him."

"You don't suppose he's been helping some stranger, then decided the man was killing women, do you?" The sheriff looked hard at Nan.

"Who knows? As far as I'm concerned, Reverend Mulhaney is a questionable person to begin with."

"But he's done a lot of good."

"Maybe, but I wouldn't lay odds on it."

"You're damned skeptical, Nan."

"And you aren't?"

He nodded. "Let's get in there and find out what's going on." He crushed his cigarette out in the ashtray.

They got out of the car, locked the doors, then walked to the reverend's car. They glanced inside. It was empty, so they continued down the road, pushing aside branches, stepping over fallen tree limbs until they came to a huge spider's web.

Nan stopped. "Beautiful, isn't it?"

"You like that?"

"Just think of all the work and skill that goes into a web, and it's all genetic."

"I guess that's one way to look at it. But come on, let's get on up to the house."

They pushed through pine branches to get around the web, then continued down the road. Soon they came to the edge of the woods. Before them was a boarded-up house, twined with ivy and camouflaged with tall shrubs.

"That'd make a damned good hideout, wouldn't it?" Sheriff Barker said softly, watching the area for any sign of movement.

"It sure would," Nan agreed, feeling a shiver run through her. "You think it's safe to go in?"

"To be on the safe side, let's go in with our guns drawn." He snapped out his gun and nodded at her.

She smiled grimly and took out her revolver.

They walked through high grass and around tall shrubs to get to the front door. It was boarded shut, so they circled the house, making their way carefully through more tall grass and wildflowers. The back door was standing ajar, and they froze.

"I'll go in first," Sheriff Barker said softly. "Cover me." He flattened himself against the side of the house, then moved silently to the edge of the doorway.

Nan took a deep breath, raised her gun with both hands, and aimed it at the open door.

The sheriff raised his revolver, then stepped fast into the open door. "Police!"

Silence greeted him.

He glanced around and saw Reverend Mulhaney lying on the floor of the kitchen. There was no other movement or sound. "Nan, get in here."

"What happened?" she asked, stepping inside. She gagged at the smell, then saw Reverend Mulhaney on the floor. "Oh, no!" She hurried forward.

"Check the Reverend."

She knelt, waved flies away from his face, and put two fingers to his neck. "No pulse." She took a deep breath, trying to calm herself. "He's dead, but I don't see any wounds. Do you suppose his heart gave out?"

"We'll let the coroner decide, but that's what it looks like." He looked grim. "Are you all right?"

"Yes, I guess. Death is never easy."

"Right. And we've seen a damned sight too much of it lately."

Nan glanced around. "But look at that kitchen drawer. It was jerked out and dropped. Do you suppose there was a scuffle?"

"There could have been, or he might have accidently pulled out the drawer trying to keep himself upright as he fell."

"That's true."

"Let's check the rest of the house."

Nan looked down at Reverend Mulhaney's still form again and shook her head. No matter what she had personally thought of him, she was deeply saddened by his death.

She quickly followed the sheriff into the living room. Dust covered everything, but there was a track of footprints leading to the rest of the house. The tracks indicated that more than one person had been in the house.

They looked in the bedroom and noticed the bed was rumpled. The small study looked untouched, but the bathroom had obviously been used, and often. Except for Reverend Mulhaney, the place was empty.

Their job done, they walked back to the kitchen.

Nan knelt and fanned flies away from the Reverend's face. "I think we ought to cover him."

"No. We've got to leave the crime scene intact."

"Do you think the killer's been living here?" Nan stood up and put her revolver back in its holster.

"Could be. Or vagrants."

"I don't like it."

"Neither do I. But let's check the sludge pit next. Maybe we'll get lucky and find something to help the case. We'll walk in from here. It's not far, and I don't want anybody alerted by the sound of a car. I'm not taking a flashlight, either, because the light would give us away."

"I wish we could do something about the Reverend."

"We'll shut the door. That's the best we can do for now. As soon as we check the sludge pit, we'll get Price to call in and get some people out here.

They retraced their steps to the road, then cut through the woods toward the sludge pit. It was dark now, but their eyes adjusted somewhat to the lack of light, and they managed to push their way past low tree branches and brush.

When they came to the edge of the woods around the sludge pit, Sheriff Barker motioned for Nan to be silent, and they crept forward. Hiding behind trees, they looked at the pit. Price was lying still on the banks of the sludge pit, and a woman was being strangled by a man in an overcoat.

Nan started to run into the clearing, but the sheriff clamped a hand over her mouth and jerked her back into the woods.

"Nan!" he snarled, holding her still. "Go call for backup. Price's car is hidden on the south side of the pit."

"No! I've got to save that woman." Nan was suddenly seeing visions of her sister and countless other women being murdered by men. She had to save this one!

"I'll save her. You get help. That's an order. Hurry!"

Nan nodded once, then disappeared into the woods.

Sheriff Barker pulled out his gun and ran for the sludge pit. He couldn't shoot from a distance for fear of hitting the woman, so he ran up behind the man, his arms outstretched, his gun clasped in two hands. "Police! You're under arrest!"

The man ignored him.

The sheriff stopped behind the murderer, just out of arm's reach, fired into a tree across the pit, then pointed his revolver at the man's back. "Drop her! You're under arrest! Stand up slowly with your hands behind your head."

Suddenly the murderer dropped the woman and, with incredible speed, wheeled around. The sheriff fired, but the man somehow avoided the bullet, grabbed his arm, and twisted it, cracking the forearm. White bone broke through the sheriff's shirt-sleeve, and his gun fell from his limp hand. In shock from the pain, he still managed to kick his gun away from the murderer.

Both of them went for the revolver, and they struggled, falling to the ground. Sheriff Barker's right arm was useless, and the pain was almost more than he could stand. Still he struggled, trying to reach the gun with his left hand. But the killer was unbelievably strong.

Sheriff Barker knew he couldn't hold out against the murderer for long. Before his strength faded, he gave one last push toward the gun, touched it with his fingers, and sent it spinning into the sludge pit. It disappeared into the murky waters.

The murderer jumped up, seemed to scent the wind coming from the south, then stepped a few feet from Sheriff Barker and picked up a huge butcher knife.

The sheriff managed to get to his feet and run a few steps, but the murderer grabbed him by the shirt collar and jerked him back. He tried to slash the sheriff's jugular vein, but Sheriff Barker threw up his left arm, defending himself. The killer slashed across his forehead, barely missing one eye, then across his forearm, then down the side of his face.

Blood was running into Sheriff Barker's eyes; he could hardly see or stand. His ears rang, but he had to fight as long as he could to give Nan a chance to get help. She'd be safe in the car, or she could drive the hell over the murderer if he came after her.

Suddenly the killer looked to the south again, sniffed the air, then turned back to the sheriff, a gleam in his eyes. With unbelievable speed, he slashed Sheriff Barker's stomach open, threw the knife toward the edge of the pit then ran off into the woods to the south.

The sheriff pressed his good arm across his stomach and crumpled to his knees. Where had the murderer gone? After Nan? No. She had to be safe. If as sheriff he had to die, at least let him have saved one woman on this case.

But everything was suddenly darkening around the edges. He couldn't see or think straight. He was losing too much blood, and knew it. He was in the worst pain of his life, and he couldn't take much more. He wasn't at all sure he was going to come out of this alive.

"Sheriff Barker!" Nan cried, running out of the woods, her revolver clasped firmly in two hands.

"Killer's gone. South. Careful."

"All right. Don't worry. Backup's on the way. I'll call for an ambulance and get the emergency kit."

She glanced over at Price and the other woman. They were still, too still. She wanted to check on them, but she had to help the sheriff first.

She quickly holstered her gun, then helped him lie down. She unbuttoned her shirt and jerked it off, glad she had worn a T-shirt underneath. His gut wound smelled like the lining of the stomach had been perforated. There was no time to lose. She bound his middle with her shirt, slowing the flow of blood. She quickly checked his other wounds. He looked bad, but as far as she could tell, if he got prompt medical attention, he would live.

"Okay, Sheriff, you'll do till I can get the medical kit."

She didn't know if he heard her or not, but she didn't want him to worry. She had to appear calm and in control. Above all, she was not going to panic. Taking a deep breath, she stood up and hurried over to Price. Neither he nor the woman were moving.

Gently she turned Price over. She gagged and swallowed hard. His throat had been cut deep, right through the jugular. He'd lost a lot of blood, maybe most of it, for his face was white where it wasn't streaked with sludge.

Damn! He'd been a good cop, and he'd loved women. In fact, he couldn't get enough of them. Maybe that wasn't even bad. Loving them was a hell of a lot better than hating them.

By now she didn't have much hope, but she checked the woman's pulse, anyway. No response. Dark bruises ringed the young woman's throat. She was too young to have been robbed of life, but then there was no good age to die at the hands of a murderer.

Tears stung Nan's eyes and her stomach heaved. Would the murders never end?

301

But she couldn't think about that now. She had to get medical help for the sheriff and get it fast. She checked on him. He was unconscious, but still breathing. She pulled out her revolver and hurried toward Price's car.

33

As Sunny walked toward Miriam's house, she felt more and more uneasy. Something was definitely not right. The path seemed to twist and turn in all sorts of odd directions, and the familiar landscape was gone. Maybe it was because the woods were dark, but she'd walked through the forest at night before and never had this problem.

She felt a rising fear, almost a mindless panic trying to overwhelm her, making her feel less and less like the strong, determined Sunny Hansen back at the house, and more and more like Dan's victim. Suddenly she wanted to cry, to cower, to run home to safety. She tried to fight the emotions, but they kept hitting her in waves, growing stronger and stronger.

Finally, she stopped and stood shivering, feeling the fear rush through her, along with a growing hatred of herself. And then the thoughts began to come. She was weak. She had no friends. She could not be loved. She was ugly. She had no talent. She would never be a successful illustrator. She would always be alone, unloved, unwanted, a failure terrified of her own shadow.

Tears began to stream down her face. She crumpled to the pine needles of the forest floor. She curled up into a fetal position, rocking back and forth, moaning, unable to move because she was so weak and life was so hopeless.

A thick fog began to roll in, quickly covering the ground, shrouding her in luminescence. The temperature dropped, and she shivered, noticing her tears had grown cold.

Cold? In August?

Confused, she roused slightly and glanced around her. She could see nothing but thick fog, and the cold seemed to be penetrating to her very soul. She could die here, in the cold and in her pity, and what would it matter? Perhaps it would be best for her, for the world. It would be no loss to anybody, especially her.

Her head fell back against pine needles. Yes, it would be easy to lie back, to let the horror of the world flow past her. She didn't care. Why should she? She had been used, abused. It would be easy, so very easy to die here and now. All she had to do was not resist.

Suddenly a peace came over her, and she knew she was doing the right thing. Yes, she would welcome the peace of death, welcome it with open arms. Then she could fly free and finally be happy.

But something tugged at the edge of her mind, something not quite satisfied with her decision, for somehow it didn't seem exactly right. She moved uneasily and touched the medicine bag around her neck. Instantly, she felt dizzy, disoriented, and sick to her stomach. She felt so nauseous she knew she was going to be sick. She was so tired, she could hardly move, and yet she had to throw up.

Forcing herself to her knees, she leaned away from the trail and emptied her stomach. She felt dreadful. Her head pounded, and she couldn't see right, for little pinpoints of light kept flashing in her eyes. Then she gagged again and heaved over and over, though there was nothing left in her stomach. She wiped her lips clean with pine needles, then started to lie down.

But she didn't, suddenly afraid if she did she would never

get up again. Instead, she clutched her medicine bag, and this time it didn't make her sick. In fact, it steadied her, and she stood up, despite the waves of horrible, negative emotions sweeping through her.

Suddenly a vision of a white owl seared through the pain of her emotions, and she remembered Spider Grandmother. She clutched the medicine bag hard and began to chant, "Spider Grandmother, help! Spider Grandmother, help!" She chanted louder and louder as she began to feel stronger.

The fog began to recede, the horrible thoughts in her head began to go away, and she began to feel better. The headache eased, her stomach settled, and she took one step, then another toward Miriam's house.

Yes, Miriam. And Billy Joe. Nan, too. She did have friends. She was loved, and she loved. She was not alone. "Spider Grandmother, help!" she chanted again. And she did have talent. She was worth something. And she did not want to die. She wanted to live, work, and love. She was no victim! Never again. "Thank you, Spider Grandmother."

She walked faster, feeling stronger all the time, until finally she felt positive again, unafraid. The headache and nausea disappeared just as the fog receded, and the land became familiar again, though it still remained cool.

Then out of the dark, a white owl flew to her, circled her once, then headed back down the trail toward Miriam's. Sunny smiled and felt her heart beat fast with joy. Spider Grandmother had sent a guide.

Following the white owl, she suddenly felt fleet-footed, as if she had wings that would carry her quickly to safety and to friends. She hurried down the trail, holding the medicine bag tightly in her left hand and chanting, "Spider Grandmother."

Finally the white owl flew out of the woods into Miriam's back yard, circled the area, then flew off into the forest. Sunny watched it, gave silent thanks, and stepped into Miriam's yard. Billy Joe and Miriam were standing there, anxiously watching the woods.

"Sunny!" Billy Joe exclaimed and hurried to her. He enveloped her in a warm hug. "Where the hell have you been? We've been out of our minds with worry!"

"I'm sorry. My car wouldn't start, so I walked."

"Walked! You walked through the woods at night with that killer on the loose!" Billy Joe looked at Miriam in disgust. "Don't that beat all!"

Miriam smiled. "Come here, child. We're not mad at you. We've just been worried." Sunny threw herself into Miriam's arms and was comforted by the familiar scent of tobacco and blackberry wine.

"Well, I'm mad," Billy Joe insisted. "That was a damned fool thing to do!"

"He's upset because you scared us," Miriam explained, looking into Sunny's face. "Are you all right?"

"Now, I am. I can't tell you how glad I am to be here."

"Did you see the killer?" Billy Joe looked worried.

"No. But it was very strange on the trail."

"Strange?" Billy Joe eyed her more closely.

"Come and sit down," Miriam insisted, leading Sunny to the porch and into a rocking chair. She poured Sunny a small amount of blackberry wine. "Drink that. Rest a moment. Billy Joe, do you want some?" Miriam held out the jar of wine.

"No. But I could use a cold beer."

"I'm sorry, I don't have any."

"It's better if I don't drink now, anyway. But when that killer's in jail, I'm going to buy a case and get roaring drunk."

Miriam chuckled as Sunny handed the empty jelly jar back to Miriam. "That warmed me."

"Good."

"Are you going to tell us what happened, now, Sunny?" Billy Joe asked, sitting on the edge of the porch.

"I'm not sure what happened."

"The Spirit Stalker almost devoured your spirit, Sunny," Miriam explained. "But because you fought back and won, you're now stronger than ever before. And he knows it."

"But how could he get inside my head like he did? And how do you know what happened, Miriam?"

"The battle was in a psychic dimension. Your spirits were struggling, and what you felt in your mind and body was but a pale shadow of what you were really experiencing. How did I know? I watched, giving you all the strength I could."

"Psychic dimension?" Sunny shook her head. "You watched? Oh, Miriam, I just don't know how to take all this."

"Miriam has a way with the truth," Billy Joe said thoughtfully. "But this whole Spirit Stalker thing is beginning to stretch it."

Miriam smiled. "Neither of you have to believe right now. Just don't back down."

"I won't ever do that again," Sunny said, clenching her fists.

"I'm with you on that," Billy Joe agreed.

"But what happens now?" Sunny wished the night was over and the sun already rising.

"The Spirit Stalker didn't win that battle, so now he'll want you to come toward him. You can feel the way is clear, can't you?" Miriam looked intently at Sunny.

"I'm not sure what I feel."

"The Spirit Stalker didn't want you aligned with us, gaining more power. But now that you are, he wants you quickly, before you call on any more power."

"And now, Miriam?" Sunny asked, glancing around, feeling colder again.

"We're waiting for the full moon to rise so our power will be complete." Miriam looked at the sky. "It'll be soon now. Can't you feel her?"

"What I feel is that it's getting damned cool for August."
Billy Joe looked around suspiciously.

"That's the Spirit Stalker trying to block our power by upsetting the natural elements," Miriam explained.

Sunny shivered, watching the same area of sky as Miriam.

"Look!" Miriam exclaimed. "There she is."

Suddenly a huge, white, luminous globe rose slowly into the sky, and with it came a howling wind, the sound of rushing water, and the cry of wild animals.

"What the hell is all that?" Billy Joe glanced around, ready to defend them.

"Spider Grandmother is sending her help through Mother Earth. But you have the power here and now, Sunny. It is you who must stop the Spirit Stalker." Miriam never took her eyes from the moon, and slowly the sounds quieted until the night was still.

"I don't know if I'll be strong enough."

"You must be." Miriam nodded. "Now it's time to begin."

"Should we take a flashlight?" Sunny asked, trying to put off the inevitable.

"There'll be plenty of light from the moon," Miriam explained.

"I can get along without a flashlight," Billy Joe said, "but there's no way in hell I'm going without my sawed-off shotgun. It'll stop that murderer." He leaned down to the porch, grabbed an ammunition vest filled with bullets, slipped it on, then picked up his shotgun.

"You can take a gun," Miriam agreed. "But it won't stop the Spirit Stalker tonight. He's reached the peak of his power, as has Sunny, so don't expect them to be totally human."

Billy Joe glanced at Sunny. "Don't worry. You look just fine. Miriam, stop trying to frighten her."

"I'm not, but it's amazing how frightening the truth can

be. Come on. It's time to go to the sludge pit. The Spirit Stalker will be drawn there by our medicine shields and Sunny's presence. Tonight he must kill her and devour her spirit if he is to complete his destiny."

Sunny shivered, but kept her fear down. After all, the man was probably already captured by Nan and Sheriff Barker, and there was nothing to worry about. But just in case they hadn't caught him, Billy Joe had a shotgun.

"All right. Let's get on with it," Billy Joe said impatiently. "I hate waiting around once the game has started."

"Just a moment." Miriam reached down and picked up two objects beside her rocking chair. "Sunny, I want you to have this powerful medicine totem. My grandmother made it, as well as the one I'm going to carry. I've had them in a trunk for years, never needing them before."

"But, Miriam, the totem might be destroyed, and it's irreplaceable."

"No, Sunny. You are irreplaceable."

Sunny took what appeared to be part of an antler hung with various feathers, dried herbs, strips of leather, claws, shells, and bits of wood. The one Miriam kept for herself was very similar. "Thank you. I'll be careful with it."

"Use it, Sunny. Don't be careful with it."

"Are we ready now?" Billy Joe asked.

"Yes." Miriam smiled grimly.

They stood up and left the porch. Light from the full moon lit their way as Billy Joe started down the path that led to the sludge pit. Sunny followed him, and Miriam brought up the rear. They didn't speak as they walked, for they were listening, but all was silent around them. The night was still cool, but oppressive like the calm before a storm.

Sunny held up her totem as she walked, looking from side to side, dreading the dark force she had encountered earlier in the woods. But nothing seemed wrong, and she began to

309

relax, thinking of the beauty and power of the white owl in flight, and the full moon rising.

"Did you hear something?" Billy Joe hissed.

Sunny gripped her totem hard and glanced around. "I don't think so."

"The Spirit Stalker!" Miriam exclaimed.

A tall man in an overcoat leaped from the woods. He grabbed for Sunny, but Billy Joe pushed her out of the way. She fell, losing her totem, and hit her head against a tree stump. Stunned, she lay there, trying to clear her head so she could move.

Miriam quickly stepped in front of Sunny and held up her grandmother's medicine totem. She chanted protective Comanche words. The man backed off. Turning toward Billy Joe, he attacked.

Billy Joe emptied both barrels of his shotgun at the man's gut. But the man moved with incredible speed and only his right arm caught a spray of bullets. Astonished, Billy Joe didn't have time to reload before the man was upon him. He grabbed Billy Joe's shotgun, broke it in half, then picked up Billy Joe and tossed him against a tree. Billy Joe fell against his bad knee and lay unmoving while he tried to recover from the pain.

Then the man turned toward Miriam and Sunny. Miriam chanted harder, shaking the totem at him. But he wasn't stopped this time, only slowed.

Sunny realized that if she didn't do something quickly, they were all going to be slaughtered. The man seemed to have superhuman strength just as Miriam had predicted, for even though his left arm was ripped open and bleeding, it didn't seem to bother him. And what he had done to Billy Joe was almost unbelievable.

"Spirit Stalker!" she shouted, standing. She had to get him away from her friends. If what Miriam said was true, he wanted her, so she was counting on him following her.

"Catch me if you can!"

"Sunny, no!" Miriam exclaimed. "We must stay together."

But Sunny had already started running down the trail toward the sludge pit. She felt more swift and powerful than she ever had in her life, and she could see well despite the darkness. Maybe Miriam was right. Maybe she would be superhuman for one night. Maybe she could even be Wonder Woman.

And her ruse worked. The man chased her, but soon she realized he was catching up with her, despite his wounds. She had to get him to the sludge pit where she would, hopefully, have more power. It was her only chance to survive, because he was looming closer and closer behind her. If he caught her, she was dead.

Suddenly, she felt him touch her, trying to bring her down. His hand was like an icy claw against her back. With a burst of speed, she got away. But he stayed with her, and again began to draw closer.

Finally, she saw the sludge pit and raced for it. But before she could reach it, he grabbed her, cutting off her breath as his arms came around her middle. His arms were cold, as was his breath against her neck, and she shivered as they fell together and rolled toward the sludge pit. She suddenly realized he wore a coat because he was unnaturally cold.

She struggled against him, arms flailing, feet kicking, but he held on to her. Yet his wounds were finally beginning to weaken him, and she could feel his power ebbing. If he weakened enough, maybe she could win. Then he grabbed a bloody knife that lay on the bank. She tried to kick it out of his hand, but instead he cut her, leaving a long gash down the shin of her right leg. Horrified, she kicked out and sent the knife spinning to the edge of the pit.

Now she was also losing strength as the wound bled freely. She knew he had gotten what he wanted, a weakened woman he thought he could overcome. But she was not giving up and continued to struggle, despite his superior strength and size.

They slipped and slid in the oily muck until he finally forced her onto her back and pressed a knee against her chest. He grabbed her neck with both hands and pressed. She thought of Dan and how he had tried to strangle her. Desperately, she fought back, thrashing back and forth, causing him to lose his grip because his hands were slick with oily sludge. She gasped for breath before he was able to tighten his hold again.

She had to get free, but how? Suddenly she heard her name called. Looking to the left, she saw Nan running toward them, a revolver clasped in both hands.

"Stop!" Nan shouted. "You're under arrest!"

But the man ignored her and kept choking Sunny. Nan couldn't shoot for fear of hitting Sunny, and she was no match for the murderer's size. She glanced back at the trees. She had managed to pull the sheriff away from the pit and hide him in the woods, not knowing if or when the murderer might return. Now he was safe, but Sunny was in trouble. If only the backup and ambulance she had called would get to them in time.

Suddenly a howling wind whipped through the clearing, and Miriam walked in from the woods. A white owl flew from her, circled the sludge pit, then flew back to Miriam and landed on her shoulder. Miriam held up her totem, then pointed it toward the sludge pit.

The waters of the pit boiled and Sunny began to fight the man with renewed strength. Tossing her head back and forth, she noticed his knife had fallen nearby. She reached for it, but couldn't quite touch it. She was seeing red, moving toward blackness as he squeezed off her oxygen, but suddenly she could hear Miriam chanting inside her head. Spider Grandmother, help! In one last, desperate attempt, she twisted her body and grabbed the knife.

She tried to stab him in the back, but he released her

neck and jerked her arm back. She gasped, drawing in lungfuls of air as they fought, rolling into the sludge at the edge of the pit. She ended up on top, which gave her greater leverage. Both her hands grasped the hilt of the knife, covered by his large, oily hands. They pushed the knife back and forth between them, each trying to end the battle.

But they were both weakening. They couldn't last much longer. Sunny shook her head, trying to clear it, and noticed a crumpled form farther away on the banks of the sludge pit. She looked closer. Another dead woman!

Suddenly she was seized by a wild fury, like nothing she had ever experienced before in her life. She began yelling Comanche medicine words, incantations coming from an unknown source. And she drove the knife deep into the man's heart. Blood spurted upward, drenching her T-shirt.

Feeling sick, she rolled to the side as he splashed into the sludge pit and sunk beneath the surface.

Nan ran to Sunny and aimed her revolver where the murderer had disappeared. "Did you get him?"

"Yes." Sunny sat up, crying, hardly able to believe she had killed a man. But he had given her no choice, no choice at all.

Nan holstered her gun, then pulled Sunny, bloody and dripping with sludge, to her feet. She hugged her close. "Are you okay?"

"Yes." Sunny clung to Nan a moment, trying to orient herself, trying to believe it was really over, that the murderer was dead and could never hurt anybody again. Then she saw Miriam hurrying toward her, the white owl on her shoulder.

When they reached Sunny, Miriam bowed her head in respect and the owl took flight, dropping one white feather which slowly spiraled downward to land at Sunny's feet. She picked it up and handed it toward Miriam.

"No, Sunny. You earned it. Wear it proudly, for it denotes wisdom and strength."

313

"Oh, Miriam! I was so afraid." And Sunny threw herself into Miriam's arms.

Miriam held her close, stroked her hair, and patted her back. "You did well. Never fear. It's always hard to kill, especially when you value life so much. But sometimes we're forced to kill to save our very spirits. And you saved not only your own but many more besides."

"Then I was right to kill him?" Sunny asked, stepping back, her eyes haunted.

"It was the only way."

Sunny nodded, her eyes slowly clearing.

Billy Joe came hobbling out of the woods, supporting his wounded knee by leaning on a tree branch. "Sunny!" he called. "Are you okay?"

She smiled and started to run to him, but her leg hurt. She suddenly remembered the cut and glanced down.

"Sunny!" Nan exclaimed. "That leg needs to be bandaged. I'll get the medical kit."

"Let me have a look at it," Miriam added.

"No, not now. It can wait." Limping slightly, she hurried to Billy Joe. They embraced, then she put an arm around his waist and helped him join the others.

"It's all over," Miriam said, nodding at Billy Joe. "Sunny killed the Spirit Stalker."

"She killed the murderer," Nan objected. "There was never anything to prove he was more than a mortal man."

"He was terribly strong," Sunny explained, stroking her white owl feather.

"Strength of the mad," Nan said as sirens wailed in the distance. "At last, out backup and the ambulance."

"Ambulance?" Sunny asked.

"Sheriff Barker's been hurt, but Price is dead," Nan said simply, motioning toward the deputy sheriff's still form on the other side of the sludge pit.

"Oh, no!" Sunny looked at Billy Joe for comfort, and he pulled her close.

"We paid a high price," Nan said. "But this case is closed. Let's go home." She started to turn away.

Suddenly a wild wind sprang up, and women's laughter filled the air. The sludge pit boiled furiously. Surprised, they all turned back to stare at the pit. As the water turned from black to blue, two bodies popped to the surface.

The Spirit Stalker was embraced in the arms of the woman with the long, blond hair.

ESPIONAGE FICTION BY WARREN MURPHY AND MOLLY COCHRAN

GRANDMASTER   (17-101, $4.50)
There are only two true powers in the world. One is goodness. One is evil. And one man knows them both. He knows the uses of pleasure, the secrets of pain. He understands the deadly forces that grip the world in treachery. He moves like a shadow, a promise of danger, from Moscow to Washington—from Havana to Tibet. In a game that may never be over, he is the grandmaster.

THE HAND OF LAZARUS   (17-100, $4.50)
A grim spectre of death looms over the tiny County Kerry village of Ardath. The savage plague of urban violence has begun to weave its insidious way into the peaceful fabric of Irish country life. The IRA's most mysterious, elusive, and bloodthirsty murderer has chosen Ardath as his hunting ground, the site that will rock the world and plunge the beleaguered island nation into irreversible chaos: the brutal assassination of the Pope.

WARBOTS by G. Harry Stine

#5 OPERATION HIGH DRAGON   (17-159, $3.95)

Civilization is under attack! A "virus program" has been injected into America's polar-orbit military satellites by an unknown enemy. The only motive can be the preparation for attack against the free world. The source of "infection" is traced to a barren, storm-swept rock-pile in the southern Indian Ocean. Now, it is up to the forces of freedom to search out and destroy the enemy. With the aid of their robot infantry—the Warbots—the Washington Greys mount Operation High Dragon in a climactic battle for the future of the free world.

#6 THE LOST BATTALION   (17-205, $3.95)

Major Curt Carson has his orders to lead his Warbot-equipped Washington Greys in a search-and-destroy mission in the mountain jungles of Borneo. The enemy: a strongly entrenched army of Shiite Muslim guerrillas who have captured the Second Tactical Battalion, threatening them with slaughter. As allies, the Washington Greys have enlisted the Grey Lotus Battalion, a mixed-breed horde of Japanese jungle fighters. Together with their newfound allies, the small band must face swarming hordes of fanatical Shiite guerrillas in a battle that will decide the fate of Southeast Asia and the security of the free world.

#7 OPERATION IRON FIST   (17-253, $3.95)

Russia's centuries-old ambition to conquer lands along its southern border erupts in a savage show of force that pits a horde of Soviet-backed Turkish guerrillas against the freedom-loving Kurds in their homeland high in the Caucasus Mountains. At stake: the rich oil fields of the Middle East. Facing certain annihilation, the valiant Kurds turn to the robot infantry of Major Curt Carson's "Ghost Forces" for help. But the brutal Turks far outnumber Carson's desperately embattled Washington Greys, and on the blood-stained slopes of historic Mount Ararat, the high-tech warriors of tomorrow must face their most awesome challenge yet!

Available wherever paperbacks are sold, or order direct from the Publisher. Send cover price plus 50¢ per copy for mailing and handling to Pinnacle Books, Dept.17-271, 475 Park Avenue South, New York, N.Y. 10016. Residents of New York, New Jersey and Pennsylvania must include sales tax. DO NOT SEND CASH.

ESPIONAGE FICTION BY LEWIS PERDUE

THE LINZ TESTAMENT   (17-117, $4.50)
Throughout World War Two the Nazis used awesome power to silence the Catholic Church to the atrocities of Hitler's regime. Now, four decades later, its existence has brought about the most devastating covert war in history—as a secret battle rages for possession of an ancient relic that could shatter the foundations of Western religion: The Shroud of Veronica, irrefutable evidence of a second Messiah. For Derek Steele it is a time of incomprehensible horror, as the ex-cop's relentless search for his missing wife ensnares him in a deadly international web of KGB assassins, Libyan terrorists, and bloodthirsty religious zealots.

THE DA VINCI LEGACY   (17-118, $4.50)
A fanatical sect of heretical monks fired by an ancient religious hatred. A page from an ancient manuscript which could tip the balance of world power towards whoever possesses it. And one man, caught in a swirling vortex of death and betrayal, who alone can prevent the enslavement of the world by the unholy alliance of the Select Brothers and the Bremen Legation. The chase is on—and the world faces the horror of The Da Vinci Legacy.

QUEENS GATE RECKONING   (17-164, $3.95)
Qaddafi's hit-man is the deadly emissary of a massive and cynical conspiracy with origins far beyond the Libyan desert, in the labyrinthine bowels of the Politburo . . . and the marble chambers of a seditious U.S. Government official. And rushing headlong against this vast consortium of treason is an improbable couple—a wounded CIA operative and defecting Soviet ballerina. Together they hurtle toward the hour of ultimate international reckoning.

Available wherever paperbacks are sold, or order direct from the Publisher. Send cover price plus 50¢ per copy for mailing and handling to Pinnacle Books, Dept.17-271, 475 Park Avenue South, New York, N.Y. 10016. Residents of New York, New Jersey and Pennsylvania must include sales tax. DO NOT SEND CASH.